Prais

Neil Douglas-Klotz

The Sufi Book of Life:
'One of the outstanding books I always keep at hand…
a good guide for the confused like me. These 99 doors
lead to a palace.'
  Elif Shafak, author of *The Forty Rules of Love*

'His inclusive spirit should appeal to readers within
many religious traditions.'
  Publishers Weekly

'Written simply, tenderly and with great wisdom.'
  Charlotte Kasl, author of *If the Buddha Dated*

'Warmth, wisdom and common sense…practical guid-
ance for any spiritual traveler.'
  Llewellyn Vaughn-Lee, author of *Sufism,
The Transformation of the Heart*

Prayers of the Cosmos:
'Reader beware: though this book is brief, it contains the
seeds of a revolution.'
  Matthew Fox, author of *Original Blessing*

Neil Douglas-Klotz is a rare jewel; a brilliant scholar
with heart whose words have the power to reconnect us
with our sacred source.
  --**Joan Borysenko**, author of
  Seven Paths to God

A MURDER AT ARMAGEDDON

A. K. A. Chisti is the pen name of Dr. Neil Douglas-Klotz, a world-renowned scholar in religious studies, spirituality, and psychology, specializing in the languages and culture of the ancient Middle East. A frequent speaker and workshop leader, he is the author of several books on the Aramaic words of Jesus, including *Prayers of the Cosmos*, *The Hidden Gospel* and *Blessings of the Cosmos*. His works on Native Middle Eastern spirituality and Sufism include: *The Genesis Meditations*, *The Sufi Book of Life*, *Desert Wisdom* and *The Tent of Abraham*, with Rabbi Arthur Waskow and Sr. Joan Chittister. Douglas-Klotz directs the Edinburgh Institute for Advanced Learning and served for many years as cochair of the Mysticism Group of the American Academy of Religion. He also cofounded the International Network of the Dances of Universal Peace in 1982 (dancesofuniversalpeace.org). In 2004, he helped begin the Edinburgh International Festival of Middle Eastern Spirituality and Peace (mesp.org.uk), and in 2005, he was named Kessler-Keener Foundation Peacemaker of the Year for his work in Middle Eastern peacemaking. For information on his work, see the website of the Abwoon Network: www.abwoon.org.

a MURDER at ARMAGEDDON

A Judas Thomas Mystery

A.K.A. Chisti

ARC Books

Published by ARC Books, a project of the Abwoon Network, Edinburgh, Scotland, UK and Columbus, Ohio, USA: www.abwoon.org

Interior maps by: Joyce Carlson, Accentials Art Services at: artwithadifferentview.com
ISBN: 1481870971
ISBN 13: 9781481870979
Library of Congress Control Number: 2015901465
Createspace Independent Publishing Platform
North Charleston, South Carolina

Table of Contents

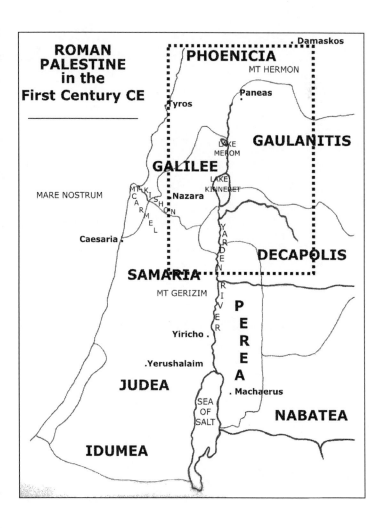

ROMAN
PALESTINE
in the
First Century CE

PHOENICIA

Damaskos

MT HERMON

Paneas

Tyros

LAKE
MEROM

GALILEE

GAULANITIS

MARE NOSTRUM

MT
CARMEL

Nazara

LAKE
KINNERET

KISHON

Caesaria

YARDEN RIVER

DECAPOLIS

SAMARIA

MT GERIZIM

Yiricho

PEREA

Yerushalaim

JUDEA

SEA
OF
SALT

Machaerus

NABATEA

IDUMEA

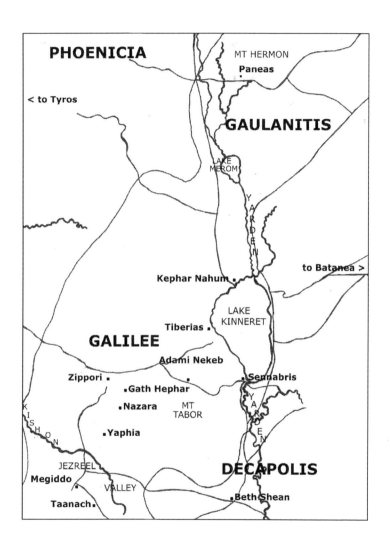

Chapter 1

Megiddo

Shemuel ben Yahayye sat down heavily in the dust, hearing a waterfall that didn't exist.

The old scribe's breath was labored as he took refuge in the shade of a small fig tree, his back to the ruins of a dry stone wall behind him. The late-afternoon light was waning. So was his life. There was no waterfall, no water at all, just a roaring in his ears as his heart raced. He wished he were back at home, up north in Paneas, sitting near the spring of Pan and the headwaters of the Yarden River as they rushed down the slopes of Mount Hermon.

Only by keeping his mind on that cool, refreshing oasis had Shemuel managed to trudge up the hill of Megiddo to a spot near one of the ancient temples. As he looked at the ruins around him, he was conscious of sitting on top of generations of abandoned and now-buried towns and fortresses, all of which had guarded the strategic pass overlooking the Jezreel Valley. *This isn't a hill; it's a cursed burial heap*, he thought. *I'm sitting on the bones of my ancestors, and many other people's, too.*

As the sun descended toward the horizon to his left, he looked north over the flat valley. The so-called Great Plain, which divided Samaria in the south from Galilee to the north, cut a wide path between the sea and the interior of Israel. By tradition, this border country belonged to the king, whoever he happened to be at the time. The land was too important to be without some rich or powerful person controlling it. Foreign troops always ended up here, wanting to either conquer the land or march through it to Syria and points east. "Capturing Megiddo was as good as capturing a thousand cities," one of the old Egyptian pharaohs had said.

And they should know, he grumbled to himself. Shemuel visualized the ancient Judean king, Yoshiah, one of King Dawid's descendants, foolishly meeting the Egyptians in battle here as they rode north to support the Assyrians in their battle against the Babylonians more than six hundred years ago. *Total disaster. Why didn't he let them ride through? Yoshiah died and lost his battle, but also he weakened the Egyptians, so the Assyrians lost their battle. And the winners—the Babylonians—invaded Yerushalaim not long after. It was none of Yoshiah's damned business, and his whole people suffered for it.* Many of Israel's major battles for survival had been fought here. And except for the judge Deborah's, most were lost.

More recently, the Romans had marched through again, splitting the land in two with the help of King Herodes—the so-called Great, the mad Idumean—about a hundred years ago.

Shemuel closed his eyes and visualized the plain again, as it could be—or might be. Another huge battleground with the Romans pitched against the Israelites, who were again fighting for survival. He shook his head and willed himself to see a different outcome, forcing his breath heavily into his chest, as if to see things the way his heart wanted to. But his head told him it was impossible.

Shemuel began to feel his heart and lungs struggling even more. He was losing his own battle. It wasn't the climb or the exertion. He was old, and his heart was failing. He was running out of time. All of his hopes depended on a gamble. Either he would meet someone here, or he would reach Yerushalaim and the one person who could carry on his work and guard the secret that could restore the hopes of his people. But Shemuel was several days away from Yerushalaim, and the person he hoped for wasn't here. In addition, he had lost his servant and bodyguard, who had disappeared sometime during the night as they had journeyed down from the north. *The breath of the Holy One had blown him somewhere. Who knew where?* He felt that same breath becoming shorter and shorter as his heart and lungs ached.

Looking west toward Mount Carmel, Shemuel remembered the story of his Israelite ancestor Eliyah, who sat there in a cave listening for the voiceless voice of the Holy One. According to some, Eliyah never died, and he returned whenever he was most needed. *Eliyah, at least, had someone to pass his work on to,* thought Shemuel grudgingly. The Holy One had sent a chariot to take Eliyah home, without pain, without all this effort. *I could use Eliyah's help now!* The true Israelites, the people of the northern lands—his people—had continued to resist, no matter how many kings and emperors tried to suppress them. The prophets had always stood against the false claims of the rich to rule by the authority of their own power or wealth, or by the authority of their fathers or grandfathers. The old ways were those of Moshe and Eliyah. No one needed to rule anyone unless the people needed to be delivered from oppression. Then the Holy One would provide someone, a *shofet*, a judge, to bring things back into balance. Or a temporary hero, or a "son" or "daughter" of the prophet Moshe, who would lead the people and then return to tilling the land or watching the sheep. Not, for God's sake, yet another king.

But the Divine One is taking a divinely sweet time sending someone now, thought Shemuel bitterly. His people had freed themselves from the descendants of King Dawid, the Judean oppressor. They had survived the Assyrians, who only carried the rich away into captivity with them. Then the Babylonians had rushed through to Yerushalaim, but they had helped things out by destroying Shelomoh's decadent temple, which was never part of Moshe's vision, anyway. They had been free for several generations from the damned Judeans. They had lived free, like their Samaritan cousins, and managed life by themselves, high in the Galilean mountains and in the heights of Gaulanitis above the sacred waters of Paneas, near his home...*Paneas, will I ever see you again? Your living waters remind me of Hanuch, the more ancient Pan, the sacred son of man who, like Eliyah, never died and returns when he is needed.*

I'm wandering, he thought. *Maybe all these deathless green men are the same, anyway. I could use anyone's help right now.* Shemuel closed his eyes. His heart was beating quickly. Too quickly. Calling upon all of his training, he refined his breath so that he could barely feel it, and at the same time, breathed as deeply as he could. That took away much of the pain in his chest. Then he visualized the ladder of Ya'aqub, his most reliable technique. He willed himself to imagine placing one foot after another, rung-by-rung, slowly climbing. He was in no hurry. His vision-place had always been available when he needed it. Only by rushing could he push it away. He gradually felt his breath becoming lighter.

He opened his eyes very slightly and saw the late-afternoon sun approaching the horizon somewhere off to his left. Turning his head gently from side to side, he received its light through the slits between his eyelids. Breathing with the flashes of light, he used its life energy to climb the ladder higher. He was approaching the holiest place, the place of vision where all the worlds meet and begin. *Then I will know what to do!* He began to hear the sacred sounds inside, sounds that would help him travel the rest of the way. Sounds of his own breathing mixed with the sounds of his ancestors:

YYYYHHHHWWWWHHHH—
Healing Emptiness,
Focused Spaciousness,
Pivot of the worlds.
YYYYHHHHWWWWHHHH—
Breath of the Being of beings
in my own breath.
Life energy of all the worlds and levels,
reveal your light and guidance!

Shemuel felt a space in the middle of his forehead open, his eyelids relaxing and spreading toward the back of his head, a smile forming, a fire rising from the darkness within him, uniting heaven and earth. The bottom of the sides of his ribs opened. The *kevod*, the glory of the Holy One, rose from underneath him into his heart. *There was a way ahead! He could see it! Maybe he* would *make it to Yerushalaim! Maybe that* was *part of the plan…*

Or maybe not. His breath faltered. He sensed a shadow pass quickly to his right, too early to be the setting sun, and from the wrong direction, surely. He continued to focus on the breath of the Holy One that he felt flowing through him. *Nothing to do now but let go.* He began to lose any sense of himself.

After a while, the back of his head began to hurt. Or was it *his* head? Then he felt a short, sharp pain penetrate the side of his ribs, and a warm liquid began to flow down his side. *This was not the feeling of his breath, not the* kevod. *It was his life force draining away. But it must all be the Holy One's breath! Alaha, the Holy One, is the only source of breath. Ameyn. There is only the earth of the Holy One under and within me.*

As he lost consciousness, he felt the earth rising to embrace him. He only wished he had been given a bit more time.

Chapter 2

A Body on the Road

"He looks dead to me, Master."

Ioannis Vivis peered over the edge of the bluff at the body lying facedown ten paces below him. As the sun began to peek above the horizon, he felt the salt air from the sea sweep over the hillside above the plain near Megiddo. It was just after the first rains of spring, a few weeks before the Israelites celebrated their annual festival of being perpetual travelers, which they called *Passover* for some reason his mother never explained. In the distance to the northeast, he could just about make out Mount Carmel through the morning mist. Part Roman, he would always be a foreigner in this land, but after five years serving the Roman prefect, he knew his way around, for survival's sake, if nothing else. Except for the body on the road below them, it was just another beautiful day in his country of exile.

Crossing the plain of wheat fields below him, he saw an eastern spur of the ancient network of roads running up the coast from Egypt. From there, one could travel straight north to Tyros in Phoenike or northeast to Damaskos. From Damaskos everything connected to the caravan trails heading farther east, through the empire of the Parthoi all the way to the Indus. *And maybe to a new life for me*, Ioannis thought hopefully. But from what his master had told him, the Megiddo plain had already seen a lot of death. Ioannis didn't like being there and finding a dead body. As a professional bodyguard, he had already seen far too many corpses in his relatively short life.

Ioannis glanced behind him. He had to admit that he originally thought he had been given an easy job. His current master, Yehuda Tauma, a scribe from Yerushalaim, sat cross-legged, leaning against a boulder, out of sight. His eyes were closed, and he was breathing like he was half asleep. Ioannis knew that Yehuda was not sleeping, but maybe this was carrying his meditation practice a bit too far. Flecks of gray in his short black hair, Yehuda was lean with delicate features and hands. He did not look used to living outdoors. *Hardly surprising,* thought Ioannis, *considering that he lives in a big house in Yerushalaim and spends most of his time looking at scrolls.* His olive eyes were clear and looked right at people, when he bothered to look. Overall, Yehuda was in good shape for someone probably just over thirty, nearing middle age. *Strange. He seems unconcerned that a corpse lies directly in our path,* thought Ioannis. *Shouldn't he be a bit more worried?* They had left Yerushalaim under the cover of darkness two nights ago and headed north, on the run, at least according to Yehuda.

From their perch on the hillside, Ioannis continued to watch for any signs of life in the body. Finally, Yehuda opened his eyes, shook himself and looked at the slave.

"Ioannis, how do you know he's dead? It could be a trap...And by the way, don't call me master!"

"Well, first, he hasn't moved for at least a quarter of an hour, judging from the length of an hour at this time of year. Second, he doesn't seem to be breathing. Third, there's a dark, bloodstained spot about one palm wide on the back of his head, if my eyes don't betray me."

"All right," said Yehuda, fluttering a hand. "But that is insufficient evidence. It could still be a trap. There are many bandit groups around these days. We don't want to run into any of them right now. We already might have the temple guard from Yerushalaim looking for us. They don't just let a high-level scribe walk away, especially if something valuable has gone missing." Yehuda sighed and levered himself to his feet. "All right. Let me take a look."

Yehuda crawled closer to the overhang of the bluff. He could see the whole road for half a parasang— two *mils* to the Romans—in either direction. Yet there were plenty of hiding places for thieves in the mixture of scrub and small oak trees that lined the valley. Farther away to the east, he could just about see the outline of a garrison, one of many built by the old Herodes to control his territory and collect taxes.

"It would be just like bandits to operate in sight of the fortress garrison," said Yehuda, "simply to tweak the Herodians' noses. You see, Ioannis, many bandits consider their work to be reverse tax collection."

"Yes, I've been here awhile, Master," said Ioannis, a bit bored. "I understand."

For some reason, thought Ioannis, *Yehuda sometimes regresses to the idea that all slaves are uneducated.* Ioannis was young, barely twenty-one years, but he had certainly given the scribe plenty of evidence to his education over the year they had been together. Or probably Yehuda just liked to lecture, from his work teaching young scribes about Israelite history and the culture they were supposed to maintain. Ioannis admitted to himself that he sometimes learned something new from Yehuda at times like this, something actually valuable for survival. He was young enough to believe that he might even get out of this godforsaken, backwater border country alive. In any case, Yehuda was continuing with his impromptu lecture.

"You see, Ioannis, old Herodes imposed impossible taxes on the peasants, both to support his huge building projects and to pass along a good income to his overlords in Rome, supplemented by many bribes to their local representatives here. The idea that the insane amount of taxes he imposed was killing his people never crossed Herodes's mind, probably because he had largely lost the use of it—likely the result of some inbreeding in his Idumean family. He spent most of his latter years combatting intrigues and plots against him, both inside and outside his family, mostly products of his insanity, but a few real. The few sons he didn't manage to kill—Antipas, Philipos and Archelaos—carried on just where he had left off. Archelaos was so incompetent that even the Romans didn't want to keep him as a client, so Judea and Idumea went back to direct rule by Caesar's prefect only two years after the old Herodes's death. That was about thirty-four years ago…"

Suddenly Yehuda broke off the lecture, became quiet and gazed with half-closed eyes at the body lying below them, the arms and legs splayed as though they had been carefully arranged.

"He certainly looks dead, probably stabbed," he said. "But the clothes are not those of a peasant. On the other hand, they aren't those of someone very wealthy either. Bandits usually choose one of the rich elites to murder, either for retaliation or profit. Linen tunic, wool mantle, embroidered sash. He's dressed like a priest or scribe, actually."

A few seconds later, as the sun rose farther above the horizon, the dawn light glanced off something on the man's back, a flash of silver dangling from a chain around his neck.

"This isn't the work of bandits," Yehuda said, jumping up quickly. "He's still wearing jewelry. Let's go down."

As they climbed down the bluff, both men kept their ears open for anyone in the vicinity. They had taken care to cover their tracks once they were out of Yerushalaim, but they were exposed on the valley floor. Yehuda stood looking down at the man while Ioannis stooped to examine him.

"Yes, a blow to the back of the head there," said Ioannis without emotion. Even though he had become inured to dead bodies, he still gently turned the body over. A large red stain showed around the bottom of the ribs on the left side. *It looks like a bloody crescent moon embracing him*, he thought as he kneeled down next to the body to take a closer look.

"The blow to his head just knocked him out," said Ioannis, pointing to the red crescent. He opened the slit in the man's clothing near the wound. "Here's what killed him. Done with a long narrow blade, some kind of stiletto rather than a pugio or dagger. Good steel, a very clean stab directly up and into the vitals. Small hole, big damage—an assassin's weapon, not a bandit's. Not much sign of a struggle either. Someone knew what he was doing. The corpse is not more than a half day old," he said, finally looking up. "What's the matter, Master?"

Yehuda was staring white-faced at the body.

"I know him," Yehuda said, trembling, with tears in his eyes, and then the words tumbled out. "Shemuel.

My maternal uncle, also a scribe, from the north of Herodes Philipos's territory near the Syrian border. He was my adopted father, taught me everything about being a scribe. He retired and went back home to his village a few years ago. I had something to tell him, was going to visit him on our way out of the empire. What was he doing down here? Why would anyone want to kill him? He wasn't wealthy, and his only jewelry—this…this…silver amulet—is still here!"

Yehuda kneeled down next to Shemuel and gently lifted the chain and medallion carefully from the body. It was a tiny filigree hand, palm facing forward, intended to ward off evil.

"So much for good-luck charms, Master," Ioannis said. "It doesn't seem to have helped him very much. I'm sorry; I don't want to be insensitive. I know it's your uncle. It could have been an accident. Maybe the thieves, or whoever they were, made a mistake."

"No, I don't think so," said Yehuda, forcing his voice to be steady. He looked toward the sun rising over the plain and placed his hand gently on the dead man's chest, as though he were listening to something, or someone. He looked across at Ioannis over the body. "As you said, this isn't the work of bandits. And Shemuel always traveled with a bodyguard. Also, I don't see any sign of tracks, besides yours and mine. It's as if the body just appeared here and was arranged to look like the work of thieves. Don't you think that's a bit odd?"

"I know he was your uncle and all, Master," repeated Ioannis, unwilling to complicate their journey. "But what can we really do?"

"I told you, Ioannis, don't call me master!" said Yehuda, forcing himself to look away from Shemuel's body and think of something else. He looked up at Ioannis. "If we meet strangers, we're two merchants from Idumea in the south traveling north on our way to Syria. That's our story. Anyway, I provisionally freed you when we left Yerushalaim. If we get out of Roman territory, you're free as far as I'm concerned. You decided to come with me of your own free will. The danger is on your young head."

"Sure, I know. So what *shall* I call you?" said Ioannis, happy that Yehuda was still talking about leaving the empire.

"You can call me Ioudas in Greek, or if we're in Aramaic-speaking company, Yehuda. I prefer that. You're my assistant; that way if I give you orders, no one will suspect anything. Your name is Yehohanan in Aramaic, by the way."

"Thank you. Somehow you've managed to make my name longer and more difficult than it is already," said Ioannis, smiling. "And you know, my former master, under Roman law, if you free a slave, you become his patron and he becomes your client. So we're still family. We have obligations to each other. Maybe I should call you *father*?"

Yehuda grimaced a bit and sniffed. "No need to be disrespectful, Ioannis. And you don't have to tell me Roman law. I may have been born here, but I was good at my job, rotten though it was, and that involved knowing Roman law backward and forward. Back to the present, please. We need to bury Shemuel, at least temporarily. Then I will send word to someone from his family who can bring him back home and bury him properly."

"All right. Where do they live?"

"Not they, he: his son Mikhael. He lives just near Caesarea Philippi; most people still call it Paneas. We're heading that way, anyway. We will probably have to go to Darmsuq to get rid of this damned pearl I found. The sale should free us both to choose our own life. Or we'll end up on a cross like every other thief who steals from a top elite."

"You didn't steal it. You found it," said Ioannis.

"Yes, and where did I find it?" replied Yehuda acerbically. "In a corner on the floor of the inner temple. It's enormous. It had to belong to one to the elite's wives, maybe of the high priest himself, or someone on that level. Stealing from the patron of a patron, they'd call it."

Yehuda looked back at Shemuel's body, beside which he was still kneeling. After some hesitation, he began to look through the old scribe's clothes and shoulder bag.

"His temple identification papers, plus a purse still containing fifty silver dirhams," he said. "Something's really not right here."

"Mas—Yehuda, I think I saw some dust rise just over that hill to the east!"

"We had better get out of sight...back up the hill! We'll have to leave Shemuel for now."

Yehuda and Ioannis scrambled back up the bluff and hid behind a large rock a little farther away from the road, but still close enough to see what was happening. After some minutes they saw a group of Roman horse soldiers gallop over the rise from the garrison.

They headed straight for Shemuel's body. *Just as if they knew it was there,* thought Ioannis.

Chapter 3

Backtracking

As Yehuda and Ioannis watched, the soldiers dismounted, stretched lazily and then ambled casually around the body. *They're acting like this is just the usual rubbish disposal job,* thought Ioannis. He understood the attitude, having been drilled the same way when he first came to Palestine. Any Roman stationed out here would not feel any pressure to pay much attention to a dead local. Two of the soldiers picked up the body and dumped it over the back of an empty horse, and then the troop remounted and trotted back east to the garrison. *How did they know to bring an empty horse?* he wondered.

Yehuda waited a bit until the soldiers were out of sight. He looked back to where Shemuel's body had been and again looked with half-closed eyes toward the sun, which was now well above the horizon. His face was drawn with concern.

"Finding Shemuel's body changes things," he said. "We'll wait a bit to cross the Great Plain and go farther north into Galilee. I know a man in Taanach, a small village near here, who is discreet and might know something about Shemuel. He also might be able to help us avoid the Romans safely."

They headed down a path southeast into the foothills, away from the plain. They had traveled up the main Via Maris from Yerushalaim to make better time and avoid suspicion, spending the previous night at an inn just to the west of the Jezreel Valley. Now they walked down a minor path deeper into Samaria. The rolling landscape alternated rich farmland with oak and myrtle trees perched on gentle hillsides. After about a half hour, they stopped for rest and some food: dry bread, olives and figs.

Lost in thought, Yehuda considered the day's events. This was one complication that he hadn't planned for when he found the pearl and decided to leave Yerushalaim. A new life seemed like the best plan, a complete break with the past. Somehow, though, he felt that this was part of some larger plan, over which he had no control. And he really didn't like that feeling.

Ioannis saw Yehuda frowning and decided something was wrong. He needed more information. It was his safety at stake, too, and knowing Yehuda, he wasn't really convinced that the scribe was used to a life on the run.

"Former master, err…Yehuda, why *did* you invite me to go with you? We don't know each other that well. I've only been your bodyguard for about a year."

"I trust you, Ioannis," said Yehuda. "And after more than ten years working in the temple, where all men are watching their backs, I am usually pretty good at knowing whom to trust. Also, as you showed back there, you know your job. You know weapons, hand-to-hand fighting. They didn't teach us any of that. By the way, how *did* you learn all that? You're young but well spoken, and you don't look…well…fully Roman. Your features, for one thing, are a bit too much like one of Shem's children, although you are tall with curly, dark hair. I never asked you before, but I suppose it would not have been proper when we were master and slave— much too intimate."

"My father was a Roman general, but my mother was Israelite. I know what you're thinking, but it wasn't like that. My father really loved my mother. He married her and took her back to Rome with him when he was detailed home. That was after the civil war that broke out when Herodes the Great died. So I was raised in Rome. Standard Roman military education, until I was about fourteen."

"Then what? How did you become a slave? You should be a Roman citizen."

Ioannis sighed and leaned back against the scrub oak tree underneath which he was sitting. "My father backed the wrong side in a plot against the emperor. The winner takes all, of course. He, at least, was executed with some dignity, but my mother and I were sold into slavery." He looked away from the scribe and rubbed his eyes, as though protecting them from the sun. "I never saw her again. I don't even know if she's alive," he said with some waver in his voice. Then he quickly regained his composure. "One of my father's friends with some influence secretly sent me here as part of a group shipment to Valerius Gratus, the former prefect. When he found out that I was trained and educated, I became one of his bodyguards. When I worked for him, he treated me like a normal soldier, not a slave.

"But when Gratus was sent back to Rome, he didn't take me with him. Pontius Pilatus replaced him as prefect, but he had his own bodyguards and didn't trust anyone else. So I became just another slave again. Fortunately, he sent a group of us as a present to your high priest Kaiapas, whom you call Qayapha, last year. When Kaiapas found out I had protected Gratus, he gave me to you as a bodyguard. By the way, now that I can ask you, why do scribes need bodyguards?"

"Ah, you see, not all scribes are equal, Ioannis," said Yehuda ruefully, wiping some sweat from his forehead. He was sitting under an outcrop of rock, but nonetheless the midmorning heat had begun to beat down relentlessly. "I was one of Qayapha's personal scribes, so really a private secretary and accountant. I did my share of the usual temple work for a scribe—teaching young scribes, recopying texts, testifying at trials as a legal expert and so forth. But I also had to keep Qayapha's personal accounts—particularly who owed him money, crops and favors. That required much of my time. Also, Qayapha used to send me on special trips to collect from rich landowners who owed him rent on large pieces of property or money for licensing rights, like the fishing concession on certain parts of the Galilean lake. Fortunately, I haven't had to do that while you've been with me."

Yehuda coughed and cleared his throat. "My last bodyguard was killed defending me on one of those trips, Ioannis. That's how I got this gray hair. We still don't know if it was a random attack by bandits or one of the families who owed the high priest money and wanted some back. Anyway, I got away and was only too happy to leave the money behind. Later Qayapha had Pilatus send a small army to the area. They killed some innocent peasants and roughed up the elites, as the usual symbolic warning. The next payment to Qayapha came in early."

"So you've been a bit of a tax collector, youself," said Ioannis, laughing grimly. He looked around at the rich countryside and imagined farmers constantly ducking one tax collector after another. "But if that doesn't happen very often, why don't they just give you a bodyguard for the trips, or a whole bunch of them? I had to meet you every day when you left the temple compound, sleep in your house and take you back in the morning."

"Yes, and I'm grateful," said Yehuda, shrugging his shoulders. "You're also a better cook than my previous bodyguard. You must have learned some Roman cooking from your father. You see, at my level, I also know secrets some people don't want known, like the ruling temple circle, Qayapha and his friends. He doesn't want me getting captured and revealing any information, such as how much of the people's tithe to the temple the top priests keep for themselves, or how much of the commission due to the Romans gets shorted. So that's where you come in. You were supposed to prevent me from getting kidnapped."

"Was it really such a bad life?" asked Ioannis. "You had clothes, food and a house in one of the best areas of Yerushalaim. Seems relatively little danger, considering what life is like in the empire: cheap and generally short."

"Yes, but I'm fed up. I'm thirty-three years old. According to the records I keep, I might expect to see fifty, maximum. I saw the priests, and Qayapha in particular, getting richer and richer, mostly from peasants being driven off their land through fabricated debt and all sorts of swindles in the name of God. The old texts I recopy in my spare time, and our whole cultural heritage as Israelites, say that things should be very different. The priests should serve the people, not vice versa. I saw my chance—a very large pearl lying in a corner in the inner temple chamber two days ago—and decided to take it."

"So, where to now?"

"I was planning to go to Zippori, Sepphoris, in Galilee first. It's one of the old garrison cities that Herodes Antipas rebuilt into a model city to cozy up to his Roman patrons, as well as to collect taxes for himself. Now people in Galilee are supposed to pay some of their crops to the Romans, some to Antipas and some to the Yerushalaim Temple. How can they have anything left? As you can imagine, most people hate all three about equally. My family was originally from one of the villages near Sepphoris, and then we moved to the city itself. I need to see my brother there before we leave Israel and the empire."

"A city, Yehuda!" said Ioannis, raising his hands in disbelief. So were you also raised as one of those 'damn elites' you always go on about?"

"No, a sub-elite, if you ask me," said Yehuda wryly. "I was only seven when my father died. After his first wife died, he had married again, and I was the child of his old age. Being the eighth son, at the end of the pecking order, meant that nothing of his wealth or land came to me. I had the wrong constitution for the army. So my mother sent me to live with my uncle, Shemuel, in Paneas, who was a scribe and became my second father. He taught me history, mathematics, holy texts, astronomy, dreams, inheritance custom, accounting, diplomacy, how to talk to a rich elite and how to keep quiet when necessary. I was trained as an expert talker. Maybe when I get to where I'm going, I can still try my hand being a merchant, if there is any trade in the Parthian Empire.

Anyway, we should probably get on; the day is getting old."

Ioannis looked around them at the open country-side. Not a sound except birds. They were relatively sheltered here in the foothills that spread out from Mount Carmel, towering in the west. "Do you really think anyone is after us, Yehuda?" asked Ioannis, scratching his chin with a bit of disbelief. "We're in the wilds of Samaria, after all."

"You never know in this country, Ioannis. I bought some time by leaving a note for the high priest saying my brother was sick and I needed to go home urgently to attend to him. It was an extra cover story, so that if the pearl were reported missing, they wouldn't automatically link it to me. There were, however, only a few people in the inner temple yesterday, so it wouldn't take a genius to figure things out."

"That should work. So we can relax a bit," Ioannis said. "Now where is this village we're heading for?" He turned to pick up his knapsack and sword, relieved that they had some clear plan. When he turned back, however, Yehuda was sitting very still, with his eyes rolled up.

"Master? Yehuda?"

Chapter 4
Trance and Consequences

Ioannis had seen Yehuda go into a trance like this before, when he guarded the scribe at his home in Yerushalaim. It was a nice enough house, he recalled, reminding him a bit of his childhood home in Rome. Ioannis did have to get used to Yehuda suddenly going into some kind of strange state at any time of the day or night. *At his home was one thing. Here in the open country-side, anyone might turn up!* Ioannis breathed and tried to relax, fingering his sword nervously.

As he watched Yehuda, he again felt the same, strange atmosphere that had led him to trust the scribe in the first place. Yehuda was definitely somewhere else when he went on these journeys. And when he came back, he seemed somehow more present than before. The whole house felt different, more peaceful, for hours afterward. Gradually, Ioannis had learned to shrug off the eerie feeling this atmosphere first caused in him. It was one more eccentricity of living with a scribe from a strange, pagan religion. *A religion that is partially my own, at least by birth,* he thought. *Anyway, guarding Yehuda was better than living in constant fear while serving a Roman prefect; one serious mistake could be your last.*

Ioannis looked back at his six years in Roman Iudaea. He had told Yehuda the truth about his background, but not the whole truth. After Gratus left Israel and Pilatus arrived, it was true that Ioannis had been demoted back to being a normal slave for the prefect. But Pilatus was never one to overlook an advantage. Just before Ioannis had left for the temple with the rest of the prefect's "presents" to the high priest, Pilatus had ordered the slave to a private audience. *With a man like Pilatus,* thought Ioannis, shivering, *it's really better to be ignored.* Gratus had considered the common people in Iudaea, and especially the temple officials, unpredictable, superstitious, prone to hysterical frenzy and frankly a bother to have to rule over. He would much rather have been in Rome. But at least while Gratus was in Iudaea, he tried to be fair and honest. In Pilatus's personality, Ioannis sensed something else. Pilatus seemed to enjoy tricking and hurting the people he was supposed to rule. Ioannis supposed that Pilatus considered it his payback for being sent to the hinterlands, where success meant just keeping a lid on things, and a big mistake probably meant execution by whoever the emperor happened to be at the time.

When Ioannis entered Pilatus's chambers, the prefect was leaning sideways, slouched on his throne with a bored look on his face. He eyed the slave like a hawk sizing up a mouse. Ioannis saluted quickly and stood at attention.

"So, Ioannis. I had a report from Valerius Gratus before he left that you were a good bodyguard. In fact, a much better bodyguard than a slave had any right to be. So I had a look into your background." The prefect paused for effect.

Ioannis cursed silently but said nothing. He called up all his training to not show any emotion, including what he had learned playing cards with the other bodyguards.

"I just want you to know, Ioannis," Pilatus drawled, "that I don't hold a man's background against him. As long as he knows where his loyalties lie."

"Yes, Master," Ioannis said, beginning to sweat.

"Yes, Ioannis. You know, I am sending you with a group of other slaves to Kaiapas, the high priest here. As you also probably know, the Yerushalaim high priest and the temple officials are in charge of collecting the tribute due to Rome from the peasants. They collect their own tithe also, which is supposed to either support them in a modest fashion or be used as a sacrifice in their curious rituals. It would be natural for a person in Kaiapas's position to take a bit extra for himself. We know that old King Herodes did it, since we had accountants go over the estimated and reported income from Iudaea during his years. Farming, which is where most of it came from, isn't all that complex. We still haven't found out where he kept all of his extra wealth. It could be as much as several years' income from all of the Roman-controlled areas here.

Ioannis shifted uncomfortably. Slaves often found it helpful to know secrets, but when your master told them to you, it usually meant trouble. As if reading his thoughts, Pilatus sighed and continued.

"Why am I telling you all this? Ah, well, Ioannis. The other slaves I'm sending over are far too ignorant to understand, or care, really. Little better than animals. But *you*. I'm sure you understand. You *must* understand about secrets. How to discover them, when to disclose them and to whom. That's why we're having this little conversation. I'm sure you understand."

"Yes, Master."

"Yes. So I'm giving you to the high priest, but a young man like you, Ioannis. How old are you? Probably early twenties. With your background and training, you could be a free citizen again—in the Roman army with an honorable commission, maybe a centurion, maybe even an officer. Only with the right friends, of course. One must always know who one's friends are. Am I right?"

"Yes, Master."

"Of course I'm right!" he said, slapping his knee, obviously very pleased with himself. "So go back to the slaves' quarters and get ready to go to the temple. But if you should hear anything that might be useful, which pertains to our conversation, I'm sure you'll know what to do."

Ioannis saluted again and left. Of course, he couldn't believe his luck when he had been assigned to Kaiapas's chief secretary. But after hearing Yehuda's words, he realized that it couldn't have been luck. Probably Pilatus had delivered Ioannis with a helpful suggestion about how to use him. Pilatus wouldn't have overlooked the information that Yehuda's last body-guard had recently been killed defending him. *A slave is always expendable, especially in the Roman army,* thought Ioannis grimly. After his father had been executed and his mother sold into slavery, Ioannis held no illusions about the virtues of the Roman empire or its rulers.

Yet whenever he remembered his father, he felt proud of his Roman blood. He was torn. What he knew of Roman politics from his father made him sick. When he came to Roman Palestine, he had decided that the only person he would trust was himself. *I am my only friend,* he reflected. *That rule has kept me alive so far. Yet when Yehuda took his chance and left Yerushalaim, he was fair enough to offer me a chance, too. That is unusual. But a door is still open back in Yerushalaim...*He looked over at Yehuda. Still breathing, it seemed. He could barely see any movement in the scribe's chest.

A few moments later, to Ioannis's relief, Yehuda opened his eyes and began to stretch. His eyes looked glazed, and as he stared at Ioannis, he looked through him, at some point in the middle of his forehead. *This is different,* thought Ioannis. *He is not totally here.* Yehuda spoke in a quiet, urgent voice.

"Ioannis. I know you know how to read and write. But I know your memory is even better. To save time, I'm going to dictate to you what happened while I was away. Don't ask any questions now. Just listen and memorize. I may forget all this later and need you to remember."

Ioannis looked quickly around them to make sure no one was in sight. All was quiet. Several bearded vultures circled just overhead, as if checking to see whether either of the men would be expiring soon. Ioannis shivered, but there was no more time to find a safer place. Yehuda had already begun speaking, the words rushing out.

"It is midnight. I am sitting under a tree in the Paneas gorge, next to a fire with my uncle, Shemuel. I hear the rushing of water from the sacred springs all around us. No one else is there. Shemuel is sitting hunched over, wearing a long robe with a hood. Suddenly he stands up, and his eyes blaze like fire. He calls:

The chariot is coming for me! The chariot is coming!
Do not go back to your home! Your home is burning!
Follow me. Find me. You were born for this.
What you are looking for is not lost!
What you have found is not worth looking for!
The treasure lies in the holiest place.
Beneath. In the darkness. In freedom.

"Then Shemuel vanishes, and I am wandering in the storage vaults underneath the temple with an oil lamp. As I wander farther in and descend into more passages, my light goes out. I realize I'm lost. Suddenly someone grasps my wrist, and the next thing I know, I am flying high over Yerushalaim. I fly north and see the Galilean Lake Kinneret beneath me. I fly just over the surface of the water toward a small fishing village on the upper west side of the lake. Nahum's village. I see all the fish in the lake swimming in the same direction, each with a pearl in its mouth. Then I wake up."

Yehuda continued to stare at Ioannis as if looking at a stone wall. Then his eyes gradually cleared until he was truly seeing Ioannis again.

"Did you get all that?" he asked, breathing hard.

"Yes, Yehuda," replied Ioannis, a bit relieved that the vision wasn't longer. *I hope he doesn't begin to make this a habit*, he thought.

"Then repeat it back to me, please."

Ioannis did so and then added, raising his hands in front of him, "But what does it all mean, Yehuda?" He hoped that there was some practical message buried in what seemed like nonsense to him.

"It means that Shemuel sent me a message, partly in the trance, but also before. That's what I was going to talk to him about. He sent me a letter two months ago, suggesting that I recopy an old, crumbling Aramaic manuscript in the temple vault. He said he forgot to do it before he retired. It was supposed to be a commentary on one of the Levitical law books. But when I finally had time and found the manuscript in the vault, the codex seemed in perfect condition. It didn't need recopying. As

I leafed through it, a scrap of newer parchment fell out. It was a short summary of the document in Shemuel's handwriting. In the middle of the summary, however, one phrase didn't make any sense, and it was clearly out of place. He had put exactly the same phrase in the letter he sent me. And it didn't make any sense there, either. Maybe the phrase was a code."

"What kind of code?" Ioannis asked, a bit disappointed that the subject had again turned to ancient manuscripts.

Yehuda raised his voice as he began to piece things together. "This is important, Ioannis! In Hebrew or Aramaic, each letter also corresponds to a number… one, two, three and so forth. If Shemuel had left me this message, it might be the key to what we call a *pesher*, a coded document. You line up the place of the letters in the sentence with a new sequence of numbers or letters and then retranslate the words in the document according to the substitution code. One word becomes another, you see. You need to find the key, of course, and the key could be in the strange phrase. I had begun to decipher it the day before I found the pearl. I took the codex with me, because I still hadn't made any sense of it."

"The vision I just received," continued Yehuda, waving his hands excitedly, "must be saying that there is a treasure buried under the temple, old Herodes's lost riches. When he began remodeling the temple before his death, he had many hidden passageways built and the architects killed. Very few people know about the hidden areas, and it's easy to get lost. The pesher might be a key to find the treasure! I can't imagine what the last part of the vision is about, though, with the Galilean lake and fish."

"Yehuda...about these trances," said Ioannis, look-ing away uncomfortably. "Aren't they just dreams? You have the pearl. We both have a chance for a new life. Shouldn't we just be getting on our way?"

"No, Ioannis!" said Yehuda pacing back and forth angrily. "I owe it to Shemuel to understand what he's telling me. Especially now that he's dead, or his flesh is, anyway. Some of our prophets become even more alive after they leave their flesh behind, so he could be sending me these visions directly. When I told you that he taught me everything, I didn't mention that he also taught me about visions and trances. It isn't part of the usual scribal training, but Shemuel told me that it is the most real part of our heritage. He had the visions, too. He told me that a few of our people must travel in the other worlds to receive messages to help the commu-nity. That's what our prophets really did, not predict the future."

Yehuda stepped toward Ioannis and put his hand on the younger man's arm, trying to convince him. "For the last hundred years," continued the scribe, "we've had the Herodes family, damned Idumeans from the south, sitting on us in one way or another. First old Herodes's father, Antipater, who tricked the Hasmoneans into calling in the Romans, and then Herodes and now his sons. The Romans killed a huge number of us after the old Herodes died. We were meant to be a free people, with no king! That's what Shemuel taught me. His namesake, Shemuel, in our history, was the last of the *shofetim*, the judges. These were ordinary men and women like Yoshua and Yhudit, temporary leaders who surfaced whenever our freedom was endangered, not permanent rulers.

But since then, for at least six hundred years, it's been all kings and captivity, the rich ruling the poor, in one form or another!"

"OK, OK, Yehuda," said Ioannis, patting him on the shoulder gently. "But that's the way the world works, isn't it? The rich and powerful rule, and we get along as best we can. Be practical. Look around you. What can we do about it? We're just two people."

"I'm not sure what we can do," said Yehuda. "But this vision means something. I need to find out what happened to Shemuel. Korah, the person I know in Taanach, might be able to help us. He knew Shemuel. He used to direct the guards in the temple before he returned home to his village. Then, after I see my brother in Sepphoris, we will talk to Shemuel's son up north in Paneas. Why did Shemuel leave home, and what was he doing in Megiddo?"

They headed up the path, and in the near distance, they saw a small village on a bluff.

"Taanach used to be a much bigger place, important in trading, almost as large as Megiddo was," said Yehuda, easing back into his comfortable habit of lecturing Ioannis, or just thinking out loud, perhaps. "The whole area was devastated by the Egyptians a thousand years ago, and then the Babylonians or maybe the Assyrians nearly finished it off a few hundred years later. It's been a small village since then. According to our history, the judge Yoshua gave Taanach to a branch of the *Lewiyyim*, the Levite family. Later, when the Babylonians invaded six hundred years ago and destroyed Shelomoh's temple in Yerushalaim, they didn't carry away the people in Taanach. They weren't rich or important enough. So the Levites who stayed behind were not part of the group that returned and set up the new temple in Yerushalaim a few generations later, when the Persians kicked out the Babylonians. The Judeans look down on the Samaritans here because they stayed behind and established their own traditions when there was no temple in Yerushalaim."

"And the Levites are who again?" Ioannis asked. "I'm not that acquainted with all the technical stuff of your temple and history. My mother wasn't that interested in it once she moved to Rome."

"The Levites are the descendants of Levi, one of the sons of Ya'aqub," said Yehuda patiently. "They're supposed to be the ritual experts, depending on what branch of the family they're from. Some were singers and chanters, some legal experts and some gatekeepers. The most privileged collected the annual tithe for the old temple. That's the official story, anyway. Shemuel told me that they were from the families of the old northern kingdom. After Moshe led us here, we had two kingdoms, north and south, which Dawid united for a while. But around seven hundred years ago, the Assyrians invaded the north, and some of their elite families and ritual experts fled south. They were absorbed into the Yerushalaim temple cult in the last years before the Babylonians conquered Judea, the southern kingdom. But of course, the Levites were considered second-class citizens even then, according to the fabricated history that Ezra later wrote. According to his 'official' story, they must have sinned for the Assyrians to conquer them. So today, the Levites mainly run the police force for the temple, or are still gatekeepers, or even worse, cleaners. The Judean elite who returned from Babylonia took all of the important and lucrative jobs.

Of course, the Maccabees, the Hasmoneans, replaced that group, and the Herodes family, who are Roman clients, replaced them. The priestly positions are some of the most profitable, you understand."

"Sure, just one elite after another," said Ioannis. "How is a priest who defrauds a poor man better than a king?"

"It wasn't supposed to be that way. That's why I left," said Yehuda. "When we get to the village, let me do the talking. We're in Samaria, always a bit of a wild place, even for a Galilean native like me. And when we find Korah, as I remember, he can be a bit volatile."

Too much information, thought Ioannis. He reached under his cloak. All it meant to him was: keep your sword and dagger handy.

Chapter 5

A Less-than-Warm Welcome

As they entered Taanach, Yehuda knew they were in trouble. It was midmorning, in early spring. The air was fresh with dew and the aroma of wild herbs and flowers. It was the kind of day when everyone should be out, including all of the chickens and goats. Instead, the lanes were dead quiet. Yehuda felt that they were being watched from the huts on either side of the path. *Someone should be up and about, either welcoming or challenging us*, he thought. Quiet was not good. Yehuda called out something in Aramaic, but they heard only silence. Finally, after several minutes, a very tall man in rags, looking unhappy, appeared from one of the huts they had passed.

"*Shalama*," said Yehuda in Aramaic. The tall man did not reply. That also was not promising. If the word *peace* did not elicit a response, thought Yehuda, they could only expect the opposite.

Ioannis didn't need to know the cultural background; he just watched the way the tall man held himself. It looked as if the stranger knew how to fight and was ready to, and Ioannis felt himself tensing.

"We're looking for Korah ben Izhar," said Yehuda, ignoring the man's failure to respond. "We're friends of his."

At the word *friends*, the tall man seemed to collapse internally. *A 'friend' means something more than just a personal acquaintance*, reflected Yehuda. In an interlocking web of patrons and clients, a friend was someone you shouldn't harm if you didn't want trouble from the friend of the friend, the patron. Ioannis relaxed also. *It seems like this Korah has some power around here*, the younger man thought.

"Villa at the top of the village," the man mumbled in a surly way. He turned away abruptly, not waiting for thanks.

"Good thing you mentioned Korah when you did, Yehuda," said Ioannis as they walked uphill. "That Samaritan looked ready to skin us alive. I guess it was our city clothing."

"Sometimes it's better not to wait for the *shalama*," Yehuda said dryly. "But yes, I suppose he did misidentify me as a Judean, even though I'm from Galilee. Probably couldn't place you exactly…from your features, that is."

"Thanks, Yehuda. I've never been called a half-breed so politely," said Ioannis.

"Don't mention it," said the scribe, smiling wryly. "Let's find Korah."

They headed farther uphill into the village. Around a corner they saw what looked like the largest house, with a high stone wall around it.

"It must be that one," said Yehuda. As soon as they neared the gate, three armed men appeared from within and challenged them with drawn swords. *Just one friendly experience after another in this village,* thought Ioannis.

"Shalama. We are friends of Korah ben Izhar," said Yehuda, again not waiting for a reply. "We would like to see him."

"Name?" asked the stockiest of the guards, biting off the word as if he could hardly spare it.

"Yehuda Tauma ben Yohanan. This is my body-guard, Yehohanan. Tell him we have news about Shemuel ben Yahayye, and it's important."

So I am back to being a bodyguard again, thought Ioannis. *At least I won't have to pretend to know about Idumean pottery or something like that.*

The stocky guard walked back inside while the other two watched Yehuda and Ioannis carefully. Ioannis eyed them closely in return, his hand resting on his sword, which he made slightly more visible. Two he could probably take if need be, he thought. Yehuda simply stood still, looking unperturbed.

After a few minutes, the first guard returned and motioned them through the gate to the front door of the house. The rest of the welcoming party put their swords away, relaxed and went back around the corner of the building, talking casually. Once through the door, two servants met Yehuda and Ioannis, bowed in front of them and presented a basin. The servants proceeded to wash the visitors' feet and then rubbed them with oil. *At least we aren't going to be attacked,* thought Ioannis. *They wouldn't have bothered with all this if we were.*

The preliminary hospitality over, the servants escorted the two into a large room in the middle of the villa. Mosaic tile in the Greek style, with symbolic pictures of the constellations, decorated the floor. Yehuda noticed some Roman slip pottery, or at least good imitations, on the table in front of them. Behind the table sat a short but very stout man with a dark beard dangling in ringlets. He was dressed in an expensive yellow linen robe over a black wool tunic. He looked bemused, neither overjoyed nor disturbed, to see the two.

"Yehuda, so it really *is* you?" rasped Korah, breathing heavily. "What are you doing so far from Yerushalaim? Aren't you afraid to go out into the countryside again? It can be a dangerous place, especially for anyone who looks like they might be collecting taxes, either for the temple or for the Romans."

"I'm not collecting anything," said Yehuda firmly. "I've quit the temple and am heading back to Zippori. I decided to stop and see you on the way. I know we were never that close in Yerushalaim, but you were a friend of my teacher, Shemuel."

"Finally come to your senses, have you?" said Korah. "The guard did say something about Shemuel. But first, who is this with you? He doesn't look familiar to me."

"This is Yehohanan, my bodyguard. His mother was Israelite, so by the old ways, he is too. He was a slave of the Romans for a while, but now he is free. We can talk in front of him."

"All right," said Korah, turning his hand over on the table and shrugging one of his large shoulders. "If you trust him. Probably safer for you if he knows everything that goes on." He gestured for the two to be seated in chairs on the other side of the table.

After both men sat, Yehuda leaned forward a bit. "Korah, on our way north, we found Shemuel's body lying near the road below Megiddo. He was dead." Yehuda stopped speaking suddenly and watched Korah's reaction. Ioannis observed him also. They were not that far away from the murder scene. Korah blanched. For the first time, his expression changed from what had been polite boredom, and he brought his right hand down hard on the table.

"No! How can it be?" he exclaimed angrily. "Why was he down this far south? I thought he was safely home in Paneas. His death is a huge loss to…well, to many people, friends…"

"So you don't know anything about it?" asked Yehuda evenly, continuing to watch him closely. "I notice that you keep a secure camp here. More than I would expect an ex-temple Levite to have."

Korah levered himself to his feet and began pacing back and forth behind the desk. "Then you haven't been out and around very much," he replied sharply. "As you know, this village was given to my ancestors by the early Israelite judges. All of the other tribes got territory, but the Levites only received grants of stray villages here and there. We were supposed to serve the temple in Yerushalaim full time, and the rest of the community would support us. That was the *idea*. But then Moshe's community split, and we were part of the northern kingdom. Later, some of us were called Samaritans, as though it were a curse! We were pushed out when the priestly offices in Yerushalaim became colonial plums under the Persians. Then came the Egyptians and the Syrians, who fought each other for Alexander's leavings. Then the Maccabees, the Hasmoneans, who were worse, because they were supposed to be 'our own people.' Bah! They destroyed our original temple on Mount Gerizim here. Judeans! They made such a mess of things that Herodes and his lot were able to bring the Romans in to help them keep order. And the Romans always come to stay, never just to help."

Korah sat back down at the table, collapsing into his oversized chair. He sighed and grimaced. "So yes, I'm now a headman in a nowhere place in Samaria, and even though my ancestors have been here for eight hundred years, we're still incomers. The people here are a mix of old families from way before the captivities, some with Canaanite blood. They used to practice human sacrifice, you know," he said, shuddering. "If my family and I didn't hold things together, they would all fall to fighting each other over the little bit left after the Romans take the lion's share and the priests down in Yerushalaim try to take the rest. I don't enforce the temple tax. But outside of juggling my reports about how many people live here, I can't do anything about the Romans and their extortion. They're too efficient, so I have to collect it to keep my life livable. That means I have to have some protection, and I have taught people in the village to appear like the Roman ideal of a typical Samaritan—dangerous, unfriendly and unstable."

Korah leaned toward Yehuda, his eyes bulging. "Anyway, how can you suspect me of having anything to do with Shemuel's death? I was on *his* side. Didn't he tell you?"

"What do you mean?" asked Yehuda, looking confused. "I didn't know Shemuel had a side. He was a scribe—as I am, or was—trying to keep our heritage alive in the best way he knew how. He wasn't involved in politics."

"No? Are you sure?" asked Korah, half closing his eyes. "Didn't he tell you about the chariot?"

"Chariot? What chariot? That's just a vision-image from our prophets, like Eliyah. A teaching tool to help students visualize the realm of God coming to earth."

"All right. Forget I mentioned it," said Korah, changing the subject quickly. "What happened to Shemuel's body?"

"We only found it early this morning, and then some Roman cavalry showed up," said Yehuda, still keeping his matter-of-fact tone. "They took the body back to the garrison while we hid, and then we headed this way. I thought you might know why he was down here."

"Didn't I already ask you that?" said Korah, pointing at the scribe angrily. "Look! I was a friend of Shemuel. Despite being from different families, Shemuel and I shared many of the same interests. He wanted to bring back a simpler life, closer to that of our ancestors before all of the kings appeared. Unless you're an elite, life has never been that great for anyone here since we started having kings. That's the problem. That's why we've had one empire after another squeezing us dry for the past seven hundred years."

"I agree, and I am sorry," said Yehuda, looking down. "Shemuel was my uncle, my adopted father, as well as my teacher, so I am still upset. There were no tracks near his body, and thieves didn't kill him. The knife wound done with a stilleto told us that, and he still had silver and jewelry with him. Then I had a vision on the way here. Him being at Megiddo was not an accident."

"A vision?" asked Korah with raised eyebrows. "Personally, I don't know about that kind of thing. That was Shemuel's world. I am only interested in the results. So what do you plan to do now?" asked Korah.

"You knew him. Can't you give me any help?" pleaded Yehuda. "I am going to see his son in Paneas after I see my brother in Sepphoris."

Korah relaxed a bit and looked at Yehuda with compassion. "Yes, I can, Yehuda. Shemuel was a very old friend. His son Mikhael…he's an odd one, as far as I'm concerned. But he has to be told, so the body can be recovered from the Romans and buried properly. I'll send a messenger to the commander at the garrison today. He knows me, and he owes me a few favors in return for extra supplies I procure for him personally. I'll send another man to Mikhael also. If I were you, I'd ask Mikhael what Shemuel was studying or writing just before he left. Probably he won't know, but his reaction might be interesting. Shemuel knew how to keep secrets. One other thing…you said that Shemuel was still wearing jewelry…"

"Yes," said Yehuda, fishing around in his knapsack. "He was wearing this silver talisman."

Korah took the chain with the small hand from Yehuda and looked it over slowly. Then he handed it back, pointing to something on the reverse side.

"What do you make of this inscription?" Korah asked in a slow, even voice.

"I didn't really notice it," Yehuda responded, looking at the amulet. "I suppose it's just the silversmith's mark. But yes, I see, too many letters for that. They're Aramaic letters, anyway: A-L-H-W-A-L-Sh, *alhwalsh*. Not any word I can think of."

"Yes, strange, isn't it?" said Korah, looking at Yehuda curiously. "Anyway, before you go, please stay for a meal. It is time for me to eat, and I insist you join me. You look hungry." He clapped his hands, and another servant appeared. Korah asked for the midday meal to be brought, and the servant rushed off, calling out some orders to those in the rear of the house.

"If you need to wash your hands again, please do," said Korah casually. "I don't know where you stand on that issue. For ordinary food, I don't bother. But I know that some of your scribal brothers consider all meals sacred and wash their hands and sometimes their feet before eating, even if they are clean already."

"Yes, I've heard that, too," Yehuda responded. "Some extreme group living near the Dead Sea. I think Shemuel mentioned them, but I never paid that much attention. I'm not one of them."

In a few minutes, half a dozen servants reappeared with wine, olives, bread, smoked fish and fresh Phoenician pomegranates. As they ate, Yehuda and Korah conversed in Aramaic, and Ioannis was just as happy that they did. He could understand a bit of his mother's language if he put his mind to it. At the moment, though, he preferred not to so he could concentrate better on the meal. The wine was excellent, and it was good to have something besides the trail food they had been living on for the past two days. He was beginning to feel almost human. If Yehuda had friends like this along the way, or better yet, "family," maybe they could make it out of the empire to something resembling a new life. When they had almost finished, Korah began to speak Greek again and glanced sideways at Ioannis, although he was still speaking to Yehuda.

"Excuse me for asking, Yehuda. But, as I know from Shemuel, your birth family didn't leave you with much, and Shemuel had very little in that way. So why did you quit the temple, and how do you expect to live?"

"I was just fed up with my work," replied Yehuda carefully. "I knew too many secrets. Too much information that made we wonder why I had agreed to spend my life there. Shemuel convinced me that I could do some good at the temple, but frankly, it seems hopeless.

The priests no longer have any sacred function. They're just glorified tax collectors, and most of what they are supposed to sacrifice, they keep for themselves. As far as how I'll live, I just trust in the Unseen One, I suppose."

"Yes, that would be the way," Korah said slowly. "Look, maybe I can help you. I was disillusioned with the temple too when I quit. But if you know the high priest's secrets, he won't let you go so easily. He will send spies after you. You will either need an armed camp, like I keep here, or plan to get 'lost.' Your hill country of northern Galilee is relatively good for that. Better yet, get out of the empire entirely. But even for that, you need friends. People who feel the same way we do. Shemuel knew some people who can help you. They know how and when to appear and disappear, to be heard or not heard."

Korah reached inside his robe and brought out a small chain with something on the end of it, a small silver hand.

He handed it to Yehuda, who looked at it in surprise. It seemed identical to the amulet that Yehuda had taken from Shemuel's body. Just to be sure, Yehuda checked in his own robe, but Shemuel's amulet was still there. The scribe looked back at Korah. "But what…?"

"Yes. It means something, Yehuda. A-L-H-W-A-L-Sh, the first letters in Aramaic for: *ayna la hazor wa adna la shemat*. 'What eye has not seen and what ear has not heard.' Sometimes the best protection is to disappear. But who or what disappears? You were Shemuel's closest student. Maybe he was coming south to see you, to tell you something. Did he write to you recently?"

"He did," Yehuda admitted, startled. He paused for a few breaths, sighed and then continued. He had decided to trust Korah. "He wrote to me about recopying an old Aramaic commentary on one of the Levitical texts. In his letter, he described the importance of the text for our culture and heritage, all the usual encouragements he used to give me, so I hardly paid attention. Then he added words that didn't make sense, and I found the same words in a short summary he had inserted into the manuscript he asked me to find: 'Learn what eye has not seen and what ear has not heard.'"

Chapter 6
Secrets

Korah leaned back in his chair, clasped his hands over his large belly and then closed his eyes. When he opened them again, he leaned toward Yehuda, beads of sweat appearing on the Levite's brow.

"Listen to me carefully, Yehuda. I'm sure you are intelligent enough to know that none of these things are coincidences. I am going to trust you, and may the Holy One preserve us both if I'm wrong. I will help you find out what happened to Shemuel if I can. For safety's sake, I seldom leave my house, but I have friends in various places with very good ears. You need to do your part, too. I am sure now that Shemuel was coming south to see you, and someone found out about it. Shemuel was not a simple scribe. He was part of a larger family of people who believe that we can change our lives for the better and free ourselves from the endless round of oppressors. As you probably know, there are many clans or family groups like mine. Some are bandits, some are people who follow those who say they are prophets, or who claim to be messiahs—"anointed" to lead Israel out of the mess we're in, mostly by armed rebellion. But Shemuel continued an ancient line that uses real power. Power from the unseen world as well as practical power in this one. You were one of his people in the vision world, it seems. Didn't Shemuel tell you any of this?"

"No, he didn't," said Yehuda, shaking his head stubbornly. "Why wouldn't he tell me about some secret group of people dedicated to changing the world, if he were part of it? I can't believe it. I don't believe it!"

"He wasn't just part of it. He was the head of it, my friend!" insisted Korah. "Whatever you believe or don't believe, it's important that we find out what Shemuel wanted to happen next if he were no longer here. Don't you want to know? Go to Paneas. Do what you can to find out, and keep me informed. I will find out what I can through my people also."

Yehuda felt all of his plans slipping away. He had made a clean break, or so he thought, from the temple and his whole past life. He had hoped the pearl in his knapsack was the ticket to a new life. And now Korah was dragging him back into the same mess again, only it was even more complicated. Should he trust Korah? Yehuda closed his eyes briefly and imagined that he was sitting and looking into Shemuel's eyes, as they used to do before their lessons together. He saw the old scribe nodding his head and smiling.

"All right," said Yehuda. "I owe at least that much to my teacher. I will find out where he was going and what he wanted to happen after his death. I still don't believe this whole secret-society business, but maybe I can discover something at Shemuel's house. How was Shemuel's work supposed to change things here? What was he, or this group, planning to do, exactly?"

"I can't help you there," replied Korah, shrugging helplessly. "Not because I don't want to, but because I can't. Shemuel was the key to it all. He worked in the other worlds to bring back the vision, and then told the rest of us what we were supposed to do and when. But each of us only knew pieces of information, not the whole picture. He said that the web of families we were involved in was called the *merkabah*, the chariot. I supplied him with specific information that he wanted, mostly about the disposition of the Roman positions in Samaria. I never knew the whole picture or everyone who was involved. Shemuel held everything together himself. If there was someone else, I don't know who it could be. But why did he direct you to that particular manuscript in the temple archives? Don't you have any idea?"

"It's obvious, isn't it?" answered Yehuda. "When old Herodes rebuilt the temple, he added a new artificial hill under it with many secret passages. Most of them still haven't been discovered. People have gotten lost down there and died trying to find where he might have hidden some sort of treasure."

"Sure, I know that old story," said Korah. "I thought it was just the Herodes family boasting as usual. It could be true. Old Herodes stole so much money that in his will he could leave Caesar and his family a whole year's wealth from Iudaea—one thousand five hundred talents, a million or so in silver—just as a good-bye gift. There's also the question of how he managed the cost of rebuilding the temple, or Caesarea on the coast, or his many fortresses. He could have stashed wealth any-where, or maybe everywhere. He was so crazy at the end that he wouldn't even care if no one ever found it. No wonder the Romans divided his kingdom in three. If his sons had inherited his grandiose paranoia, they would have given the empire no end of trouble. The Romans really only want these lands as a buffer against the Parthians to the east. Anything else is a bonus. They don't want to waste a lot of resources on a place that is only a border, a middle ground, a "middle east." Sure, it's another of their many income streams, but compared to Syria and Egypt, it can't amount to much. So you think that manuscript may be the key to some of Herodes's hidden treasure, if it really exists?"

"Maybe," replied the younger man, looking out the window behind Korah. "But part of me doesn't really want to know. I just want to leave the empire and start another life. Maybe I'll go to Parthia and try being a trader. I like to talk, and I like to travel."

"Don't be ridiculous, Yehuda!" exclaimed Korah, raising both hands in exasperation. "Is that what Shemuel trained you for? Where is your loyalty to our land and our people?"

"I could ask you that as well," replied Yehuda, looking back at Korah and frowning. "You sit here comfortably in your fortress as the headman of a village. You got out of the temple. That's all I want to do, too!"

"OK, let's leave it there, Yehuda," said Korah soothingly. "We shouldn't argue. But if we did find old Herodes's treasure, it could fund a proper revolution. We could not only arm the men ready to rise against Rome, we could buy enough men from outside the empire, from Nabataea or Arabia, to defeat them. That's what the Romans do when they wage a real war, hire men. If we did the same, we could drive them out, once and for all. There are plenty of us who would give everything we had if we knew we had a fighting chance. I know that some of Shemuel's students in Nazara were working with their relatives in Batanea east of the Yarden River, people there are skilled with horses and weapons."

Since it was already midafternoon, Korah recommended that the two stay the night, but Yehuda wanted to be on his way north. He was impatient to fulfill his promise, to find out what happened to Shemuel and then leave as soon as possible. Korah offered to send some of his men with them until they had crossed the Jezreel Valley and were safely into Galilee. With luck they could do it by nightfall, camping in the foothills. Then they would have only a short hike to Sepphoris the next day.

As they left the villa, Ioannis asked Yehuda, "So you're sure you can trust this Korah? It's still possible that he had something to do with your teacher's murder. He had the means and the men, and he's nearby. Maybe he's just trying to distract you for some reason."

"Yes, I know that. You're right, Ioannis," replied Yehuda. "But we have to head north anyway, and he's not suggesting that we do anything I wasn't going to do already. All this about a secret society and the silver amulet puts things in a different light, though."

"Korah must be a member of that secret society, isn't he?" asked Ioannis. "He had one of the amulets. But if he is, why couldn't he tell you more that would help, rather than just offer up vague suggestions?"

"I don't know," said Yehuda. "The amulet could, of course, have been planted on Shemuel. I don't remember seeing it before. But Korah has given us some real help." Yehuda nodded to Korah's three armed men walking ahead of them, the same three that had met them at the gate.

"If it is help and not an ambush," said Ioannis grudgingly. As they walked through the village, he decided that he would have a talk with their guard while it was still daylight. *Will we need guarding* from *them?* he wondered. At least he could assess how capable they would be in a fight against him. At best, he might find out something that could help him and Yehuda.

As they descended from Taanach back through the foothills toward Megiddo and the valley, Ioannis quickened his pace until he was walking alongside the three guards. They weren't saying anything to each other, and his presence didn't seem to make them any more talkative. He decided to wait a bit before speaking, and he fell into step with them. One thing Ioannis had learned in the Roman legion was that men who marched together, in rhythm, were more likely to trust each other. After walking about a *mille*, they still hadn't said a word, so he decided to try a question or two.

"So," said Ioannis. "Korah a good chief to work for, then?" asking the usual question that servants and slaves first asked each other. They did not open discussions with questions about the weather, because it didn't matter to slaves. Life was what it was, good or bad, depending on the masters' treatment.

"Not bad," the portly one replied. They walked another hundred paces in silence. Then he asked, "Yours?"

If this one rations his food the way he rations his words, he would be as skinny as a ghost, Ioannis thought. Still, it was something.

"Not bad," he replied. "You know how it is with these temple or ex-temple types. You been with Korah long?"

"My family has served with his family for centuries," the portly man replied proudly, touching his fist to his chest. "I am Shimeon ben Itzak. We come from these hills; this is *our* land."

Ah, yes, the subject of honor and land will always make a man here more talkative, thought Ioannis. *I suppose it wasn't so different with Romans.*

"So you were with Korah in Yerushalaim, when he was at the temple?" Ioannis asked casually, hoping he could wring a few more details out of Shimeon.

"My father and then me," Shimeon replied. "We were farmers, but Korah trusted us and saw that we could help protect him, so he made us bodyguards, soldiers for the Levites. Our uncles and brothers continue to work the land. We share everything in common, as was the old Israelite way."

"Probably a better life as a bodyguard," Ioannis agreed easily. "Not so much physical labor. But there's danger…"

"Yes, a bit," Shimeon said. "Several people have tried to kill Korah, but my father and I stopped them all," he bragged.

"Clearly!" Ioannis said enthusiastically, inviting him to go further. "Why would a Levite be in any danger? Was it an honor or money thing?"

"Honor? No, not on your life! Korah's family has always been held in the highest regard in this part of Samaria—like my family. And yes, Korah is wealthy, but he has always done right by those in his larger family, which includes us—me and my two cousins," he said, gesturing to the two young men who were now on the other side of Ioannis as they walked together. They were listening proudly to their older cousin hold forth.

"So what was it, then?" Ioannis pressed a bit further. "As a bodyguard, I like to know the danger I'm up against, and I expect you do, too."

"Oh, yes," agreed Shimeon. "But it's always the same danger. The Romans, or people who collaborate with them." He glanced suspiciously at Ioannis.

"Yes, I hate the damn Romans," said Ioannis with feeling. "They killed my father and sold my mother and me into slavery." *Well, it's the truth,* he thought. He didn't have to tell them that his father was Roman.

"So you know," said Shimeon. "But what about your master? I'm told he was working for the high priest. These so-called priests have been betraying us to our oppressors for centuries. It's all a sham."

"My master has quit the temple," Ioannis said. "Same reason. So you don't go there for the festivals?"

"To the Yerushalaim Temple? I'd rather go to Gehenna, where they used to sacrifice babies in the time of the damned Judean kings. We go to Mount Gerizim, our own sacred place. It doesn't matter that there's no building there now. It's where we've worshipped for more than five hundred years. The high places in nature have always been the holiest. They don't require buildings, or maintenance, or a bunch of priests leeching our blood year after year."

"But you worked for Korah at the temple in Yerushalaim, I guess."

"Of course, because that's where our master was working," said Shimeon. "He was doing things there, undermining the priests and trying to help our people in secret."

"OK, I got it," Ioannis said. "And your two cousins were there, too?"

"No, they're young, just fresh from the village. I'm still training them, but they're fit and willing. Don't worry. We'll get you safely across the Jezreel Valley. The Romans patrol there often, but we know when and where they usually travel, as well as the trails they use. Also, they don't usually bother a small Samaritan group heading into Galilee. They have their eyes out for groups going the other way—smugglers and bandits. We're not on that list of theirs, so they don't bother us. The Romans are really very lazy. I'm surprised they have an empire."

For Shimeon, that was almost a philosophical sermon, thought Ioannis. He decided to leave his questioning at that. It seemed they were in safe enough hands, unless Shimeon were a lot better at dissembling than Ioannis thought he was. Which he doubted.

Ioannis ambled along with them for a while longer. They did get into the subject of the weather, plus the crops in Samaria, and what food he and Yehuda could expect to find on their way north, either in the villages or on the land itself. By that time they were almost back at Megiddo and the Great Plain, but this time farther to the west than Yehuda and Ioannis had been. They came to another bluff overlooking the valley and sat down to rest a bit. Shimeon and his cousins surveyed the valley beneath for activity, as Ioannis casually walked over to sit beside Yehuda.

"We can trust them, Master," Ioannis said quietly. "I've had a talk with them."

"Yes, I know, Ioannis," said Yehuda evenly. "I have been breathing and looking into their hearts. They are good men." He glanced at Ioannis, who looked a bit disappointed. Then Yehuda added, smiling, "Of course, I'm interested in what they said."

Shimeon was clearly in a hurry and motioned for them to continue almost immediately. As they walked down into the valley, Ioannis repeated the entire conversation quietly for Yehuda. By the time he finished, they were midway across, and the sun was nearly to the horizon in the west. They had just crossed the Kishon

River, which ran through the western part of the valley, when instinctively Ioannis looked back east toward where they had found Shemuel's body. He stopped short. Another cloud of dust was nearing them, arriving from the direction of the Roman garrison.

Chapter 7
Intelligence

Earlier that afternoon High Priest Yauseph Qayapha was napping in his chambers at the temple. A knock on his door interrupted a particularly pleasant dream of him being surrounded by heavenly angels, all of whom looked a bit like his wife's beautiful new maidservant. As a member of the Zaduqya sect, the Sadducees, he wasn't supposed to believe in angels, he thought, shaking himself awake, but he might make an exception for this one.

Upon entering his chambers, one of his secretaries announced that a temple Levite identifying himself only as a "close family member" wished to see him immediately. Qayapha motioned disgustedly for the scribe to admit the man, who entered a few moments later.

"Yes, Sakaryut? Why are you bothering me in the middle of the day? I told you to only come here in the evening, when most people on my staff have gone home."

"Sacred Father, I would disturb you only in a situation of extreme necessity," replied the man. Of medium height, medium build and with medium-length brown hair, his features made it difficult to identify him as a Samaritan, Galilean, Judean or Idumean. Despite his unremarkable appearance, he stood confidently before the high priest as if he were the equal to any man. As a Levite, Sakaryut felt himself the elder of any of the newcomer priests who came to the temple after the Persians sent Ezra to refurbish it.

Impertinence personified, thought Qayapha. *Yet if one saw this man a dozen times at close range, one might still miss him in a crowd.* Whether by design or the luck of family blood, he was excessively average looking.

Sakaryut continued speaking without waiting for acknowledgement to proceed, as might befit an inferior.

"Honored Sir, a year or so ago, you asked me to keep an eye on your personal scribe and secretary, Yehuda Tauma."

"I know that, Sakaryut. After Pilatus imposed various gifts on me, including a new bodyguard for Yehuda, I became worried about all of the secrets the man knows, mostly secrets of the temple, and some to do with my personal affairs. Which are also God's work, of course."

"Of course, Father. You should know, then, that two days ago, Yehuda left Yerushalaim with his bodyguard and headed north on the Via Maris toward Samaria."

"I know that already. He left a message for me saying that he was going to visit his brother on a family matter for a few days."

"Sir, what do you know of Yehuda's relationship with his brother? From what I discovered by asking around, Yehuda hasn't seen him in a decade at least. They are hardly on friendly terms."

"Now that you mention it, Sakaryut, I do know his brother a bit. We have certain, ah, dealings together, and in return for a modest allotment of my friendship, he collects a bit of temple tax for us up there in Galilee. Most of his peasants don't support us, of course. They believe we're betraying Moshe or some such nonsense. But in Zippori, where he heads one of our loyal elite families, there are many who understand the moderating influence that the temple has on Roman rule for the average villager in the whole land of Israel."

Qayapha stretched out his arms effusively and then remembered that he was not speaking to a crowd of Israelites, potential contributors. He looked closely at the spy. "You're right. His brother is a very different sort of person from our Yehuda. Although Yehuda is good with numbers and that sort of thing, I'd prefer that he had a bit more of his brother's practical intelligence when it comes to contemporary political challenges and the many ways they can be met by applying the appropriate financial incentives."

"Bribes, you mean, Sacred Father," interjected Sakaryut drolly.

"Yes, ah, just so. In any case, perhaps it would be best if you trailed after Yehuda a bit. If you can't find him immediately, then I'd like you to remain in Galilee on another little errand. This actually cropped up at just the right moment. There is yet another prophet up in Galilee saying slanderous things about us here. Perhaps you could drop in on this prophet and see what is really going on. Name of Yohanan, from what I hear. Between the Hasmoneans and their kin, we've had enough Yohanans to last a lifetime…always troublemakers, if you ask me."

"Happy to do it, Father. Shall we follow the usual arrangements, including my standard extra compensation for frontier work?"

"Oh, all right, yes! I swear, what one has to pay for proper intelligence these days is just outrageous…"

Not coincidentally, on the same day, one of Prefect Pilatus's informers was giving a similar report concerning Ioannis to his superior. But in this case, the spy was standing at full attention, afraid to move a muscle out of place.

"Do you want me to follow him, Prefect?"

"No, no. He may return; he may not. It was always a long shot anyway whether the little half-breed could dig anything of value out of that nest of religious charlatans over there at the temple. We can't waste our time and the emperor's resources if there is no reasonable reward in sight. First, report all this to my aide-de-camp, Aristeaus. Tell him to send word to our friends in the north to keep an eye out for a Yerushalaim scribe and his bodyguard stumbling through the great hinterland of Israel. The gods help them! That will be all."

＊＊＊

"Tetrarch, sir, honored of the Holy One, there has been an incident in the valley below Megiddo."

"Megiddo? That ruin?" asked Herodes Antipas, looking down at his chief minister, the Roman advisor Gaius Metallus, from his throne in Tiberias on Lake Kinneret. "I didn't think that was in our territory. How is it a problem of ours?"

"It is not, of course, tetrarch. But it *is* just on our border. And the victim of what seems to be murder was a well-known resident of Paneas in your brother Philipos's territory just to the north."

"I know where my brother Philipos's territory is, you idiot! If it weren't for my insane father, the damned Romans probably would have given all of Israel to me to rule. Excuse me," Antipas said, flapping his arms around him. "I know you're Roman and that Rome sent you to help me, but how much can you divide a little land like this? My brother, Archelaos, of course, was clearly incompetent and had to be removed. And Philipos has always been a bit too close to the Parthians, if you ask me. So if there were any justice, it should have all come to me. Anyway, what do you mean by *well known resident*? Was he some kind of revolutionary, or terrorist?"

"He was a retired scribe, my liege," explained Metallus patiently. "He was found stabbed to death this morning at Megiddo."

"A retired scribe, Metallus!" Antipas slapped the arms his throne in exasperation. "Why are you bothering me about some secretary-cum-historian who didn't even live in my territory and was murdered in Samaria? Sometimes I wonder why our friends in Rome sent you to be my chief minister…I mean, really!"

"But some of these scribes, sire…"

"Oh, yes, yes. There has been a bit of trouble in the past." Antipas shrugged. "Renegade scribes with underground networks reciting arcane incantations to bring about some kind of divine judgment on their betters. A lot of superstitious nonsense, if you ask me. Nothing ever really came of it, did it?"

Metallus persisted. His job was to prevent Rome having to send in more troops due to one of its client kings' incompetence. "The people can be easily roused by some of these so-called prophets, my tetrarch, as you know from the past."

"Yes, yes…but a prophet, not someone with his nose in a scroll most of the time. Anyway, he's dead now, so one less to worry about… Antipas scratched his head, as though trying to remember something. Finding it, he raised a finger. "But, Metallus, what's this I'm hearing about someone down at the bottom of the lake where the Yarden flows out? I hear he's pushing people under the water and then, when they're good and confused, yelling to them about redemption and judgment and corruption in high places, meaning me. That sounds like torturing my subjects and brainwashing them into sedition. Get me a report on what's happening down there as soon as you can!"

Just what I was trying to tell him, thought Metallus, sighing to himself. He bowed to Antipas with a wry smile and left the throne room.

Chapter 8
Speaking and Listening

Shimeon had also seen the cloud of dust. "Let's just keep moving," he said. "We don't have anything to be afraid of. I know these people, and they know Korah. He's a good friend of the garrison commander."

That meant, thought Ioannis, *that Korah paid a substantial enough bribe, probably in wine or other smuggled luxuries, to guarantee the safety of his family.* Ioannis still had a feeling of foreboding, however. As a half-dozen horse soldiers rode into view, the five men kept walking across the plain. Ioannis looked toward the Galilean hills, which were only about two Roman *millia* away.

The captain of the troop rode up to the group and stopped in front of Shimeon. The other five stretched a bit in their saddles and then unsheathed and resheathed their swords. *Five against six,* thought Ioannis. But the six had horses, a big advantage unless Simeon was an even better fighter than he had boasted.

"My friend, you're out a bit late today with your cousins, aren't you?" asked the captain in a proud voice.

"We know our way around," said Shimeon proudly in return. "Our ancestors have been here for a thousand years."

Mistake, thought Ioannis. *Romans don't like to be reminded that they are far from home and not wanted in places they end up conquering. Their little peninsula is not that much larger than this country, after all.*

The captain ignored the gibe. "Yes, I suppose you do. But who are these two men with you? I don't recognize them. They're not part of your family, are they? Their clothing looks like they are from the south."

Shimeon looked a bit nervous.

Romans love that nervous look, thought Ioannis. *Shimeon should have spent more time playing cards. Now what would he say?* Ioannis began to think that Shimeon's fighting skills might be tested after all.

"Look, you know how things work," said Shimeon, trying to reassert himself. "The friends of Korah are our friends. Your commander is also a friend of Korah. We don't want any trouble. We're just taking our friends from the south over into Galilee to visit their relatives."

"So they *are* from the south? Where in the south?" asked the commander sharply.

This Roman doesn't miss anything, thought Ioannis.

"You know, we had word from the prefect in Yerushalaim to watch out for any suspicious persons who left Yerushalaim in the past day or so," the commander said.

Ioannis thought the commander was bluffing, but Shimeon again looked stumped. He was clearly out of his depth negotiating with Romans. Korah must have handled that side of things himself. *So here we go,* thought Ioannis, flexing his wrist. He looked over at the two cousins. They didn't look ready for a sword fight with six mounted Roman professionals. What to do when outnumbered and outmatched? According to his boyhood Roman army training, he should pray to Mithras, a popular new sun god who helped soldiers in difficulty. Ioannis wished that he had paid more attention to the necessary chant when they had learned it.

Just as he looked over to Yehuda, the scribe had already stepped forward.

"Hail, Caesar!" he called confidently in high Latin. "Captain, my name is Yehuda ben Yohanan, and I am the chief secretary of High Priest Kaiapas of Jerusalem. My bodyguard and I have come north on a personal mission to do with my family. Korah, and *these* men," he said, gesturing rhythmically back and forth more times than necessary to Shimeon and his cousins, "have offered their help to us. We know that bandits plague the Great Plain, and that the noble Roman army cannot be expected to deal with all of the brigand groups that infest our country." He continued to move his hand back and forth, pointing to all of the Romans. "That is why the prefect in Jerusalem works closely with the high priest to maintain order in the country."

The captain nodded, looking a bit dazed, and waited for Yehuda to continue. *That's a good sign,* thought Ioannis. *That means he knows he's outclassed in terms of status and protocol.* Ioannis noticed that during his speech, Yehuda had gradually shuffled around so that the Roman captain was looking into the setting sun, with Yehuda's face in the shadows.

"So," continued Yehuda in a slow, rhythmic and monotonous voice, "we are extremely grateful that you have stopped us to make sure that we cross the Great Plain safely. All hail, Caesar."

The Romans responded, "All hail!"

Yehuda continued without taking a breath. "We can assure you that if we see anyone who looks suspicious, we will send word back with these men, whom you know already, or through Korah, whom your commander knows, so then you will know everything that needs to be known. Hail, Caesar."

"Hail, Caesar!" the Romans replied.

"There are so many dangers in the world when there is no law and order, and we understand that you are only upholding the great principles of Roman order and society, for which we are grateful. We are, of course, not the sort of men you are looking for, not bandits; we do not know them, and we do not ever want to know them, and we do not want to remember them in case we do meet them. Hail, Caesar."

From his side, Ioannis could see that Yehuda had said the last words while looking directly at the Roman commander's chest, where his heart would be, rather than into his eyes. *To the Roman, it probably seems like Yehuda is being deferential,* thought Ioannis. But Ioannis noticed that Yehuda's eyes were a little crossed and that his voice sounded different from his usual speaking voice, like an incantation. His long speech in complicated, official Latin had caused the commander's eyes to glaze over.

The Roman captain shook his head a bit as if to clear it. "Uh, hail, Caesar. Yes, well…not remember… you're clearly not bandits…not the men we're looking for," he said. "We should be on our way to patrol, to keep order…Hail, Caesar!" He turned his horse abruptly, and the rest of his men followed him as they rode further west.

Shimeon and his cousins looked a bit stunned. They hadn't understood the language, but they saw how the Roman reacted. They turned to Yehuda and nodded with renewed respect.

"You'd be dangerous in the Roman Senate, Master," said Ioannis. "Is that what they teach you in scribe school? How to outtalk the Romans?"

"The Romans have been here for nearly a hundred years, Ioannis," replied Yehuda. "So, yes, learning the words they respect or fear is how we have adapted and learned to survive. But the language is only part of it. It doesn't work without training the voice and breath a bit, which we do for our ritual chants. Admittedly, using my voice as I just did was manipulative. But judging our chances of survival in a fight, it seemed the most humane thing to do. Even if we had defeated them, there are many more Romans where they came from. We need to move, as Korah said, unseen and unheard. Also, I only told them the truth, although not all of it. We don't *know* that they were looking for us. As Shemuel once told me, the partial truth told in a boring, hypnotic manner is the easiest way to defeat a mind habituated to obeying commands in an empire."

The group hiked on until they entered the foothills just over the border of Galilee. There was no border outpost, but they were now in Herodes Antipas's territory. So in addition to the Romans, they also needed to be on the lookout for any of his men. By this time, the sky had begun to turn dark. Shimeon and his cousins found a campsite they had used in the past and started a fire. From their shoulder sacks, they produced a leg of lamb they had brought with them and began to roast it. Ioannis helped them set up camp, which consisted of unrolling some blankets and gathering brush wood for the fire. Everyone was in good humor after the successful encounter with the Romans.

A short while later, Ioannis sat down by the fire, contentedly munching on a piece of the lamb. *Life could be bearable with the right friends*, he thought. *Maybe these Israelites are not all uncivilized peasants.* Then he checked himself. He was part Israelite, after all. He thought again of his mother and began to feel very sad. He usually tried to avoid thinking about her for that very reason, but something in this countryside seemed to remind him of her. She had said she was from the "mountains in the north." There were some foothills here, but in the dying light, Ioannis had seen the ridges of higher peaks in the distance farther north. Maybe this was part of *his* home, too. He looked at Shimeon and his cousins with envy. *They are simple men, but at least they know where their home and family are. What do I have? No home, no family, no purpose.*

After he had eaten with the others, Yehuda sat by himself looking out over the Jezreel Valley with its many wheat fields. The main sowing had taken place five months ago, and then another late sowing took place during a break in the winter rains. By now some of the crops would be ripe enough for the animals. *Only the late-spring rains are needed to make them full enough for us children of Adam and Hewa.* The moon was rising, still a waxing crescent.

Yehuda remembered all the times he had sat with Shemuel under the same rising crescent moon. Once they had traveled a half day south from Paneas to the area around Lake Merom, a dense, uninhabited wetland. It was one of the areas called in Aramaic *madbara*, wilderness, someplace where human beings didn't live. He loved it. Shemuel had first taken him there as a young man, after a particularly intense period of studying sacred texts. He remembered that the sun had set and the waxing moon had begun to rise early, just as it did tonight.

"I want you to stop thinking and just listen, Yehuda," Shemuel had said. "Listen to the sound of the water, the wind in the reeds, the birdsong, animals, snakes, nature around you. Don't be overwhelmed. First isolate each sound and listen to each with the ear of your heart. When you have made friends with each one, then begin to bring the sounds together. This chorus is the real sacred scroll." They spent some time listening, and then Shemuel had continued:

"All your study of the written word won't help you if you don't inscribe this on the tablet of your heart. Written words only served human beings when we moved into cities, when we began to create kingdoms and empires. Most of life happens without any written words. A few of us, like you and I, need to learn texts and languages, but only to help our people. These days life is more complex than it was for our ancestors. We need not only Aramaic and Hebrew, but also Greek and Latin to help our people survive under the yoke of the Romans. But none of it is worth anything if you forget to listen more deeply.

"Feel around you. Feel in your skin and in your heart how the light changes as the moon rises. Now listen to the moon in your heart. Feel your heart expanding with the light, just as if you were the moon reflecting the light of the sun. You can't see the sun, but you know it's there. Feel your connection to the Holy One the same way. Feel yourself riding on the light rays of the moon, flying, just as the text you've been studying tells the story about the 'son of man' riding on waves of glory."

With Shemuel guiding him, Yehuda had closed his eyes and felt the earth under him and the water around him, becoming part of his body. Then he felt himself rising toward the moon, floating on the air, until he was inside the moon, bathed in its cool light. He flew through the sky, looking down on the earth beneath him. Then he perceived himself exploding into light. When he opened his eyes again, Shemuel was looking at Yehuda with love.

"You're on the way there, Yehuda," Shemuel said. "You've had a blissful experience, but in order to help our people, you need to learn how to bring a vision back rather than simply dissolve into the light. Then you will learn how to bring actual power back from the other world, the power to change things around you. But remember: that power only works if you know it comes from the Holy One and that it serves the people—our people and our land."

Yehuda looked out over the Jezreel Valley under a similar moon and wondered, "And who are *our* people? Galileans, Samaritans, Judeans, Romans, mixtures like Ioannis? Whom do I include? And what helps *them*?" He half closed his eyes, taking in the reflected light, and again breathed, feeling his heart becoming the moon. He asked inwardly: "Send me what I need to know, Shemuel. I can't ask you in person anymore, so I'm asking you now. If what you taught me is true, what am *I* supposed to do?"

He felt his bones rooting into the earth, and at the same time, his spirit rising into the sky. Then he heard the scribe's voice say, "Go further. Find where I have come from and where I have gone. Then you'll know what you need to do." He felt a tingling at the top of his head as light flooded from the moon down to the bottom of his spine. A spark of energy rose like fire through his whole body. He was in the right place, going in the right direction. He felt free for the first time in ten years, since he had left the north for the city.

Yehuda opened his eyes and smiled wryly to himself. *Just like Shemuel to be cryptic. I wish I had asked him something more specific, like, "Who killed you, and why?"*

Chapter 9

A Village Meeting

The next morning, dawn brought mist from the sea, followed by the first hint of the late-spring rains. The hills of lower Galilee had already begun to bloom with wildflowers—anemones, tulips and poppies, all in red—followed closely by white lilies blossoming in fields of wild mint, cumin and dill. The fragrances of wild rose and mandrake also scented the air, reminding Yehuda of the sights and smells of his youth. Since he had moved to Paneas in Gaulanitis to live with Shemuel, he had not spent much time back in Galilee.

The party climbed through the foothills via pathways that became more and more familiar to the scribe. In the distance to the northeast, he could see Mount Tabor rising above the Yarden Valley, its wooded slopes providing numerous places of refuge whenever invaders entered the land. Deborah the judge had prepared her forces for the battle against Yabin and the Canaanites on Tabor. It was also one of the ancient high places, sacred to the long-forgotten, original inhabitants of the land.

Finally, the small band came to the end of the path, where it joined the main trail heading north. The road led to Yaphia, a medium-sized village of about eight hundred people about seven Roman millia south of Sepphoris, according to Shimeon.

"We will leave you here," he said. "I'm sure you know your way, and we need to get back to Korah. His protective guard is a bit shorthanded when we're away.

We'll tell him about the encounter with the Romans, since he will want to know."

"Brothers, we've been very grateful for your help and company," said Yehuda, giving each a warm embrace. "Please also tell Korah that if we learn anything of interest to him, we will send word. Shalama! May you and your families prosper!"

Shimeon and his two cousins turned around and marched back down the path toward the Great Plain.

"Honorable Israelites," said Yehuda to Ioannis. "Samaritans, Galileans, Judeans, Canaanites. We were all once nomads, some children of Abraham, Sarai and Hagar, some those whom Moshe led out of Egypt. The Canaanites who were here then became part of our families, too. Who can separate blood from blood? Everyone came from somewhere else once upon a time, according to our earliest stories. And we all come from Adam and Hewa."

Ioannis felt vaguely comforted by Yehuda's latest short lecture. *Half-breeds are people too*, he thought, chuckling to himself. *It all depends on who you feel your family really is.* As they walked on, he began to breathe more easily. *I had forgotten how much I despise city air. Maybe that's my mother's lungs in me.*

As they entered Yaphia, they found people flooding into the town, and Yehuda remembered that it was the day before Shabbat. He reflected that villagers might attend meetings on this day and also possibly trade goods with each other. Because the Romans tried to tax transactions using money, most villagers didn't use it, preferring to trade whatever extra small handcrafts or other goods they had—a cup here, a piece of clothing or weaving there. Originally, most families raised all of their own food and produced whatever else they needed for sustenance. Commerce for money was virtually unknown. It only entered the picture when taxes were due, and in case someone, maybe Antipas or the Romans or a Temple tithe collector, didn't want goods in kind—sheep, oil, olives, wheat or grapes. If a village did contribute to the Yerushalaim Temple—and by no means did most of them in Galilee do so—then some foodstuffs wouldn't keep until they were sacrificed. They would have to be turned into something else that could be traded for sacrificial goods by the priest—money of some sort. As far as Antipas's tax went, he mostly took as his share the extra food that a family raised. He could use it to feed his retainers in the city, or he could turn it into money for building projects or luxury goods by trading the crops to the Tyrians or Nabateans. Like most kings, Antipas felt that he was due his tax for the services of government, keeping the peace and so forth.

Most villagers, Yehuda knew, resented the increasing levels of tax that Antipas required, and many considered it a family duty to hide as much food and land as they could. If they somehow fell behind, Antipas's soldiers could easily appropriate some or all of their land, making it even more difficult to survive. Tax had so impoverished some villages, like Kefar Hanania in the north, that the residents had become tenant farmers on their own ancestral lands. Or they had been driven off their land entirely and turned to making pottery, since fortunately, the earth near the village was suited to it. Most Galilean villagers didn't understand what services Antipas provided, since they kept their own peace and solved all of their own disputes at village councils, *knessets*, like the one that might be happening in Yaphia that day. The Greeks sometimes called such a council a *synagogue*, which was not any fixed building, just a gathering of the elders of the village to sort out any trouble that had surfaced.

"I would like to see what is happening at the village meeting here," Yehuda said to Ioannis. "I could catch up on some of the news from the area before I go to Sepphoris to see my brother. I may also be able to find out if Shemuel came this way. By the way, here you are Yehohanan and back to being my servant and assistant buyer. It's better not to mention either the temple or Yerushalaim. We're traders on our way through to Darmsuq. We're taking the long way so we can see beautiful lower Galilee."

"OK, Yehuda." Ioannis smiled. "I'll try to look commercial and astute, rather than like an armed thug."

All of the men were heading toward a large central house, probably that of the headman of the village. The two entered through a portico and found themselves in a room with decorated columns running along a north-south axis. Stone benches lined three sides of the room with the entrance facing south, as was usual. The room was made for a gathering. One day it might be a banquet or a wedding celebration, another a community meeting. It was a sign of honor for the headman's family that they were able to offer this room to the community to use. Ioannis thought that it didn't look very different from the large house of a Roman village leader.

Yehuda went over and introduced himself to a small group of men at one side of the room, whom he reckoned to be the village elders. It was the proper (and safe) thing to do if one expected any hospitality. As he looked Galilean and spoke Aramaic with their own dialect, the small group was interested in his background and family. They were disposed to accept him as a Galilean expatriate.

"My name is Tauma ben Yahayye," said Yehuda. "Although I was born here, I was raised in the rocky heights above Paneas. Maybe you have heard of Shemuel ben Yahayye, my uncle, whose family has lived in that area for generations."

"Yes, we've heard of him," said one of the elders, a short, stocky man with a long beard. Yehuda presumed he was the headman, since he assumed control of questioning a newcomer. "We hear that he is a scribe, but one who serves the people. Not the usual scribe," he added, raising his eyebrows. "My name is Felayah ben Abitub, and my family has lived here since before the Assyrians. I can hear from your accent that you are one of us. But why did you move from Galilee? Most people stay in the land of their forefathers."

"I was a burden on my family, not enough land to support us all," replied Yehuda honestly.

"Of course," said Felayah, "The cursed Romans and the Herodes family have made all our lives a Gehenna. We had some chances with the Maccabees, since at least they kept their corruption localized in Yerushalaim and mostly left us alone up here, as long as we paid lip service to the temple. Well, anyway, you are welcome to join our knesset today. Maybe you can offer some wisdom for the troubles facing us, Tauma ben Yahayye."

"I would be happy to help in whatever way I can," replied Yehuda. "One other thing before you begin. You haven't by any chance seen or heard of Shemuel passing through this way recently?"

"No, I haven't," replied Felayah quickly. "But if he had, he would likely have stopped in Nazara rather than here. That's where he visits most often and where people say he has students or family."

"Thank you. God willing, I can offer some help at your meeting."

"God has little to do with it," the headman replied. "The trouble is everything that is tearing us away from the ways God told us to live, the healthy ways."

Felayah turned away and spoke to his fellow elders, preparing for the meeting to follow. Ioannis asked Yehuda quietly, "Master, why did you give a different name? Is there something I should know?"

"Later, Ioannis," said Yehuda from the side of his mouth. "The meeting is about to begin. Just watch and listen. In particular, notice anyone who looks nervous when I mention Shemuel. If I have the opportunity to do so, that is."

The meeting was called to order, and immediately men vied for the right to speak first. Felayah called on a thin, dark-haired villager, who looked like he had been fasting for a week.

"My family can't take any more of this!" said the thin man with a screech in his voice. "We're just about at the end of what we can raise from the small plot of land we have, and we don't want to ask for more charity or loans from our friends here," he said, gesturing around the group passionately. "The temple people in Yerushalaim want their tithe, and I've put them off. The Romans are here, seemingly for good, so I've gotten used to their tax. But now we have Antipas breathing down our necks not far away. First he rebuilt Zippori and needed food for the builders. Then he built a new capital, Tiberias on Lake Kinneret, close to the hot springs at Hammas. A resort for his rich friends. He didn't have enough people to run the city, so he stole some of our sons and their families to be his slaves there. So now he's stealing not only our crops but also our people. And he has raised the tax again. For what? We don't see any benefit. We only see more of his rich friends coming to live in Tiberias. And we still have his tax collector in Zippori, just a few millia away, sucking our blood for God knows what. What can we do? My family is desperate!"

"The only thing for it is revolt!" called out a tall, well-fed man in ragged clothing, a long scar on his left cheek. Breaking protocol, he didn't wait to be recognized by the headman. "Some of us have already gone to hills to join the bands there. Maybe we should all do that!" Some men expressed shock that he had spoken out of turn, but others nodded in agreement. Arguments broke out in small groups around the room, and soon the din of voices overwhelmed any semblance of a meeting.

"Brothers, we need to keep the order of our village knesset!" yelled Felayah, waving wildly for attention. "Our families have lived here for many centuries. How can we keep our land if we head to the caves of Arbel, or wherever else the bandit brotherhoods are living? Once we abandon our lands, the Romans or Antipas will confiscate them. Then we're lost." Gradually, the tumult in the room subsided.

"But what do you recommend?" continued the well-fed raggedy man, still standing and holding the floor. "As our brother said, we can't go on as we are. It's one thing when the oppressors are days away in

Yerushalaim. It's another when they are camped on our doorstep, with all of their hired mercenaries."

"Maybe we should follow this prophet I hear about from Nazara, Yohanan," chimed in the thin man. "I heard that he has started a protest down near the bottom of the lake. He's saying that we should just ignore all the tax collectors and return to the old ways of our villages. That means that all debt gets forgiven every seven years, at least between us. All property goes back to the community every forty-nine years. We need to take care of one another and ignore the Romans and Antipas. No rich or poor, no slave or free, at least in our own villages. Wasn't that the way of Moshe, even if it wasn't the way of rich elites like Dawid and Shelomoh?"

"Our brothers down south are also oppressed by the Romans," replied Felayah, who had begun to shift his weight uncomfortably at the mention of forgiving debts and no rich or poor. "The temple is an innovation, yes, but it's not our biggest problem. Our biggest problem is the Romans, who are propping up the damned Idumeans like Antipas, who are impoverishing us all. They have soldiers. We can't simply ignore them."

"The prophet from Nazara says just the opposite," replied the thin man, clearly emotional and desperate enough to stand up to the headman. "He says we should just ignore them all and take care of ourselves, our own debts and differences. Know the way of truth, and the truth will free us."

"That's just mystical nonsense," said the well-fed ragged man. "It's easy for the Nazarans to say. They're very cozy with the rich. The only way is armed rebellion. We're up against hardened steel, real power."

A Village Meeting

The meeting descended again for some minutes into chaos, with various voices trying to be heard. The headman held up his hands for silence.

"Look, friends!" Felayah cried. "Let us not fight among ourselves. Everyone agrees: we have to find some way through this together. Extreme solutions can't help. I propose that we send a delegation to Zippori to negotiate with Antipas's main tax collector there, Benyamin ben Yohanan." This suggestion reignited the uproar, and several men began to curse when they heard the name of Benyamin.

"All right!" said Felayah. "Yes, he hasn't been very flexible in the past. But I'm sure if we send the right delegation with the right approach, we can make him understand. No one will get any tax if we're all completely impoverished."

"We've tried delegations before," said the well-fed ragged man. "It's a waste of time. We need to tell the bastard that if he doesn't lessen the tax, and then we will all go on strike. There will be no food raised this season, so there will be nothing to pay tax with."

"Yes! Yes! That's it," cried several voices. "Strike!"

"OK, all right," said the headman, trying to calm everyone down. "It could be part of our negotiating strategy. Now, besides myself, who should be in the delegation? I propose people whom Benyamin will respect: Matthai and Yiremayhu."

"Sure, his cousin and son," muttered a man to Yehuda's left. "Same old story."

"All right, that's settled then," said Felayah, not waiting for more suggestions. "For us to have the best chance, we have to appeal with reason to the old ways, and even Benyamin will have to listen. Now, brothers, we have a visitor from the south, but he is one of us who had to leave his village in Galilee a generation ago for the same reasons we've been talking about. As a merchant in Idumea, he hasn't done badly for himself, so that proves we can come through this as well. His name is Tauma ben Yahayye. Having spoken with him briefly, I sense a commitment to our ancient Galilean ways. Maybe he can offer us some wisdom."

Everyone turned to look at Yehuda, and Ioannis wondered what his master would come up with now. *Probably too many men to put into a trance, or whatever he did to the Roman cavalry*, Ioannis thought.

"Friends, yes, I empathize with your troubles," said Yehuda, standing up and looking around slowly. "I have spent many years down south, so I didn't know how bad things have become here in your villages. All I can say is what my uncle Shemuel of Paneas, whom some of you may have heard of, used to teach me. When we act, we need to recognize that all real action comes from the Holy One. That doesn't mean we sit around and pray all day. No, the Holy One created the universe with force, with substance, with light. So we need to find solutions that work practically but also have insight and wisdom. As a stranger to your village, I can offer no more than that. You know your own circumstances best, but I do offer you the hand of friendship and pray that you can come through your troubles in a better condition than you face now. My servant and I are on our way to Syria, and perhaps we can discover how other villages have handled this problem. When we return, we could report to you."

Some of the village men had begun to yawn at this point, which may have been what Yehuda was hoping for, thought Ioannis. But at the mention of Shemuel, he noticed that the well-fed ragged man became suddenly alert and watched Yehuda carefully. Looking more closely, Ioannis noticed that the man's ragged clothing seemed calculated, too neat, as though he had dressed to appear poor rather than because he actually was.

"I sense a wisdom in you, brother," said Felayah. "You are a man of the world. Perhaps you could join our delegation. Surely Zippori is not much out of your way?"

"No, it isn't," replied Yehuda quickly, "but I have some other stops before we get there. If it turns out that we are there at the same time, however, I am willing to add my voice to yours." Many heads nodded at this, and the meeting broke up quickly. Felayah clapped Yehuda on the back and thanked him effusively for his contribution, which seemed a bit excessive to Ioannis.

"Seems he's more impressed with your supposed status as a merchant than anything," said Ioannis to Yehuda as they left the building. "I don't really see how you can help them. Any anyway, why did you give them that strange name rather than your own?"

"You're right. Maybe I can't really help, but I feel I should try anyway," replied Yehuda. "The deception about my name was a bit of forethought. That bastard tax collector Benyamin they're all cursing? He's my brother."

Chapter 10

Stories

Yehuda and Ioannis walked back through the village toward the path heading north to Sepphoris-Zippori. Villagers from Yaphia were standing around in groups, catching up on news, or gathering around makeshift markets with goods for sale or exchange by their neighbors. Yehuda was thinking about how easy it had been to lie about his identity, and he didn't like the feeling. Everything had become much more complicated than he thought it would be. *I imagined a simple, mildly dangerous story. Just escape with the pearl, walk away and start a new life. But my past turned out to be heavier than that. Why did I think I could cut myself free of it—from Shemuel, my family and my homeland?*

Yehuda was still lost in thought when he noticed that the well-fed ragged man with a scar on his left cheek had appeared suddenly out of the crowd of villagers and was walking beside him. Ioannis, on his other side, immediately moved toward the man, blocking him. The three stopped and stood close together at the side of a village lane.

"Shalama, brother," said the ragged stranger to Yehuda, standing his ground. There was more challenge than peace in his voice, and he ignored Ioannis completely.

"Shalama, brother," replied Yehuda. "I noticed you at the meeting. Do I know you? Can I help you in some way?"

"Perhaps I can help you," said the stranger. "And no, you don't know me; neither do you need to know me. But I think I know you."

"How could that be, friend?" asked Yehuda.

"At the knesset you mentioned Shemuel from Paneas," replied the stranger. "I presume you mean Shemuel ben Yahayye."

"Yes, that's right," replied Yehuda, giving out the minimum of information. He did not trust the stranger, given the lack of courtesy.

"Please excuse my directness," said the stranger, as though reading Yehuda's thoughts. "It's important to know whom one can trust these days. Aren't you one of Shemuel's students, rather than a merchant from Idumea? He described you to us exactly at one of our recent meetings. You were one of his inside people. I don't blame you for deceiving the men at that village meeting. I would have done the same. But if I don't mistake you, and I don't believe I do, then you would find it valuable to go to Nazara. Ask for Eliyuhena ben She'atiyel. He can help you find what you're looking for."

"And what would I be looking for, friend?" said Yehuda, his face blank.

"What we're all looking for," hissed the man. "Freedom! Freedom and an answer to your questions about Shemuel. Look, I overheard you talking to that headman. He's just another of our rich, ignorant Israelites, happy to keep things as they are. Some of us see things very differently. So did Shemuel."

"What do you know about Shemuel?" asked Yehuda, moving closer to the stranger and staring with fire into the man's eyes. He directed all of his breath through the middle of his own chest, as Shemuel had taught him to do, in order to hear the real truth, rather than just words.

"What do I know? I know what eyes can't see and what ears can't hear," said the stranger quietly, standing his ground and meeting Yehuda glance for glance. "And I know that he was killed by enemies of our movement. I know that we're also waiting to find out what comes next. And when the Power will come. Do you know?"

"No," said Yehuda suspiciously. "Shemuel didn't mention anything to me about a movement. He taught me about power from the unseen, from the Holy One, not power from the blade of sword. Or a dagger," he added, watching the stranger for a reaction.

"Power is power," said the stranger without expression. "We relied on Shemuel for the next steps. He could see. Most of us can only act, but that may be enough, if we know how and when. Listen, go to Nazara and ask for Eliyuhena. Give him this sign." The stranger put one of his hands quickly to his ears, as though it were a nervous gesture, and then winked an eye. "Maybe he can tell you where their family is meeting next and what they're going to do about Shemuel's murder. Our own brotherhood is waiting to hear about the next step."

Yehuda shook his head and put his hands on his hips impatiently. "To know what to do, one first needs to know who killed Shemuel, right, friend? So who killed him? Maybe it was you and your brotherhood. What do I know about you, after all? Nothing."

The ragged stranger stepped closer to Yehuda, challenging him. "Don't mistake your friends for enemies or your enemies for friends," he retorted menacingly. "Shemuel was playing a much more complex game than any of us knew. You have the same look in your eyes as Shemuel. You have been to the other worlds. But you don't seem to be a man of action. You have one with you, though, I see," he said mockingly, glancing toward Ioannis for the first time. "Maybe you need to know how to use a dagger yourself."

"Why would I need that?" asked Yehuda. "If the Holy One doesn't help us, then what can a few daggers or swords accomplish against either Antipas or the Romans?"

"We don't need many," replied the stranger. "We only need a few, in the right places, appearing and disappearing in the cities of the elites, to eliminate the rich collaborators, those who cozy up to Antipas and the Romans for their own security. Here, look at this," he said, revealing a long, needlelike stiletto from underneath his cloak. Ioannis instantly stepped in front of the man, grabbing his arm. "Be at peace," said the stranger to Yehuda. "If I had wanted to kill you, I could have done it easily, even in the middle of a crowd. With a quick stroke to the side of the ribs, you wouldn't even cry out. You could even walk for a few paces. Only a sigh would escape. By the time you felt anything and fell to the ground, I would have disappeared. No one looks at a man in rags very closely. They don't want to imagine themselves in rags someday. Neither seen nor heard. So don't be foolish. Shemuel was ours. And yours too, I suppose. Maybe if you go to Nazara and meet the brothers there, we can all find out what we need to know. Shalama, and go well." The ragged, well-fed stranger walked off quickly, without waiting for a response.

Ioannis watched the stranger carefully until he disappeared into the crowd and then looked toward Yehuda for advice. Yehuda furrowed his brow and sighed, gesturing for them both to continue on their way. They walked on toward the main road and had reached the outskirts of the village when they heard up-roar behind them. Yehuda recognized the tall, thin vil-lager from the meeting as he came running out of the village center toward them.

"What's happened, friend?" asked Yehuda.

"Our headman has been killed, murdered!" the villager exclaimed, wide-eyed and waving his arms around. "No one saw anything! He just fell down dead, and then we found a small puncture wound between his ribs, like the talon of a bird. It must have been a *shed*, a demon! The Holy One has abandoned us! Now what will we do about negotiating with Herodes's tax collec-tor in Zippori?"

"I don't know, friend," said Yehuda evenly and without emotion. "I'm sorry to hear this. I will still try to plead your cause in Zippori when I'm there. Presumably your other two representatives will still be going."

"Thank you," he said, "at least that's something. I need to go home and tell my family to prepare for the worst. Our headman was the only person who Benyamin in Zippori respected. He hardly knows his son and cousin. Alaha help us all!" The thin man ran off toward the western side of the village outskirts.

"I suppose we're going to Nazara, then?" asked Ioannis, indicating in his tone of voice that he thought it was a bad idea. "Or we could just forget the whole thing and continue onward. I don't like mixing with assassins."

"Yes, it is hard to know whom to trust, if anyone. The brotherhood the stranger told us about seems to agree with what Korah said," replied Yehuda. "And we still need to find out who killed Shemuel and why. Why didn't he tell me about this brotherhood if he was supposedly the leader of it?"

"All right, then how do we get to this Nazara? Is it a village like Yaphia?" asked Ioannis.

"No, even smaller," said Yehuda. "It's a bit to the east, off the main road to Sepphoris. We should find a path just a *mille* or so from here. Nazara was always an insignificant place, despite its name, which I think means 'guardian.' It probably refers to the hill it's on, which overlooks the whole region."

"Well, as far as I can tell, I'm your guardian," said Ioannis, smiling. "You know, maybe that stranger was right. It wouldn't hurt you to know a bit about how to defend yourself. I could show you. If we're going into this brotherhood group, one knife or sword might not be enough."

"Maybe later, Ioannis," replied Yehuda. "I am getting the message that Shemuel has laid down a trail for me to follow. If that's so, then I need to trust him rather than think about everything that doesn't make sense."

"Which is quite a bit," said Ioannis.

"Yes, you're right," Yehuda said and laughed. "But this was the way Shemuel taught me. Things don't always make sense when you're following tracks into the unseen. What's true in the inner worlds is true in the outer ones as well sometimes. The prophet, he said, tries to bring the two worlds together."

"If that's the way it is," said Ioannis, "I'd hate to think of all those Roman gods and goddesses, fighting and fornicating, actually interfering in our lives, making the mundane world like the sacred one. Things are enough of a mess here already with emperors and kings making the decisions for us. Most people just want to get on with life, not have more mystery."

"True, Ioannis. But nothing ever really changes if we blindly follow what everyone says is possible. Here in Israel, that's mainly what has happened since we left things to the rich and powerful instead of taking charge of our own communities."

A short while later, they came to a path on their right, marked by a giant Tabor oak tree. Yehuda stopped a moment and looked up into the tree's branches. Then he sighed and put a hand to his heart.

"Is this the path, Yehuda?" asked Ioannis.

"Yes, it is," Yehuda responded. "But...let's stop here a moment. These giant trees, which we call *elah*, are sacred. At such places, from the old times, we used to bury our respected ancestors or honor those who had passed away. *Elah* is after the old Israelite deity, *El*, who was here even before Moshe brought us out of Egypt. It is just another name of the Nameless One, who has countless names. We couldn't see Shemuel buried properly, so I want to honor him here before we go any farther."

"Yes, of course," said Ioannis. "The dead always need to be honored. Do you need me to go somewhere else?"

"No, not at all. Just stand next to me with your shoulder next to mine, and raise your hands like this." Yehuda put his two hands together, cupped at his heart.

"Then breathe in your heart, and feel all of your ancestors, good and bad, as though they were in a caravan traveling ahead of you. Breathe with them all, all the way back to the beginning. They did their best, and we are part of that caravan. So breathe with forgiveness, thankfulness and compassion."

As Ioannis stood next to him, Yehuda felt his own heart opening further, the younger man's natural innocence and energy joining his.

"Now, just breathe with me, and I will say a prayer for Shemuel, for all our dead and for all of us. When I say 'Ameyn,' you can say it after me, or just feel it in your heart." Yehuda raised his cupped hands a bit higher and began:

May the Great Name,
through our own expanding awareness
and our more sincere action,
lift itself to become still higher and more holy.
Ameyn!

May all the names of all the beings in the universe,
including the names of those whom we can no longer touch
but who have touched our hearts and lives,
and including our own names,
live within the Great Name.
Ameyn!

May the names of all who have died in violence and war
be kept alight in our sight
and in the Great Name,
with sorrow that we were not yet able to shape a world
in which they would have lived longer.
Ameyn!

May the Great Name,
bearing all these names,
live within each one of us.
Ameyn!

Ioannis felt his shoulder touch Yehuda's, and as the older man began to say the prayer, a picture of his father flashed into his mind. He could see his father smiling at him as a boy, telling him that everything would be all right and that he was protected and loved. He felt a profound sadness and guilt that he had been powerless to stop his father's death. But then each time he said "Ameyn" after Yehuda, he felt himself releasing the guilt and feeling only the sorrow, which gradually faded. Ioannis felt himself affirming that he might yet be able to shape a world in which his father could have, would have, lived. Then Yehuda was continuing:

> *Even though we cannot give you, Holy One,*
> *enough blessing, enough song, enough praise,*
> *enough consolation*
> *to match what we wish to lay before you…*
> *And though we know that today*
> *there is no way to console you*
> *when among us some who bear your image*
> *are slaughtering others who bear your image…*
> *still we ask that from the unity of your Great Name*
> *flow great harmony and joyful life*
> *for all the God-wrestling folk.*
> *Ameyn!*
>
> *You who create harmony*
> *throughout the ultimate reaches of the universe,*
> *teach us to create harmony*
> *within ourselves and among ourselves,*
> *and to make peace for all the children of Adam and Hewa*
> *and for all the creatures who dwell upon the earth.*
> *Ameyn.*

Strange, thought Ioannis. *Now we are consoling God? What an odd idea. And yet not so strange, I suppose, if Yehuda believes that we are all part of God, a God here grieving with us.* It was not so different from some of the early Greek philosophers like Parmenides and Heraclitus, whose sayings his tutor had taught him as a boy. One of those was:

"It is necessary to speak and to think only what is;
for being is, but nothing is not.
And it is all one to me: where I am to begin,
for I shall return there again."

Yes, Ioannis thought, *I shall return there again. And my father is there, too, and his real existence was always there and always will be.*

He opened his eyes and looked toward Yehuda. The scribe was already looking at him with compassion and some curiosity. *How long have I been standing here?* Ioannis wondered.

"Shall we go?" asked Yehuda, smiling.

"Is there anywhere to go?" asked Ioannis.

"Maybe not," said Yehuda. "But the story that the Holy One is telling continues anyway."

CHAPTER 11
The Lost Branch

The path to Nazara led upward along a ridge through a mixed forest of cedar, cypress and Tabor oak trees. Their fragrance lifted Yehuda's and Ioannis's spirits as they climbed farther up the hill toward the village. The oak trees provided much of the wood for furniture, houses and boats for the inhabitants of Lower Galilee. In the distance to the east, Mount Tabor made another appearance, guarding the way toward Lake Kinneret. To the north across the Beit Netofa Valley, on a much smaller hill, they could see Zippori, the Greek Sepphoris, which guarded the route from the Great Sea, *Yama Raba*, eastward toward Kinneret. Zippori was an ideal place to garrison an army, foreign or domestic, and so control the whole region. Herodes Antipas had immediately made it his capital after his father's death, only to move about ten years ago to his better-furnished, Roman-pleasing capital, Tiberias on the lake.

To the south they could see the Jezreel Valley, through which they had come, much of it divided into large landholdings occupied by clients of the Romans. The image of Shemuel's dead body flashed into Yehuda's mind, and he suddenly felt a sense of foreboding about their journey. Then the late-afternoon wind from the Great Sea began to rise behind them, pushing them along the trail. This didn't improve Yehuda's mood. *The Great Sea in the west is the direction of Sheol, the place of the dead,* he thought. *Am I being pushed by a wind from death?* But then he felt his connection to Shemuel again. He imagined he was falling uphill, borne along by the current of the breath of the Holy One. Whatever danger awaited them must be part of his destiny.

As they entered the outskirts of the village, they again noticed the activity of many people coming and going. It was still Friday, a normal day for a market, Yehuda reminded himself, and perhaps there had also been a knesset in Nazara earlier. He wondered what had happened there. As in Yaphia, there seemed to be groups of men standing around, either talking or trading goods. But unlike Yaphia, there were also women in the village, engaged in both buying and selling at the local market. Some of the men seemed tense, looking suspiciously at everyone who passed. Because Yehuda and Ioannis were strangers, they immediately attracted attention, and one of the village men, middle-aged, with dark hair and a long beard in ringlets, walked up and greeted them cordially.

"Shalama, friends!" he said, smiling. "Can I help you? We have not seen you here before!"

"Shalama," Yehuda replied. "Yes, friend, we are strangers here, although I am originally from Galilee. I have not lived here for many years. My servant and I have been living in the south."

"Yes, I can tell from your accent that you are one of us," said the man. "My name is Eliyuhena ben She'atiyel. May I know yours?"

"Tauma ben Yahayye," said Yehuda. "I believe you are the man we have been sent to see. I was a student and adopted son of Shemuel ben Yahayye of Paneas."

"*Was*, you say," replied Eliyuhena, showing no emotion.

"Yes, Shemuel was killed, and we have been directed here to find out why," said Yehuda. "We were told you could help us."

"Who told you this?"

"Someone who didn't give his name," replied Yehuda, at the same time touching his right ear and closing one eye.

"I see," said Eliyuhena, "or perhaps I don't. But you must excuse me. I am lacking in hospitality. Would you consent to dine at my home this evening?" He then looked at Ioannis questioningly.

"Yes, gladly," said Yehuda. "This is my friend Yehohanan. I trust him with my life. On the way to Galilee, we visited Korah ben Izhar in Taanach. He also pointed us in your direction, I believe, but without mentioning any names."

"You're also welcome," Eliyuhena said to Ioannis, relaxing at the mention of Korah's name. "Again, I must ask your forgiveness. You have come at a time when our village is in crisis, and many of our men were just meeting to consider how to address it."

"May I ask what kind of crisis?"

"We'll speak more of it later this afternoon. The danger is from both outside and inside. In the meantime, please accept my belated welcome to our village." He embraced each man briefly. "You are free here. I must excuse myself, as our market is just ending, and I have a small stall here with my wife, selling and exchanging olive oil. My home is up the hill in that direction," he said, pointing. "It's on the left about six hundred paces, what the Romans call a *stadium*. You will know it by the sign on the door. There are several small farmhouses in a cluster around a larger courtyard. Please come around the eighth hour of the day. It's not long from now. We will have time then for a talk among the larger family, plus Shabbat prayers, before the meal."

Yehuda looked at the sun's position in the sky. It seemed Eliyuhena used the Roman system of time, like himself and many city people at the time. Both the day and night were divided into twelve equal hours, so the length of an hour of day was determined by how long the sun was shining.

"We will be there," said Yehuda formally. "Thank you for your welcome and hospitality."

Yehuda and Ioannis began to stroll around the village. After their talk with Eliyuhena, people no longer looked at them as strangers, but as potential customers. Yehuda noticed that even though this village was much smaller than Yaphia, it seemed that the residents were better dressed and looked healthier. Then he noticed that the quality of goods being sold in the market was also higher—pottery from Kefar Hanania, dried fish from the lake, olive oil from village presses, grapes from nearby vineyards. There was even a small bakery selling bread, the staple of the Israelite diet. The wife of the baker, or so Yehuda presumed, stood at the door of the shop selling, while the baker welcomed people inside. Yehuda noticed the usual bartering between customers. But he also saw transactions for money, mostly in Tyrian-minted silver coins. That was significant. It showed that some men in the village made their living acting as brokers, selling local goods that transported well, like wine or oil, to customers elsewhere, customers who had money to spend—like the elites in the cities. *So they must have some buyers or patrons in Sepphoris or Tiberias,* thought Yehuda. *Interesting. Whatever danger the village faces, poverty probably isn't one of them, at least to judge from the people gathered here.*

Just before the eighth hour, they found their way to the courtyard that Eliyuhena had mentioned. The gate was open, and on the doorpost in front of the entryway, Yehuda saw a small box that contained a passage from the Torah, the sign of a pious household. In addition, to the side of the box, he found the carved image of a small hand with an eye inside. It was a usual symbol of protection, of course, but perhaps, thought Yehuda, it carried an additional meaning here. *The-eye-has-not-seen group?* The courtyard was surrounded by a wall and shared by several small farmhouses with outbuildings. A stone stairway in the courtyard led to the upper floor of one of the buildings.

As they entered the courtyard, they saw a well and near it a round clay oven for baking bread. Stables were tucked into a corner of the wall on the left. Some women were finishing the day's work with the early flax harvest, in preparation for weaving linen cloth. Eliyuhena's servants welcomed them and washed their feet. They also offered the two travelers bowls of water to wash their hands. Yehuda noticed the higher standard of purity here. Eliyuhena's family seemed paradoxically Romanized in some of their customs, yet Israelite in others.

As they were washing, more guests began to arrive. The servants then led them into a larger meeting room, a *traklin*. Places were prepared for about twenty people. Unlike the usual Roman *trikla,* Yehuda noted here a mixture of couches, benches and chairs. One could recline, as the Romans did, or sit around several round tables, all of which were grouped around the

The Lost Branch

main table. The servants directed Yehuda and Ioannis to a couch near the main table, several seats to the left of Eliyuhena and his wife. As the guests gathered, Yehuda noticed that the men and women were seated together, definitely unusual. As Shabbat would begin later that evening, Yehuda expected a bit of a wait for dinner and explained to Ioannis some of the rituals to expect.

The smells beginning to come from the kitchen helped stoke the younger man's appetite. He struggled to concentrate his attention on the possible danger from those around him, as was his normal habit. *Is this a gathering of our friends or our enemies?* he wondered. *Yehuda seems to trust them, but that doesn't mean I need to.*

"Shalama, brother," said an elderly bald man sitting down heavily on the couch just to Yehuda's right.

"Shalama to you," replied Yehuda.

"Eliyuhena tells me that you were one of Shemuel's closest students, his adopted son," said the bald man, sighing. "Terrible news! We only heard about his death earlier today."

"Yes, you see, we found the body," replied Yehuda. "Unfortunately, the Romans came along, and we had to flee. Do you know anything about why he was down here in Galilee?"

"Well, he was here in our village teaching a few of his close students," the man replied, "but I believe that Eliyuhena knows more. Excuse my rudeness, but I am also anxious for news. My name is Yauseph ben Ya'aqub. I am one of the elders of the family and have lived here all my life, working as a *nagara*, a carpenter. My ancestors returned here from Assyria about two hundred years ago, when the Persians defeated the Babylonians. We were originally from the north, Israelite going back to Moshe, so we returned to this area and rebuilt this village. We could really use some of the prophet's *mesh*, some redemption or rescue, now."

"Are all of you related here?" asked Yehuda, looking around the room as it began to fill.

"Yes, although some of us are distantly related," said Yauseph. "When the Assyrians took people away about seven hundred years ago, they couldn't take everyone, so they mainly deported the professionals and some head people. The rest they left here in the north, and over time some intermarried with Canaanites, Phoenicians and other neighbors of ours. Some of us who went to Nineveh took Assyrian spouses. It doesn't really matter," he said, shrugging his shoulders "We're all sons of Moshe in heart, and that's what counts as purity here. My ancestors, who returned with the group to Nazara, were architects for the Assyrians, and then for the Babylonians who conquered them and then for the Persians. After we came here, the Greeks arrived and now the Romans. Through all of these changes, we try to keep our hearts clear and undisturbed; otherwise we can lose our way."

"But you *are* blood relations, aren't you?" pressed Yehuda, confused a bit about the group in which he found himself.

"Yes, yes," said the old man a bit absently. "But what is blood? The *dami* that the Holy One gave us is just the outer sign of our human essence. That's what the word means. So issues like blood purity must not distract us. As sons of Adam, we are all related anyway, aren't we?"

"Yes, of course," replied Yehuda. "I was just saying the same earlier today." He was going to question

Yauseph further, but it seemed that everyone had arrived. Conversation stopped, and Eliyuhena began to offer an opening prayer:

"Holy One, ruler of heaven and earth. Thank you for gathering us all here together. Thank you for the bread of the earth and all the food we share with each other. Thank you for providing for our families. As we consider tonight the dangers ahead, we thank you in advance for your guidance. Please protect our brothers and sisters who are away at this time, doing the work of the family. From gathering to gathering, may your name and light be kept sacred in our hearts' feeling and through the work of our arms. Ameyn."

"Brothers and sisters," continued Eliyuhena. "It is again Sabbath evening, but I have called us together also to face some severe challenges. Most of you know about this, but there are new developments. First, so that we can speak freely, I need to introduce our guests, who are sitting next to Yauseph here to my right. This is Tauma ben Yahayye and his servant. Tauma is the man whom Shemuel identified to us in his last visit here as Yehuda, perhaps another name of his, one of his chief students. We did not know about him previously, but Shemuel believed in keeping his own secrets."

"Speaking of secrets," interjected a portly, brown-haired man sitting at one of the outlying tables to Eliyuhena's right, "Why didn't the rest of us know that Shemuel was just here, considering that we now know he's been murdered?" The man was wearing an expensive-looking embroidered linen robe, noted Yehuda. Another proof that some of the family were doing very well for themselves.

"There was a reason for the secrecy, Yoezer," said Eliyuhena to the man. "It's part of the reason for this meeting, but only part. I'll ask Zakarya ben Abiya to tell the story, since it all begins with his son," said Eliyuhena, turning to the elderly man immediately on his left. "Zakarya was the head of this community before me," he said to Yehuda. "He was also its *kahna,* our priest, and he brought us Shemuel to replace him as our spiritual guide when he retired." Zakarya was wearing a traditional undyed linen robe, his long, gray beard flowing down the front. He breathed heavily, sighed and looked around at the group with sad, brown eyes. Then he began, as though settling down to tell an ancient story.

"My friends, as you know, some months ago, we became concerned about my son, Yohanan, whom some now call *mudana,* baptizer. About a half year ago, he went off to visit our brethren in Kochaba beyond the Yarden River in Batanea. Batanea is not part of Judea or Galilee, not under any Herodes, and administered by the Romans as an autonomous region. It is a border country, guarding the entrance to the Yarden Valley, some of the territory held by our Ammonite ancestors from the old times," he said, nodding to Yehuda as though in explanation. "Many of our kinfolk resettled there two centuries ago, when our families returned from Babylonia and Assyria. Some of our family were skilled in horsemanship, so they found work with various kings by training cavalry soldiers at the garrisons there. The Persians, Greeks, Maccabees, the old mad Herodes—their horse soldiers were all trained by our people. But some of our people in Batanea recently became involved with a radical religious sect. This group is obsessed with reforming the Yerushalaim Temple. Why, I don't know! Moshe carried the ark with him. The temple could be anywhere, everywhere. The Holy One placed the message in our hearts, not in stones or buildings.

"Excuse me, Zakarya," said Yoezer impatiently, "but we know all this."

"Yes, yes," said Zakarya, not willing to be rushed. "But out of courtesy, our guests need to know the whole story. Out of wisdom also, if they are going to help us. And the Holy One *has* led them to us to help. Am I correct, Yoezer? Doesn't all help come from *Yah?*" Zakarya's eyes and voice suddenly flashed fire as he threw the meaning of the name of Yoezer, "Yah helps us," back at the portly man. Yoezer nodded an apology with his hand over his heart.

"All right," Zakarya continued. "These radicals, this extreme sect, call themselves *Hassaya*, healers, or *Hoseh ha-tora*, keepers of the Torah. I suppose they think there is some value in keeping the Yerushalaim Temple pure. As if it had ever been pure! They believe Yerushalaim needs to change before anything else can change. They turn their back on our own Israelite heritage—the Northern Kingdom and the sacred lineage we bear. Do you understand so far?" Zakarya asked Yehuda.

"So far, yes," replied Yehuda, nodding his head thoughtfully. "But you raise other questions for me. Which lineage are you? And what is this sacred mission that Eliyuhena mentioned?"

"Excuse me. I see that Shemuel did not tell you," replied Zakarya. "He probably did not even tell you that we existed. People think we're nothing and always mispronounce the name of our village. We are not *Nazara*; we are the *Natzara*, 'people of the branch.' We renamed this place when we returned from Assyria."

— 99 —

"The branch?" asked Yehuda, puzzled. He looked around the room and noticed that all of the men and women were nodding, almost in unison, as Zakarya mentioned the word *Natzaru.*

The old man leaned forward, placing both palms on the table in front of him, as though he expected Yehuda to understand. "Yes, as the prophet Yeshaya promised, 'A shoot will come from the stump of Yishay; from his root a branch will bear fruit.' Most people think he meant one person, a messiah or annointed one, who will save us. We understand it differently, of course," he sighed, turning a hand over.

Eliyhena broke in impatiently. "Please understand clearly, Yehuda. We're trusting you with a secret!" he said warningly. "Our whole family is the lost branch of the line of Dawid, through Ruth, his grandmother, and Yishay, his father," he said, opening his arms to include the whole group gathered. "Remember, both Ruth and Yishay were children of the tribes of Moab and Ammon, who came from the family of Lot, Abraham's brother. When Moshe returned with our people from Egypt, the Ammonites were already here, living on the other side of the Jordan River in what is now Batanea. So Dawid was from a marriage of the children of Abraham and the children of Abraham's brother, Lot. Yishay had other children besides Dawid, you know, and we are from that branch. Our mission is to continue this line and bring the vision of Moshe to earth again."

Yehuda shook his head slightly, clearly not understanding.

Eliyuhena raised his hands in frustration. "Yehuda, Moshe had only one simple vision: freedom!"

Chapter 12

Underground Roots

Some murmuring erupted around the room now that the family's secret had been spoken aloud.

"Well said, Eliyuhena!" chimed in Yauseph. "Too much of this family lineage nonsense always confuses things. It is what keeps the older generation like us stuck in the past," he said pointedly, glancing at Zakarya.

Yehuda rubbed his face with both hands, trying to clear his head. "Freedom, I understand, of course," he said, allowing his voice to trail away. He looked out a nearby window and noticed the sun moving toward setting. Soon it would be time for Shabbat, and the ritual meal would begin, followed by the actual meal. The rest of the people around the table were peering at him anxiously to see how he would react. "But what I don't understand is how you can be Dawid's lost line. Wasn't he from the tribe of Benyamin, from Judea?"

"Yes, yes," replied Zakarya, shrugging his shoulders dismissively. "That's what the Yerushalaim scribes would have you believe. They write the history, and they're paid to justify their own position as the main collaborators with our oppressors. For three hundred years they've been doing this. All because the Persians chose them to repossess and colonize the land again. But Dawid, *our* Dawid, was only half-Judean. He was also half-Ammonite and Moabite. We have more claim to him. He was originally from the north, from here. He was anointed in the home of his father, the Moabite

Yishay. Shemuel the last judge and first prophet, Dawid's teacher, was also from the north, and so was the great prophet Eliyah. The Yerushalaim elite wants you to believe that Dawid slaughtered the Ammonites, our kinsmen from beyond the Jordan, but it is all lies."

Zakarya became more enthusiastic as he gestured to the women around the other tables, all set in a circle. "Look at the women of our community, sitting as equals with the men! Dawid's son Shelomoh had an Ammonite wife. All right, he had a few others, too, but Shelomoh, king or not, had the old tradition in his blood, as you can see from his love poetry, the 'song of songs.' The old tradition says that the Holy One is in all forms and names, female and male, which are worshiped with a faithful heart. Our tradition tells us that without the marriage of the male and female divinity within us, in the heart of the One, there is no new life."

"And you've been keeping this hope alive all this time—for hundreds of years?" asked Yehuda incredulously. "And the Shemuel I knew, my teacher, he was also your teacher and priest?"

"Not just priest, high priest," said Zakarya. "I was the high priest before him, but I bowed to his greater wisdom."

"But he didn't tell me any of this!" exclaimed Yehuda. "How can that be?"

"There was much he didn't tell us as well, it seems," answered Zakarya. "Perhaps he did not want all of his secrets kept in one place, or with one person, or with one group. What *did* he teach you?"

Yehuda looked around at the opulent hall in which they were seated. Tapestries from Phoenike, Rome and Greece hung from the walls. On the main table, the bread and wine were covered with a fine linen cloth, waiting for sunset. If he forgot about the conversation they were having, it could be the home of any rich elite in Yerushalaim, even that of High Priest Qayapha. He glanced at Ioannis for support, but the younger man sat without expression, looking a bit lost in all of the details of family lineage. *Probably getting hungry*, Yehuda thought. *Anyway, I warned him.* He began to make sense of what Shemuel had taught him in relation to something as practical as revolution against an empire.

"Shemuel taught me that we were carrying on the traditions of the ancient one Hanuch," he said, "Hanuch who 'walked with the Holy One' and was taken home without dying. My master and uncle taught me the meditations that allow one to ascend through the heavens to the highest, to see and feel life from the heart of the One. That was Hanuch's secret, he said. Like our ancient ancestor Ya'aqub, Hanuch climbed the heavenly ladder, wrestled with the Holy One and returned with power— not just spiritual power, but power to use here on earth. He said that a person today could become like Hanuch, part human and part divine, and that person could be Israel's salvation. Of course, he also taught me all the skills needed to work inside as a scribe in Yerushalaim, even how to talk to the *Priyeshey*, the new group of elites who want to change the old ways to accommodate our rulers. He taught me our complete Israelite cultural heritage."

"Not quite complete, it seems," said Zakarya dryly, "since he didn't tell you about us. And he sent you to Yerushalaim?"

"Yes, he said that our people needed someone on the inside of the temple," said Yehuda. "He told me I could do good there, although he wasn't very clear about what that good was. Only that 'everything has its season,' as Shelomoh wrote. I was reluctant to go, but he said that he had other work and needed me to take his place there. He didn't tell me what that other work was."

"Did he tell you about anyone else he was training to take his place?" asked Zakarya.

"No. Is there someone else?"

"We don't know. There may have been," replied Zakarya. "Let me finish my story, and then you'll know as much as we do. As I said, my son Yohanan came under the influence of this radical cult, the Hassaya in Batanea, who also have a group near the Dead Sea. You have to understand that our mission depends on remaining secret until the ripe time. 'What eye has not seen and what ear has not heard.' All of a sudden, Yohanan started preaching publicly, shouting about the evils of the temple. 'Repent and be baptized!' he is saying. It's only bound to draw attention to him and maybe to us. They will want to know where he came from. It could undermine the plans of our whole family. We have placed family members and clients in many powerful places. That's how we found out about Shemuel's murder so quickly. Also, we have contacts in other families, like that of Korah the Levite in Samaria. He has his own sources on the inside, the private secret police that he trained when he was in charge of the temple security. So there is much at stake."

"You say this problem with Yohanan all started a half year ago," said Yehuda. "What has happened since then? What have you done?"

"We did what anyone would have done. We sent another family member from here after him, to talk some sense into him and tell him to stop attracting so much attention. In hindsight, we chose the wrong person."

"Who was it?"

"Yauseph's son, Yeshua," said Zakarya, nodding at Yauseph and frowning slightly. "Yeshua was very devoted to Shemuel and spent as much time as he could with him. Shemuel always said that Yeshua and his cousin Yohanan were his closest students here. We thought he would be the best person to send, since he and Yohanan were also good friends. But Yeshua has always been a bit otherworldly. Maybe Shemuel was teaching him these ladder meditations you spoke of. That would have been a bad idea, I think. Anyway, we sent Yeshua off to find Yohanan. And what happens? Yohanan baptizes him! Then we just heard today that Yeshua disappeared into the northern wilderness and hasn't been seen since. It's all a disaster!" said Zakarya, uncharacteristically banging his fist on the table in frustration. "Now we have two of them lost that we need to deal with!" The news caused a number of family members to exchange worried glances around the table. Several began to mutter angrily.

Yauseph stood and raised both hands to get the group's attention. "Zakarya, please," he said tenderly, placing one hand on his heart and bowing gently toward the old priest. "Let's all calm down. I think we need to trust our young men a bit more. Maybe there is some greater plan. The Holy One is the best planner, after all."

"Yes, Yauseph," said Zakarya testily. "I know you have this greater-plan philosophy. It allowed you to deal with Yeshua's strange birth. We won't speak of that. But trusting doesn't mean doing nothing. Everything we have planned for generations could be ruined if we are discovered prematurely."

"Thank you, Zakarya," said Yehuda. "I see you do have a serious problem. But how would your larger plan eventually unfold? I see that your family here is not poor. Some of you must be doing business with those whom Antipas has put in charge in Zippori, collaborating with them, providing them with goods that they sell for a profit or give to the Romans to keep them happy."

"Yes, that is all part of the plan," replied Eliyuhena. "It is not just the few of us here. We have our people—including our friends and clients—everywhere. We have the elites fully dependent on us for almost everything they need in the cities, for their whole system. If we gave the signal, it would all collapse overnight. But we'd have to back it up with force, and the time is not ripe. We have contacts in Zippori and within Antipas's court in Tiberias. They don't even know how much we're supplying them. We have friends in Samaria, also in Judea. We don't know all of their names, or their real names. It's safer that way. Each branch of the family is autonomous, but linked, all united in one goal: follow Moshe to freedom from the oppressors. We need to drive the empire out in such a comprehensive, overwhelming way that no empire ever returns again."

"And you think that is possible?" asked Yehuda, shaking his head incredulously. "Maybe the Herodes can be overthrown. Maybe you can even defeat the one Roman legion stationed here. But there are more Romans where that legion came from. There are Romans all the way from here to Iberia. What then?"

"Once we drive the first group out, we will simply buy more soldiers," replied Eliyuhena. "From the Nabateans or Parthians, if need be. And we will keep the Romans out. If they try to come back, we will wage a war of attrition from the hills of Galilee, attacking their caravans, blocking all their routes to Syria and the East. After their losses are high enough, they will give up. We will make peace with whomever the Romans have left in charge of Syria, offering their caravans safe passage through to the East. They only need to pay some annual tax and let us keep our independence."

"I see that you've thought all this through," said Yehuda, amazed. "But what of the priests in Yerushalaim who collaborate with the Romans and the Judeans who follow them?"

"The priests can take care of themselves. Without them, it's just one less tax to pay, one less tribute. Who can argue with that?" said Zakarya, raising his hands in disbelief. "The temple is in your heart, rather than that abomination of wealth and privilege that old Herodes built. And there can't be very many Judeans who really believe that the priests in Yerushalaim are offering up anything other than a spectacle for them three times a year. It's just a religious form of the circus that the Romans put on to keep their ignorant people sedated. Once we enter Yerushalaim, we will present a scion of Dawid to them as the leader, and that will satisfy everyone."

"One thing that Shemuel taught me before I went to the temple," said Yehuda slowly to Zakarya, "is that there are many more ignorant people who just want to be sedated than one thinks. One needs to account for people not doing the wise, or even intelligent, thing," he said and smiled sadly.

Zakarya blanched. "God help us! I hope he was wrong in this case," he said.

At that moment, there was a commotion in the courtyard outside. Ioannis jumped to his feet and ran to the window. He saw several armed men on horseback enter. One of the horses carried a long bundle slung over the Roman four-horned saddle at its middle.

"Don't worry, my son," called Yauseph to Ioannis's back. "That must be my son Ya'aqub returning with Shemuel ben Yahayye's *pegra*, his corpse. His breath, of course, lives on. Ya'aqub will place the *pegra* in one of the family tombs built into the hillside. Then later, when only the bones remain, we will place them in a stone box, or give them to his son."

"As soon as we heard about Shemuel's murder," Eliyuhena explained, "we arranged to collect the corpse. That only required a small bribe, since no one at the Roman garrison thought him a man of any importance, just another casualty of bandits. Then we sent word to Shemuel's son, Mikhael. We need to bury our priest the first time now, before Shabbat, but he could fetch the bones later and take them home for the second burial. We just heard late this afternoon by return messenger that Mikhael is on his way; he will be here just after Sabbath ends tomorrow. He apparently doesn't travel on Shabbat, even in an emergency, although I have a hard time believing he's very pious. Shemuel told us he is a merchant."

"Yes, that's right. Very strange," said Yehuda, scratching his head. "But Shabbat is a conflicted issue in these lands. I've heard that these Hassaya, whom you say Yohanan was visiting, also don't travel at all on the Sabbath. I only know about their group living near the Dead Sea, not the one in Batanea. The Pharisaioi, the *Priyeshey,* or 'preventing ones,' also don't travel on the Sabbath. They make a living from the ruling elite by trying to keep the masses under control, busy paying attention to rules of ritual purity that they create. It's certainly a good way to prevent any revolutionary energy arising that the poor might have left after they work themselves to the bone all day. Others take the Shabbat more symbolically. Shemuel taught me to remember the spaciousness, the turning within, of the Holy One on the seventh day."

"Yes, he told us that as well," said Zakarya. "And that's what we celebrate here. We invite you to remain as our guest until Mikhael arrives. Maybe then we can find out what Shemuel told him about his last trip. It may be important for us all to know, particularly whether anyone found out about us. When Mikhael arrives, we had planned to tell him as little as possible about ourselves and only what he probably already knows: that Shemuel regularly came here to offer us religious teaching. And if he doesn't want to take Shemuel's body back to Paneas, we will bury it here properly."

Ioannis returned to the table next to Yehuda. As he walked across the room he noticed an elaborate floor mosaic, mostly composed of animals eating one another. Beautifully, of course. The most peaceful figure was a rabbit eating grapes. *I suppose I still need to remain on guard,* he thought.

As if hearing his thoughts, at that moment, a muscular, redheaded man in his midthirties burst into the room, breathing heavily. He was wearing a sword and clearly knew how to use it.

"I'm back!" he said to Yauseph. "We barely got the corpse into one of the platforms in the tomb and the stone rolled back in time. The sun is setting soon." He looked quickly around the room and stopped when he noticed Yehuda and Ioannis. "Who are these strangers?" he asked angrily, putting his hand on his sword.

ChapTeR 13
The Ways of Natzaran Men

"This is Yehuda Tauma ben Yahayye, Shemuel's student, nephew and adopted son," explained Eliyuhena. "He has come to try to help us find out what happened. I was just explaining to him our situation."

Ya'aqub exploded. "How do you know he is this Yehuda Tauma? I never heard of him. And why are you giving away our secrets to such a person? Don't we have trouble enough?" He walked over to the head table threateningly.

"Son, please put your sword away," said Yauseph soothingly. "Remember, it is almost Shabbat."

"Ya'aqub, listen a moment and calm down," said Eliyuhena forcefully. "I know that your half brother Yeshua is also missing due to this crisis. We're here to try to sort that out. Not only are we and our families at stake, but also the plans and sacrifices of our ancestors. We need to take action to safeguard them. We all trusted Shemuel, and he told me before he left here earlier this week that Yehuda Tauma was a friend, working inside the belly of the whale in Yerushalaim. We need all the friends we can get right now. Yehuda gave all the right signs when I met him. He was also in contact with Korah, who sends us information via intermediaries from his own sources."

"All right," said Ya'aqub grudgingly. "Let's get down to it. God help anyone who betrays us!"

"Where were we?" asked Eliyuhena, turning to Yehuda.

"You were explaining about how you would kick the Romans and the priests out of Yerushalaim with your claim to Dawid's lineage. But what about the northerners, the Galileans, Samaritans and others?" persisted Yehuda. "They aren't going to bow down just because you mention Dawid and the branch. Everyone else thinks he's just a cursed Judean."

"For the real Israelites, we are from the north," replied Zakarya, raising a finger for emphasis. "For those beyond the Yarden, over in Decapolis, we have our Ammonite and Moabite heritage. We have a lineage that includes *all* sides, and anyway, it's the victors who write down the history and make up the family trees. We will unite as children of Ya'aqub, whom some call *Yisrael*, the one who wrestled with the Holy One. One of our commanders here will present himself as a successor of the judges, the military leader. Another will act as the prophet, preaching a vision that stirs the people into action. Once we drive the Romans out, a third will ride into Yerushalaim as the anointed one, a king to bring everyone together."

"And do you have people who can fill all these roles?" asked Yehuda.

"We *did*," replied Eliyuhena slowly, rolling his eyes, "but as Zakarya mentioned, things have gone a bit crooked."

Yehuda thought for a bit. "You mean that Yohanan was supposed to be the prophet and…"

"And he started too early, before all of the other pieces were in place," said Yauseph, shaking his head.

"Not only that," said Zakarya, turning to Yauseph, "but the one we thought could act as the anointed one and rule from Yerushalaim turned out to be a bit…impractical. That is Yeshua."

"But we don't really need all of these different roles, if we have a strong military leader," protested Ya'aqub, hitting his chest with his fist. "And we have that."

"Yes, Ya'aqub, we know you think that," said Yauseph to his son, "and that you are he. You are a fine commander. But you aren't able to bring visions through from the unseen. And honestly, you do not have the skill with the common people to win their loyalty. For a united Israel, all three are needed."

"Yehuda, now you see our full trouble," said Zakarya. "Do you have any ideas about what we can do now?"

"I was hoping to find out what happened to Shemuel," said Yehuda, avoiding the question. "That's why I'm here. Isn't that part of the picture, too? If someone discovered who he was, your plans are also in jeopardy from whoever killed him. He could have been in contact with other groups besides your clan. Perhaps he had his own plans. Do you have any information? Did he say anything while he was here about being in danger?"

Zakarya looked at Eliyuhena, who looked back at him. Neither said a word for a while. Then finally Eliyuhena spoke, choosing his words carefully, as he looked around the room.

"Look. Shemuel spoke to only a few of us the last time he was here. He talked in riddles, and perhaps

Yohanan or Yeshua might have understood him if they had been here. I didn't. From what I understood, he hoped to visit a student in Yerushalaim. That must have been you. He also spoke about some trouble or betrayal in his family. I assumed at the time that he was referring to his son, Mikhael, to him not continuing in Shemuel's footsteps as a scribe. But now we see that Shemuel had many families, so I don't know which one he was talking about. We knew he supported us, but he must have served others as well."

"We have told you much about ourselves," broke in Ya'aqub, looking at Yehuda closely. "Why don't you tell us a bit more about yourself? For instance, what are you doing here? Why aren't you in Yerushalaim? How did you meet Shemuel? And who are your people?"

Several of the men and women stood up and moved toward the kitchen. As sunset neared, they began bringing in cooked food to tables at the periphery of the room, so that it would be ready to serve immediately after the ritual blessing of bread and wine. Ioannis's stomach grumbled as the smells of the cooking floated through the room. He noticed that a few of the men besides Ya'aqub were looking suspiciously at Yehuda and himself.

Yehuda ignored the tone of interrogation in Ya'aqub's voice and answered as briefly and honestly as he could.

"I've quit the temple," he said, turning both palms over on the table in front of him. "I was fed up with the mission that Shemuel gave me. I didn't see that things were getting any better or that I could possibly improve them. He mainly asked me to keep my eyes and ears open and to report to him occasionally. He told me explicitly to do whatever the high priest asked me to do. As Qayapha collected more and more wealth for himself, that eventually entailed keeping track of and collecting all of his secret obligations. At the time, I didn't see how that was going to help anyone but Qayapha himself."

"Did you give Shemuel information about Qayapha's debts and clients?" asked Zakarya.

"Yes, of course. He asked, and I told him everything."

"Well, that's why you were there then!" said Eliyuhena. "Shemuel used that information to infiltrate those links between the high priest and his clients."

"Of course, now I understand," mused Yehuda reluctantly. "Once in a while, Shemuel would ask me to recopy an old manuscript that was in the temple vaults and then either give him a copy or smuggle out the original and leave the copy in its place. The priests don't really care about these manuscripts, anyway, so it didn't seem important to me. My bodyguard Ioannis was also looking for a new start, so he left with me."

Yehuda looked around the tables, meeting the eyes of as many of the family as he could. He spoke from the heart. "I was the youngest son of a large family from near Zippori. When my father died, there was nothing left for me, so Shemuel, who was my uncle, adopted me and taught me the ways of the scribe. I spent most of my boyhood and early life in Paneas with him, as he prepared me to take his place in Yerushalaim. He was away much of the time, of course, but he gave me plenty to read and study. Much of what I was supposed to study was nature, the stars and planets, learning how to read them as if they were a sacred scroll."

"So you must know his son, Mikhael," said Eliyuhena. "What is he like?"

"Yes, I know Mikhael, but he is a generation older than I am," said Yehuda. "He had his own friends, and that didn't include me. Then he moved away to Darmsuq for some years to start a caravan business, from what I heard. When I moved to Yerushalaim ten years ago, Shemuel asked Mikhael to come back home to help him with the family home and small farm he had. From what Shemuel said, I don't think Mikhael was happy about coming home, but he did. After that, I didn't go back to Paneas more than once or twice. It took some years for Shemuel to get me moved up the ladder at the temple, and then I saw him mostly when he visited Yerushalaim to receive my reports or retrieve a manuscript."

"You say that your family was from near Zippori," said Zakarya. "Probably I know them. Who are—or were—they?"

Yehuda had been dreading that question, but he determined that he needed to trust the Natzara. They had trusted him. And then there was the matter of the last manuscript that Shemuel has asked him to copy—"what eye has not seen and what ear has not heard." He decided to get right to the point.

"Look. My eldest brother is Benyamin ben Yohanan," he said and then paused. As he anticipated, the room erupted in indignation. Several of the men cursed, and others leaned forward, putting their head in their hands in despair. Ya'aqub sat bolt upright and stared at him with suspicion. Ioannis looked at Yehuda anxiously.

Yehuda stood and continued to look at the whole group, breathing in his heart as Shemuel had taught him to do when he was worried about the reaction of others to what he was saying. He raised his hands to calm the group. Gradually the outburst subsided. "Look," he said forcefully, "all blood family members are not alike! Isn't that so? Not only is my brother much older, but also he had a different mother and inherited most of the little wealth my father left. Then he built it into even more. I've hardly seen him during the past twenty-five years, and he certainly has no interest in me. He always thought that our uncle Shemuel was just a useless dreamer."

"He became rich making friends with our oppressors, with the Herodes family," said Eliyuhena, shaking his head.

"Yes," agreed Yehuda. "He saw that the Hasmoneans, the Maccabee family, were only ever going to tear each other apart. When our father died, my brother threw in his lot with old Herodes. He recognized in the future king the combination of ruthlessness and cunning that would take the Idumean to the top. My brother was correct, and so he cultivated the same qualities. He never wanted to help his blood family very much, so he was happy that Shemuel took me off of his hands."

"We do a lot of business with Benyamin," said Yauseph, scratching his chin thoughtfully. "He thinks we're good suppliers and clients of his, whereas in reality, we have spies throughout his household. It could be awkward if he, or someone in his employ, found out that you were here. Questions would be asked."

"Yes, I understand," said Yehuda. "I have been thinking of that. I was going to visit him. It's part of the reason I gave for leaving Yerushalaim suddenly. But on our way here, we stopped in Yaphia and attended their knesset. I made a commitment to help plead the villagers' case—too many taxes—to my brother. They don't know he's my brother, of course. So that will give me an another excuse to visit him. I don't need to mention that I was here."

"Taxes, taxes, everyone has too many taxes," Zakarya said and sighed. "Does Yaphia think it's special in some way?"

"Well, we heard that their headman was murdered today," said Yehuda. "By the way, the man who sent me to you may have had something to do with it. He talked about a group, a movement that was focused on assassinating those who collaborate with the Herodes and the Romans. He showed Yehohanan and me his stiletto, and he could easily have killed me as we were walking together."

"What did he look like?" asked Eliyuhena.

"He wore ragged clothing, but he somehow did not look poor, said Yehuda. "Strong, tall and well fed, with hard, clear eyes. He knew your sign."

Yauseph, normally calm, smacked his forehead at the revelation. Other men groaned. "Just one more thing," moaned Zakarya.

Yehuda continued slowly, assessing the impact of the news on everyone present. "He also told Ioannis and me that Shemuel was 'one of theirs.' But his program seemed very different from yours, more like urban terrorism than building a secret revolutionary movement. He wouldn't give his name."

"We don't know him, do we, Ya'aqub?" asked Eliyuhena, turning to the redheaded man.

Ya'aqub shook his head silently, looking down at the table.

"That's not good at all," said Eliyuhena. "Who could he be?"

"Perhaps Shemuel had yet another family he was working with," offered Yauseph tentatively. "Did you see whether he had one of our amulets?" he asked, taking a silver hand medallion from under his tunic.

"This is the one I took from Shemuel's corpse," replied Yehuda, showing his own. "But no, I didn't see one on the stranger. From what he said, he would be unlikely to show it openly."

"But how could Shemuel work with such a group?" asked Zakarya. "Assassins! They only make things worse. They will attract more attention from the Romans, and then we'll end up with another legion posted here. That will only make the final revolution more difficult, and bloody."

"Not everyone believes that," said Ya'aqub, shrugging calmly. "There may be room for the element of distraction in our strategy. While the Romans and Herodes are looking in one direction, they won't be seeing what's happening in another."

"But this type of warfare is against our sacred ways," said Zakarya. "Killing the innocent. Where in scripture can you find it?"

"You mean hit-and-run war? Appearing and disappearing into the hills? How about Dawid himself, before he became king?" asked Ya'aqub.

CHAPTER 14
The Ways of Natzaran Women

"Cousins, we're not going to solve this now!" interrupted Yauseph. "It's only distracting us from the immediate problems we face. And more immediately, it is now time for Sabbath prayers. It is time, as Yehuda here reminded us, to turn within and trust the Holy One. To lay our inner and outer burdens down. Zakarya, would you lead the prayers that take us into Shabbat?"

Silence fell over the room as everyone took a breath in and out.

Zakarya stood and addressed the group. "As we sometimes do, tonight I ask that my wife Elishyba offer the blessings, as is part of our ancient heritage. Rather than repeat written prayers, she recites the prayers coming to her heart that we need to hear right now," he said, turning to Yehuda. "We listen to the voice of Holy Wisdom coming through a woman's voice among us. Shemuel confirmed that this is an important ancient tradition for us to continue."

He nodded to Elishyba, who sat next to him, dressed in white linen. She had been watching the proceedings with a slight smile—but the eyes of a hawk.

She stood and raised a light veil over her graying head. Then she closed her eyes and began to sway from side to side, as if in a trance. The whole group watched transfixed as she began to speak:

So on the seventh day
the heavens and earth are completing themselves,
with all their swirl of habits and laws.
The caravan of creation continues,
the great Beginning in front of us
and those in the future behind us
urging us on from behind.
The heavens and earth around us
are calling forth all of the possibilities,
challenges and opportunities that
the Holy One has radiated from
ahead of us in bereshith,
the mysterious beginning-moment.

The words "was" and "shall be" are echoing
through the heart of the Holy One now
as we hear them in our own hearts.

Yehuda was struck that she was retelling Moshe's old creation story as though it were all happening now, not a long time ago. But then, he reflected, the old Hebrew verbs could be heard as past, present and future, all at the same time.

Spreading through the four directions,
filling heaven and earth,
what is left for the seventh
movement of the light symphony
of the Holy One?

It can only be the mysterious
movement of returning,
of turning within.

Elishyba became more animated, as if the spirit of priestesses and goddesses of all times had taken possession of her. Yehuda didn't know what to make of this. He had only experienced Shemuel going into such states, with his everyday self displaced by some other being. Shemuel had mentioned that women, too, could access the heavenly realms, but Yehuda had never seen it happen before. As Elishyba continued more deeply into trance, she began to exert a hypnotic power on the group. She opened her eyes and looked around at them. A light radiated from her whole being.

Listen, my family!
A clear "I can!" is resounding
from the heart of the universe,
responding to the questioning void
that began creation.

Nothing can return to the way it was,
no matter what happens!

So the Holy One is now permitting itself,
through us,
the most mysterious creation of all.
It is restoring to itself
the remembrance
　　of all that has been going on
　　from the beginning of time until now.

We remember, now, in awe and mystery,
what was before the beginning.
We ride that wave
and feel deep compassion

for everything that drops its form
and returns to join the ancestors —
with all that dies.
We go that way, too!

We now touch the void
and remember that
everything we care about,
everything that seems so important,
all our plans,
at one point were not here,
and at another point will not be.

Yehuda noticed that many of the men shifted uncomfortably at this point. She was asking them to lay down their plans and their whole identity. To let them go entirely. Even deeply in her state, Elishyba seemed to sense this. Still deeply in the trance, she spoke more soothingly to the family, opening her palms in front of her:

My family, don't worry — we have help!
The Holy One is sending out another breath,
a breath of blessing and support toward us.
It is remembering, through us,
its own original state.
All of the heavens and earth
are on this journey with us,
returning to the Source,
but we forget.

This inner turning and returning,
the opportunity to pause and reconnect

with each other and with the Source,
flows through the lifeblood,
makes its tent in the very bones
of our community.
Only this is sacred —
this moment, this gathering of light,
this holy day!

Everyone responded "Ameyn!" affirming their willingness to be true to the vision she had brought through.

Elishyba recited simple blessings over a cup of wine and a loaf of bread. She then began to pass them both around the tables. Each person shared the cup or bread with the person next to him or her, adding a personal blessing of Shabbat. Next, family members brought the rest of the food from the tables at the sides and began to share it.

Yehuda reflected that the meal was simple yet strangely rich. The usual Israelite staples of bread, herbed olive oil for dipping and vegetable stew were served alongside opulent baked fish—tilapia from Lake Kinneret—as well as smoked sea bream from the *Mare Nostrum*. The latter was definitely a luxury.

After they had eaten a bit, Ioannis sighed contentedly and leaned toward Yehuda. "What do you think, Master? Will we stay here for another day or so? Can we delay our journey that long?"

"Yes," said Yehuda, "we can. It will give the people in Yaphia time to pick a new leader for their delegation to my brother. And that will give us another reason to be in Zippori, besides my personal one. Also, maybe Shemuel's son will be able to give us some information about why he left Paneas."

"I notice that you gave them a very straightforward story about why you're here, as well as your past," said Ioannis in a softer voice. "But you didn't mention a couple of points: the two items you found at the temple recently. One small and round, the other a manuscript."

"You're right, I didn't," said Yehuda, smiling wryly. "Trust opens the door to more trust. But not everything needs to be disclosed at the same time. Sometimes a little patience is the best strategy, as Shemuel taught me. Then 'what eye has not seen and what ear has not heard' is in no danger of causing anyone unnecessary difficulty."

"What they don't know can't hurt us, or them, you mean?"

"Something like that, Ioannis. Let us finish enjoying the beginning of Shabbat, shall we?"

The sun had long disappeared behind the horizon by the time they finished the meal. People began to leave the room and return home. Yehuda stayed behind to speak to Eliyuhena and Zakarya and to learn where they would be staying.

Ioannis walked out into the courtyard to wait for Yehuda and noticed that the crescent moon had risen over the horizon, slightly fuller than the night before. His head was swimming with the complexity of all the Natzara family's plans. He wondered whether some, or any of them, could actually happen. What kept coming into his mind, however, was the picture of Elishyba, Zakarya's wife, as she gave the Sabbath blessing—her eyes shining, her voice resonant, her gray hair curled around her brow like the goddess Hera. Since being sold into slavery, he had lived mainly in a man's world, a world of those who held command and power, or were trying to get it.

He knew of women as the wives of his masters, as other slaves, or as prostitutes, but nothing like this. Nor had he seen women and men sitting together to make decisions for their community. If Elishyba were a sample, the women here were unlike any others he had met.

As if summoned by his thoughts, a young woman emerged from the dinner to draw water from the well in the courtyard. As she was about to return, she noticed Ioannis standing nearby. She walked over to him. Her light veil wreathed her dark-brown hair, but her face, a thin aquiline nose and open brow, was clearly visible in the moonlight. Clear, intelligent blue eyes, bearing some curiosity, looked boldly into his.

"You are welcome here, friend. You can feel safe here," she said, as if reading his thoughts.

"Thank you," said Ioannis, a bit disconcerted, feeling anything but safe with her. "My name is Yehohanan. May I be permitted to know yours?"

"Some people say you should be permitted, since I have spoken to you. Others say you should not, since you are not of the family," she replied, smiling. "However, you have eaten and prayed with us, so to me you are part of our family. My name is Zilpah. I am the younger sister of one of the men they were talking about, the one who has gone missing, Yeshua.

"Aren't you worried about him?" asked Ioannis. "I would be if it were my brother." *If I had a brother,* he gulped. *Talking to this woman is making me speak like an idiot.*

"No, I don't worry about Yeshua," responded Zilpah, looking down and then raising her face to him. "He has always lived in another world, or maybe two others. If you count this one, it makes at least three. Even if he wandered into the wild areas on the other side of the Yarden, he would still end up making friends with the birds and lions and whomever else he met. Nature is one of the worlds he travels in easily. Only people sometimes cause him problems. They often expect him to be something that he's not."

"What would that be?" asked Ioannis.

"Well, my father first hoped he would be a carpenter. My mother thought he would be a prophet, something about visions she had before he was born. Then Shemuel hoped that Yeshua would carry on part of his work here, as teacher and priest of our community. The old scribe told a few of us that when he was here last. As you heard, the family hoped he might one day lead us into Yerushalaim, winning the people's hearts." Zilpah put down the jug of water she was carrying and stood again, raising her hands in exasperation. "'The holy remnant of the ten tribes of the north.' Hah! I don't think Yeshua was interested in any of it."

"So what do you think happened to him, or to Yohanan?"

"My cousin Yohanan…if he got involved with some kind of cult and became convinced…He has incredible concentration. Shemuel used to say that Yohanan was one of his best students. And my cousin does things with so much energy and passion, almost too much. So if Yohanan gave Yeshua some kind of baptism or took him into some kind of trance, it might have launched my brother in a whole new direction, in this world or another. Only the Holy One knows…" Her voice trailed off, and before Ioannis knew it, he was simply staring at her face. He realized that he should say something, but somehow the pause had gone on a little too long.

Then he noticed that another woman had come out of the house and was walking toward them.

"Zilpah, we are still waiting for the water…ah, I see…"

"You know our guest, Yehohanan, mother," said Zilpah, picking up the water jug again and turning toward her confidently. "We were just talking about what might have happened to my brother. Excuse me, Yehohanan. This is my mother, Mariam."

"Shalama, honored lady," said Ioannis, remembering his better Aramaic. He immediately saw where Zilpah's eyes had come from—the same still clarity, penetrating but not overly serious. Mariam's eyes had a tinge of sadness around them, however, and it seemed that she could read his thoughts. From her, the words *I see* conveyed something more than the usual meaning.

"Shalama. It's nice to meet you, Yehohanan. I hope that my daughter has *appropriately* welcomed you to our community. Perhaps you would both like to come back inside now? Yehohanan, I believe that your friend Yehuda is ready for you and him to go to your room for the night."

Chapter 15

Dreams of Heather

As the sun rose over Caesarea Maritimus by the sea, Pontius Pilatus awoke at dawn, dreaming of heather.

As a young boy in the highlands of Caledonia, he had roamed with his father along a meandering river through a long, wooded valley. *Gleann Lìomhann*, the locals had called it in their strange language. Although Pilatus had covered his tracks sufficiently, he didn't like anyone to know that his blood was as mixed as many Roman officers. He wasn't any more from Italia than Ioannis, even less so.

His mother was Caledonian; his father was originally a Gaul who had been rewarded with Roman citizenship for his service as a spy to Julius Caesar during the latter's Gallic wars. Later, on the orders of Caesar Augustus, he had posed as a trader to the tribes in the northern British Isles; however, he was really an informal Roman envoy to the local king, Metallanus. His father had tried to persuade Metallanus to support the Romans when they came. The king could increase his status, raise tribute and win powerful allies when the Romans finally, and inevitably, invaded. To the king, the Roman Empire was only an abstract idea, but he tolerated Pilatus's father because he found him entertaining. Then the Gaul fell in love with a woman from the north, in a village with an ancient, sacred yew tree. They had a child together and settled down for nearly a decade. But Pilatus's father never forgot his mission and continued to secretly supply Rome with information for a possible invasion: the location of roads, trade routes and fortified brochs, as well as the battle tactics of Celtic warriors.

As in all such villages, no one ever trusted the incomer, and the local boys used to taunt and bully young Pilatus, who had a strange name. Left to himself, he used to take refuge in the branches of the giant yew tree and plot his imaginary revenge. People told the boy that it would kill him to spend too much time in the sacred tree, but he didn't care. He would look out over the glen, feeling the cool wind and hearing the refreshing sound of the river, hoping to find his rightful place somewhere.

Eventually his father had taken him back to Rome. He couldn't gather any more information, and he realized that his son would miss a proper Roman education. When they arrived in Rome, young Pilatus, because he was clearly not local, was given a special cap, a *ponteus*, to show that although he was of mixed blood, he was a freeman and a citizen. It was for his protection, but it had been his shame. He later adapted the word as part of his name out of spite and to distinguish himself from those whom he believed to be his inferiors. Due to will power and audacity, he rose quickly through the ranks of the army. He still missed the land of his birth, however. That's why he preferred to be in the Roman fortress in Caesarea on the coast, where at least he could see water. Something in his Celtic spirit hated all the dust and earth that often shifted and rocked under your feet.

The day before, a secret messenger from Rome had informed Pilatus that an invasion of Caledonia could be forthcoming, and that he might be called back to help lead it. It gave him hope. He might be relieved of the odious job he currently held: collecting tax from religious fanatics in a place that was simultaneously nowhere and in between everywhere important. He had a chance, that is, if he didn't do something foolish that caused Rome any problems. Pilatus took stock of himself coldly. He was thirty-six years old, equestrian rank. The previous prefect, Valerius Gratus, had served ten years here. Pilatus had now served six years, and he didn't want to wait another four or more to be transferred elsewhere. He was wasting his best years here, and he was a better man than Gratus, anyway.

After some less-than-adequate local wine, he had fallen asleep dreaming of honor and prestige in the name of the empire. Strangely, he had awoken dreaming of heather. *One way or another,* Pilatus reflected, *I will get back home! And when I go back, it will be on my own terms. I will pay back those who bullied me as a child with the iron of the Roman army. Then I can settle down with a local woman like my mother...Roman culture in a beautiful wooded glen...top man in paradise.*

He pushed himself out of bed, threw on his tunic and mantle and called for his personal secretary. A few minutes later, the man appeared and presented himself to Pilatus, who was sitting in a chair near the window, looking out over the sea.

"Yes, Prefect."

"I may be leaving here soon, Aristeaus. I have been thinking that I must not leave any loose ends."

"Yes, Prefect."

"You have been reading all of our spying reports from this area. Do you see any potential trouble arising?"

Aristeaus, who had an excellent memory, quickly reviewed all that the spies had reported over the last month. He organized things in his mind from the south (closest, most tamed) to the north (farthest, most volatile) and began, raising a finger for each point:

"First, Judea: our largest problem here is Qayapha, the priest, who as you know was appointed by your predecessor. First, he is supposed to handle the civil administration of Yerushalaim, but does so badly. On feast days, there are always too many people in the city for my liking. The common people swarm into the city to get fed from the sacrifices of the priests. This is understandable, because they're providing the meat and food that is sacrificed, but there are still too many arriving for anyone to keep public order if some sort of revolt were planned for the same time. That *has* happened previously.

"Second, in addition to collecting 'sacrifice' for himself and his priests, Qayapha is supposed to help us collect tribute and taxes for Caesar. But that rarely happens. When it's time to send tribute to Rome, we usually have to send men into the temple and simply confiscate any food, supplies and valuables we find. This is a bother, and we should not have to do this. Also, we have to conduct the raids in the middle of the night, when most people are sleeping. That way we don't cause a riot by Judeans claiming that we're committing sacrilege. We could replace Qayapha, but there's no likely candidate in the wings, certainly no one who would perform better for us, anyway."

"I understand," said Pilatus, grimacing. "It is odious that we have to deal with these people, but from what I've heard from my friends, the situation is quite usual in the backwaters of the empire. And let's face it; that is where we are. The additional problem is the religious-fanatic element, as you say. Most of Rome's conquered peoples are happy when we help them build temples to their local gods, and they don't think anything of paying tribute. Here they rejected our help, again some strange notion of sacrilege. Are they still finishing their temple in Yerushalaim—the one old Herodes started remodeling?"

"Yes, of course, Prefect. It seems to go on forever. Old Herodes didn't really have much of a plan. He finished the main part before he died, but there are innumerable unfinished wings, passageways and tunnels. No one will provide us with an overall architectural design, much secrecy and the usual holiness nonsense, so we can't determine how near they are to finishing it."

"Do you think they're hiding something in there?" asked Pilatus, spitting on the floor. "That would be just like them."

"I don't know, Prefect," answered Aristeaus. "It's a loose end, certainly. Shall I have them bring in Qayapha for some enhanced questioning?"

"No, no…that could start a riot also. If we replace the man, perhaps then, but not now. OK, so much for Judea. Anything else?"

"Third, Samaria and Galilee: Mostly small villages, so no large groups gather without us knowing. Again, crowds tend to appear in sites that the locals consider sacred. In Samaria, there's Mount Gerizim. Samaritans consider that much more sacred than Yerushalaim. They think the Yerushalaim Temple is an abomination, and they are worshipping as their prophet Moshe did: in the open, on the high places. But I don't see any inclination to revolt up there. We even periodically receive tribute from a few villages via the local headmen we own there."

"That's all good, then," said Pilatus, leaning back in his chair, a bit relieved. "We want as much dissension as possible over what is sacred to whom. It keeps them all at each other's throats. And Galilee? Historically, those hills have been the breeding ground for rebels. They almost overthrew the old Herodes until we saved his skin. Hill people are always independently minded, I can tell you. I was raised among some of them."

"Prefect, so far as I can tell, things are fairly quiet on that front also. We have a headman in Zippori who regularly sends tribute. He is dishonest, but knows not to be too dishonest with us. Zippori is the main town up there, and it was the center of the last revolt, the one against old Herodes. I can understand the revolt, of course. The old Herodes built a lot, but he was a madman—killed thousands of innocents as well as most of his own family. Not a good way to increase a tax base."

Pilatus rubbed his temples in disgust. *What a country; what a history!*

"Yes, Aristeaus," he sighed, "a madman…but our madman, at least. So nothing else?"

"Just the usual banditry, but that's also normal for these poor rural areas. Rob from the rich; keep it for yourself. What else can you do if there's no land and no work? Then there is the occasional freelance religious visionary who pops up. They call them *nabiyim*, prophets. People who have lost touch with reality—well, who can blame them, either? Sometimes people gather around these men, but mostly they lose interest. Poor people need to find food and shelter, and if there's none on offer, a prophet won't do the trick. I have heard of one recently who may be getting a bit political. Besides going into trance, he also yells about the corruption of one of the old Herodes's sons, Antipas."

"Is there any truth to what he says?" Pilatus stood and began pacing back and forth. He had a bad feeling about this somehow.

"Antipas does his best not to tax people too severely, *he* says. But there are reports of him not only taking food as tax, but enslaving the children of people who he says owe him money."

"Many of our best clients do this, Aristeaus," said Pilatus drolly. "Some people are just in the wrong place or even born at the wrong time."

"Yes, but like his father, Antipas is also obsessed with luxury-building projects to impress his patrons in Rome. With more and more tax, including human tax, he's also increasing his army. He's always trying to outfox us, or his brother Philipos in Gaulanitis, to persuade Rome to allow him to rule over the whole area."

Pilatus stopped pacing and scratched his chin thoughtfully. "It would be a disaster, of course. He's a terrible administrator—throws a decent feast, certainly—drunk much of the time, distracted by women constantly. But if he were king like his father, it *might* get us out of here…"

"We might be back in soon, however," said Aristeaus, smiling, "given the factors you've mentioned."

"Ah…but given a decent interval," said Pilatus, raising a finger, "it would be a different *us*, Aristeaus."

"Is there anything else, Prefect?"

"Not for now, Aristeaus. Just keep me informed the moment you hear of any trouble on the horizon. As I said, I may be going soon, and if you continue to be diligent, I will take you with me. By the way, did you hear anything from that bodyguard of Qayapha's scribe, Yehuda? Ioannis was the guard's name...the one we embedded to get us information about funds hidden in the temple."

"Let me think...Yes, a few days ago some of our men saw them crossing the Plain of Esdraelon, the one the locals call the Jezreel Valley. They were heading north into Galilee. But they did tell Qayapha that's where they were going, according to our sources at the temple. Some family matter or other of the scribe."

"All right. Perhaps he will have something for us when he returns. He's an opportunistic lad. He may see or hear something that helps us. That will be all, Aristeaus."

Pilatus walked back to the window and returned his attention to the sea. The port city of Caesarea was just waking up, boats were being loaded, preparing to head west into the Great Sea. *If only I never had to go back to Yerushalaim! Caesarea was the model of what a colonial city should be. Clean, orderly, built along Roman lines. You would never guess that you were in a country of corruption, banditry and religious fanatics here. And escape is only a ship away,* he thought, looking at the wharf. Closing his eyes, he listened to the waves and imagined the sound of the water to be his own little, private river winding through a glen in Caledonia.

Chapter 16
Hidden Scents

At sundown the next day, Yehuda and Ioannis gathered with the community to say farewell to Shabbat. Both looked back on the day just ending. They had learned things they didn't expect, and they were more confused than ever.

The night before, Eliyuhena had shown them to a very comfortable room in the family villa, a wing reserved for visitors and guests. Eliyuhena told Yehuda they had decided to lodge the two in the same room that Shemuel used when he visited. Some of the teacher's belongings were still there, so he hoped Yehuda would feel at home. After sleeping in the open for the past two nights, they were ready for actual beds and slept soundly. It was very quiet in the villa, and only the activity of the household and its animals awoke them the next morning at dawn.

After breakfast, Yehuda announced that he was going to spend the day in meditation. He also planned to look through Shemuel's scrolls and belongings to see if he could find a clue about where his uncle had been going before getting killed.

Ioannis decided to go for a walk in the surrounding countryside above the villa. It was a beautiful, clear day. The coolness of mid-spring was beginning to give way to a hint of the warmth that would become overwhelming by summer. The wildflowers they had seen the day before, plus wild herbs like hyssop, coriander, mint, mustard and rue, were just coming into their own. As he walked uphill, he found himself in a field of flax, most of which had already been harvested.

He noticed that no one from the villa was out in the fields, even though it was midmorning. *Orthodox or not, they're at least resting from work if not counting their steps,* Ioannis thought. He had noticed several priests in Yerushalaim limiting their movement on the Sabbath. His mother had told him a little about Shabbat, which she said went back to the Babylonians resting on what they considered "evil days," days during which one should not make a wish. *Probably taking a break from wishing could be helpful,* he reflected. *Too much wishing for what one doesn't have can bring unhappiness.* His mother had said that while living in Rome she always kept Shabbat inside rather than outside. It would have attracted too much attention to just stop and do nothing, she said.

As he walked farther overland, in the direction of Zippori, he found himself in a rocky field filled with mixed shrubs and trees of the most bizarre appearance. Some trees had gray, flaky bark, like paper, which peeled off to reveal a green layer underneath. Many of the branches divided repeatedly and were tipped in spines. Other trees had a very soft texture, like cork. Some showed small branches with even smaller four-petaled white flowers. Others were yielding round, red fruit bursting in the middle to reveal inner seeds. The bushes had similar, unpredictably branching shapes, but hugged the ground. Cracks in the bark, on both the bushes and trees, revealed an oozing sap. Small insects flew around, pollinating the male and female bushes and trees, which all had different appearances. The whole area seemed to be wild, with no purpose or design. Ioannis was struck by an intense rush of aromas and smells, predominantly a mixture of licorice, mushroom and damp wood.

He sat down on a rock in the midst of the field, intoxicated by the smells and suddenly wanting to take a rest. As he breathed in the aromas and looked out over the hillside below him, he could just make out the roof of one of the buildings of the family's villa. He wondered who owned this land, but as he looked around him for any boundary markers, he noticed over his shoulder that someone was watching him from farther up the hill. He stood up quickly, turned around and saw the figure began to walk slowly toward him. It was a woman, and the gait and figure looked familiar. Zilpah.

"Shalama, Yehohanan," she said, coming up to him. "I'm sorry to have disturbed your meditation. Please be seated and continue."

"Shalama, Zilpah. I will sit if you do," said Ioannis, indicating another rock near, but not too near, to the one on which he had been sitting. Zilpah sat down, and for a few moments, they both looked out over the hillside fields together.

"I notice that you're out this morning, unlike the rest of your family," said Ioannis, attempting to make some conversation.

"Yes, I'm out," she said, still looking downhill and smiling, but offering nothing more.

"I was struck by this field, overcome really," he said. "I've never seen, or smelled, anything like it. Is it wild?"

"Wild?" she asked, looking at him slyly with a sideways glance. "Yes...I suppose it is...in a way...

partly. It's my responsibility for the family. That's why I'm out today. Just to have a look."

"But what is it?" Ioannis pressed, turning toward her. "It doesn't seem to be a crop. Just a jumble of spiky bushes and trees."

"The smells should have told you," replied Zilpah calmly, still looking over the hillside. "Maybe there are too many of them, too many smells? If so, I've done my work well. Only a few of these plants are crops, you could say. The valuable ones are mixed in with many other common varieties. Anyone without an expert eye would simply think they had happened upon a jumble, as you first thought. A tax collector, for instance."

"And I'm not a tax collector, correct?"

"Yes," she said and sighed, turning to face him more directly. "I don't know why I'm so protective. The family has decided to trust you with all of its closest secrets, and so I should trust you as well. I certainly *want* to," she said, clasping her hands together on her lap and looking at them. She looked up at him again, smiling. "If you sat here long enough, you would probably notice, underneath all of the other smells, a particular one."

"A bit like licorice mixed with mushrooms?" asked Ioannis.

"Yes, that's it! You have a good nose. You probably never mixed in the social circles where you would have smelled it before. There's a variety of it used in healing and perfumes. It is very valuable, by weight more valuable than gold. From a few bushes and trees here, we can produce the *tzori*, balsam, sometimes called 'balm of Gilead.' These few plants may be worth more than the produce of all the other fields the family owns and all the other crops or goods that we trade."

"I've heard of it," said Ioannis. "But I thought it only grew in the south, near the Dead Sea."

"Yes, that's what everyone thinks," replied Zilpah, raising an eyebrow. "That's why we don't grow more of it. It took a generation to prepare the field to create the right soil conditions, through drainage and bringing in earth from the south. We received the original plants from relatives beyond the Yarden in Gilead. You won't find a hillside like this anywhere else in Galilee."

"And you keep it a secret from the tax collectors?" Ioannis smiled. "Well, that makes perfect sense, Zilpah." He was relieved to have something to talk about that didn't involve the fact that they were talking intimately. And sitting rather too closely together.

"We have to have something, of course, to show Antipas's agents or the Romans, or whoever else comes along to tax us," said Zilpah, continuing on breezily. "So we show them the flax fields, or the flocks, or the wine business. It makes us citizens in good standing, and then we can trade with the rich and powerful as good clients. It is just part of the Grand Plan, as they told you last night," she said, looking down and frowning slightly. "We trade the distilled essences of this *murra,* the balm, secretly through brokers and other traders who don't know where it comes from, except from Israel. We have the highest quality, by reputation.

"And this? And they leave it to you, a..."

"Yes, a woman, you were about to say, Yehohanan!" said Zilpah, looking up and laughing. "Yes, to me. Less obvious that way, and I know more about plants than the rest of them put together."

"So the income from this goes to..."

"It goes to, well, to the whole plan. You'll find out more, if you need to know," said Zilpah, suddenly serious again. "They'll tell you. Yeshua was supposed to be in charge of this field, but he was never reliable. He kept running off to be with his friends in other villages, things like that. Maybe he spent too much time here as a boy, inhaling the smells. I don't know. Anyway, about five years ago, my father Yauseph told me that it was now my responsibility."

"I thought from what you said last night that Yeshua was the great hope of your extended family."

"Yes, too many expectations on him, I think. He is my favorite brother, and I love him, but he wasn't really born for expectations. He always had his own way. He went along to Shemuel's lessons only because he liked to be with his favorite cousin, Yohanan. Yeshua had natural ability, but Yohanan really studied all of the texts Shemuel was teaching to his few private students here. You understand, most people in the community just wanted Shemuel to be their priest, to offer rituals in the old northern Israelite way."

"Did you attend Shemuel's lessons, too?"

"Yes. He encouraged me, but used to tease me about my name, Zilpah, which means to trickle down. 'Let the light of the Holy One trickle down through the top of your head, Zilpah,' he used to say. Or 'I see the sap of joy oozing from you today, Zilpah.' Someone must have tipped him off about the balsam field, or more likely he just smelled it on my clothing. It does become overpowering. Not much escaped Shemuel's notice. Maybe that's why someone killed him. Sometimes I remember a few simple things that he taught us—to slow down our breathing, to imagine light in our hearts, to feel joy in our skin." She shifted her weight, as if she were uncomfortable, and then moved sideways to a flatter rock, which was just next to the one on which Ioannis was sitting. He wiped his brow and pretended to look at the balsam fields intently.

Zilpah continued unperturbed. "All those old scrolls Shemuel talked about didn't interest me. But Yohanan immediately saw how he could use the way the old prophets spoke to rally people to the Israelite cause and to independence. 'Use their enthusiasm for religion,' he said, 'and then people will follow you anywhere.'"

"You're not so sure?" asked Ioannis.

"No, I'm sure he's correct," she said ruefully, shaking her head. "But I grew up with all of this independence talk. I literally took it in with my mother's milk. I don't see that we're much closer to it than our grandparents were. Neither are we ever likely to be. Yes, we are getting ready. Always getting ready. And we are becoming richer and more involved with the culture that we say we're trying to overthrow. How does all *that* work, I wonder?" She gazed up into the sky, as though expecting an answer.

"I don't know," replied Ioannis, turning again to look at Zilpah. "I lost both my father and mother to political intrigues. So I don't get enthused about big plans to overthrow empires." He told her briefly what his early life had been like, up to the time of being posted to the temple and meeting Yehuda. Ioannis wondered why he was telling Zilpah all this, but decided not to think too closely about it. Maybe later.

"I'm very sorry to hear about your parents," she said tenderly. "To lose them so young must be terrible." She looked down and away from him, to offer him a bit of privacy. "At least I have my mother and father. I shouldn't be ungrateful for the life my family has given me. But I do worry about Yeshua and what he may have gotten himself into."

"You think it may be dangerous?"

"That's the point. Yeshua doesn't understand what danger is!" she said, throwing up her hands. "He's always been oblivious to things that are…practical. Yeshua could end up being fodder for Yohanan's desire to bring the revolution now, on his terms rather than the family's. Yohanan is tired of waiting. And other family members will do anything to keep their secrets until they feel the time is ripe."

"So who makes the decisions? Who decides when it's time to call in all the debts and start the revolution?" asked Ioannis. "Eliyuhena? Zakarya? Your father?"

"My father and Zakarya are the elders, yes. They are the patient ones. But we have a smaller council with younger voices like Eliyuhena and my other brother Ya'aqub, the redheaded one you met last night. They are pushing for action soon. And there are women in the inner council, too, like Zakarya's wife, Elishyba, and my mother also. Without the women, it would degenerate into a mess of argument all the time. They try to moderate both sides."

"Unusual to have women involved in this, if you excuse me for saying so. I'm just not used to that, being raised in Rome."

"Yes, I understand. From what I've heard, Roman women wield a lot of power behind the scenes. But here, in the old Israelite ways, women could be more public—judges, seers or even prophets. My family continues that part of our culture, at least, even while it benefits from Greek and Roman culture in other areas." Zilpah looked toward the sun. "You know, we should probably be getting back to the villa. It's almost time for the midday meal."

She looked strangely at Ioannis for a few seconds, as though not wanting the moment to pass. "Perhaps you go first," she said, standing up quickly. "I'll follow later, since I still need to visit a few more of my plants here. You might like to see where I distill the essence of the balm when you get back. There's a small door just to the left and behind the communal privy. Hides the smell from visitors."

"All right," said Ioannis, rising to his feet and turning toward her. "Thank you for...for the talk. It was a pleasure."

"My pleasure, also," said Zilpah, moving a bit closer to face him. "I hope that we can be friends." She turned away abruptly and walked up the hill. Ioannis turned the other way and began to find his way downhill slowly among the spiked branches that reached out to grab his cloak from underneath. *Things are beginning to get sticky*, he reflected.

When he reached the villa, he decided to follow Zilpah's advice and find her perfume workshop. Toward the far end of the villa complex, he found the communal privy he had visited the night before. Around the back he found a small building to the left. Knocking on the door, he didn't receive an answer, but he hadn't expected one since Zilpah was still checking her plants. He entered through the door into a darkened room with no windows, only a small skylight overhead that was partially covered. He allowed the light from the door to show him the path down a small aisle and then shut it partially behind him. *This doesn't smell like a perfume workshop,* he thought.

Reaching up, he removed the cover from the skylight. Looking back down, he saw a trapdoor under his feet partially covered in straw. *Maybe here,* he thought, lifting the door and finding a ladder going down. *I suppose they would want to hide the balsam factory.* Even as he was descending, Ioannis began to feel distinctly uncomfortable.

When he reached the bottom, he found himself in a very large underground cavern. The light from above still illuminated the ladder, but he couldn't see very far into the cavern. *Well, I've come this far, I'll see what I can find,* he thought. Not too far from the ladder, he found a wooden crib along one of the rock walls. Reaching in, he pulled out a sword in a scabbard. Rummaging around, he found another. And another. He took one under the skylight. These were excellent swords made of hard steel, probably from Iberia. Not too far away, he found stockpiles of lances, shields and armor.

Farther into the gloom, the cellar opened into an enormous cave with a dim light at the other end. Ioannis walked toward the light and found larger siege equipment, like catapults and rams. Farther on, he found chariots. All around him he smelled something he knew well, but not perfume: equipment for war. *So everything goes in and out of the cave entrance, which is hidden from view, probably part of the hillside,* thought Ioannis.

In the same moment came another thought: *Probably I shouldn't be here.* He quickly climbed back up the ladder, replaced the cover on the skylight and hurried back down the aisle to the door to the courtyard. Closing it behind him, he had just taken a few steps toward the front of the privy when he met Ya'aqub coming around the corner toward him. His confusion must have shown on his face.

"May I help you, friend?" Ya'aqub said, a fixed smile on his face.

"I was just looking for Zilpah's workshop," explained Ioannis. "She told me that it was back here somewhere," said Ioannis, waving vaguely around behind him. Better the truth, if only a half-truth, as Yehuda said.

"Oh, that," said Ya'aqub, visibly relaxing. "That's around the other side of the privy, to the right and back." He pointed the other way. "But she's probably not there now. Somewhere up with the crops, I would think. It's about time for the midday meal anyway. Perhaps we can walk there together," he said, taking Ioannis gently but firmly by the arm.

Chapter 17

Messages from the Dead and Living

Yehuda opened his eyes when he heard the sounds of someone in the courtyard calling the residents to the midday meal. He wondered how long he had been away. What was the last thing he remembered? *Yes, Shemuel's papers. His instructions for climbing Ya'aqub's ladder. And something else?* He began to bring it all back as he looked around him in the room and saw the open lid of a wooden chest…Then he remembered.

Since Ioannis went for a walk after breakfast, Yehuda spent some time with his regular devotions, just to put himself back into his regular rhythm. While they had been on the road, he had only done his meditations in the heart, as they were walking. That was the most effective way, anyway, but part of him, he guessed it was his animal self, liked the regularity of prayer at certain times, with certain movements. Didn't the psalmist say, "seven times a day I praise you," and again, "evening and morning and noon, I will pray, and you will hear me"?

Well, seven or three, it didn't make that much difference. The regularity, retuning himself to the sun's cycle, helped calm him down and tether his *naphsha*, his small self, long enough to let his higher one, the *ruha*, begin to guide him again. After the events of the past week, he felt lost in a maze of intrigue and confusion, partly of his own making.

After the prayers, he breathed and felt a connection through Shemuel to the Holy One. Oddly, he felt that Shemuel was still alive and might just walk through the door as if nothing had happened. He looked around the room and was drawn toward the chest where Eliyuhena told him Shemuel kept the private things he used while he was with the Natzara community.

Opening the chest, Yehuda saw Shemuel's ritual clothing. He had clearly used these only when he appeared as the high priest for the community, leading the rituals and prayers in their own house temple. Probably the temple was held in the same meeting room where they had dinner last night. Yehuda carefully picked up the clothes, breathed the incense he could smell in them and felt his teacher's presence even more strongly.

Underneath the layers of clothing, he found Shemuel's prayer shawl, which he picked up and draped carefully around himself. Wrapped inside the shawl, he found a small wooden box inlaid with mother-of-pearl decorations—stars, waves of water and small hands facing palm outward.

Inside the box were two small scrolls, each about two finger's length from top to bottom. They were partially unrolled to a place about halfway through the manuscript. Yehuda noticed that it was one of the Hanuch texts that Shemuel had taught him. As he lifted the small scrolls, he noticed a third roll of parchment underneath it. He opened it, and one of the words jumped out at him—*yehudim*—Judeans. *What was Shemuel doing with a note about the Judeans?* Then he realized that the word was not *yehudim* but *Yehuda*, his own name in Aramaic. He laid the other scrolls carefully aside and read the note:

Yehuda,

If you're reading this, it probably means that I am dead. It certainly means that the Holy One has led you to trace my footsteps here. I gave instructions to the community to let no one but you stay in my room. This family is a part of my work, about which, forgive me, I never told you. It was much safer for you that way, and also for the Natzara to not know about you. I have just informed a few of them today. I suppose, on the inside, we will always be nomads, people who feel that it is safer to wander, to appear and disappear into the wilderness whenever it's necessary. All these plans, who knows? Maybe we only make plans to pass the time the One gives us between birth and the door to whatever lies beyond. If the Holy One wills, perhaps I have only disappeared temporarily. Who knows?

The note in the text I asked you to copy in Yerushalaim probably led you here. You are important for the survival of our lineage. When you have understood everything in yourself, it might lead you to great wealth that can help our people in times of need, like these.

Everything? wondered Yehuda. *Was there something in the text itself or not? Is some treasure buried in the temple catacombs or somewhere else?* But the note immediately changed subjects without explaining.

I taught you about Hanuch and how he remained hidden for most of his life. Then he ascended to heaven and tried to intercede for the fallen angels, the Watchers who had inter-married with the daughters of men. They had also brought greed, profit and war to human-ity. As you know, Hanuch came back from the holy throne with the message, "Sorry, Azrael and the offspring of you fallen ones—judg-ment is coming! The Holy One is coming again in our own human form to bring justice back to the people.

Of course, I remember all that, Yehuda thought.

Yes, it's an inner story, our personal story, of course. As I taught you, all of these charac-ters—fallen angels, good angels—are part of us. How could it be otherwise when the Holy One is all that exists? Our naphsha, our human souls that we think are separate, are only relatively real.

But right now this story is happening on the outside also, around you. At a few moments in history, this happens according to the will of the Holy One. As I taught you, the prophet tries to bring the inner reality, God's reality, into action on the outside. A new reign of the Holy One's empowerment is coming. I began to get this message when I took you on as an appren-tice, so I knew you were one of the keys to the door of the new reign.

Yes, I did think it was all symbolic, simply part of our cultural heritage, thought Yehuda. *I didn't know he meant me to interpret it literally. Who are the fallen angels and their offspring, then? Or more to the point, who is going to bring the judgment, and how?*

There is also another one whom I've met here at Natzara, another key. He is half living in the other world already. He only needs a bit more training to be able to control his coming and going. His inner work can create a great storm on the outside, a storm that will sweep away the old kingdoms and bring in a new one. Please help him. Together you can change the course of life for our people, in both worlds.

So who is that? Yohanan? Yeshua?

The text you find on top of this note will help you remember. It will help you find where I have gone. Do the meditation now, with the right *kavannah*, the right intention. If you love me, do as I have done. Another message waits for you at my home in Paneas.

Remember? Remember what? Couldn't he have been a bit clearer? Always riddles! Yehuda put the note aside and picked up the small scrolls. It was opened to a central section in which the prophet Hanuch, who had previously been "hidden," ascends in vision to the highest heaven. As Shemuel had taught him, he began to visualize his way through each passage. He knew the story by heart, anyway. First he opened a door in his heart to Shemuel himself by breathing in through the top of his head. Then, with his eyes half-closed, he began to feel himself lifted up, as if the vision was happening now, not to someone else at another time:

> Clouds invite me, and a mist calls me.
> The stars and cosmic lightning hurry me on their path.
> Then the winds lift me upward into heaven.
> I fly on until I near a wall of crystal, surrounded by tongues of fire.
> Now I begin to be afraid.

During this part, Shemuel had taught Yehuda to breathe down into his heart with devotion, still remaining open above, feeling more than trying to see what might come next.

> I walk through the tongues of fire and approach a large house,
> the walls and floor are inlaid with clear crystal.
> Through them I see the ceiling open to the heavenly stars and lightning.
> Hovering there are fiery cherubim in a sky as clear as water.
> More flaming fire surrounds the walls,
> and all the doors now blaze also.
> I walk through the flames into the house.
> Inside it is as hot as fire and as cold as ice.
> Awe covers me; trembling grips me.
> I shake and tremble. I fall upon my face.

Here Shemuel had taught Yehuda to breathe through his whole skin and then down into the depths of his body, as if the highest and lowest were coming together within him. When this happened, and only then, he was ready to feel his heart as an altar and take the next step.

Then I look up and see a high throne,
made of wheels that spin like the shining sun.
More cherubim appear.
From underneath the throne flash so many
streams of fire that I have to look away.

One more chance to release any personal desires or wishes in what he might see or feel. It was all up to the Holy One now, as he entered into a vision of pure light, centered in his heart.

The Great Glory sits upon the spinning throne,
and its robes shine more brightly than the sun,
whiter than any snow.

For a long time, Yehuda remained there, merged with the light, his sense of himself very slight, insignificant in comparison to the Great Light. When he became aware of himself again, he returned immediately to the awareness of his heart. Then he performed the final part of the meditation, to see what message he could bring back.

I am prostrate on my face, trembling:
and the Holy One calls me
with his own mouth
and says to me,
"Come here, Hanuch,
hear my word!"

At this point, in the way that Shemuel had taught him, he would usually see colors or symbols, or sometimes letters or combinations of letters dancing like living beings, sending an encoded message. Each Hebrew or Aramaic letter was a particular energy, a living being and an expression of the Holy One. So one could read the letters like oracles, messages from the other side. Instead, this time, Yehuda heard a voice, giving a very mundane direction:

Roll farther. Hear your teacher!

Roll? He had been flying, not rolling. Maybe unroll…He looked downward at the manuscript and unrolled it a bit farther. Then he saw notations in his teacher's handwriting at the side of two passages a bit farther on, where Hanuch says:

I went from there to the middle of the earth, and I saw a blessed place in which there were trees with branches abiding and blooming, branches of a dismembered tree.

Next to the word *branches*, Shemuel had written "*netzach, Natzara*, the branches of Dawid."

Then a few passages later, he found another note from his teacher near the words of the prophet:

To the west there was another mountain, lower than the previous one, of small elevation, and a ravine deep and dry between them.

And I wondered about the rocks, and I wondered about the ravine.

So I asked, "For what purpose is this blessed land, which is entirely filled with trees, and this cursed valley between?"

Uriel, one of the holy angels who were with me, answered and said, "This cursed valley is for those who are cursed forever: Here shall all the cursed be gathered together who speak with their lips against the Holy One and Its glory. Here they shall be gathered together, and here shall be their place of judgment."

Next to this passage, Shemuel had written the words:

Megiddo, Har-meggedon, the mountain of Megiddo.

Yehuda closed his eyes again and found himself sitting on the hill of Megiddo, looking outward over the valley. This time, he wasn't looking at Shemuel's body. He was seeing thousands of dead bodies and the entire valley strewn with blood. His breath caught, and he called inwardly for help from his teacher…

The next thing he knew, someone in the courtyard was calling the community to lunch. *They will think I'm fasting,* thought Yehuda. *Let them.* He looked again at the scroll of Hanuch still unrolled on his lap.

Megiddo? he thought. *It was just a small hill, not even a natural hill, since it had been built up from the ruins of dozens of settlements. Yes, it was between Mount Carmel to the west and Mount Tabor to the east, both sacred mountains, and the Great Plain connected them all. To the north was Galilee, with its many trees. And the "branch" of the greater tree where he was sitting, the community of Natzara? So Shemuel also shared the community's hope that it would bring the deliverance of the Israelites from foreign rule once again. But how? Armed revolution? Visionary power from the heavens? Both, or something else? It might explain why Shemuel was at the hill of Megiddo, but why was he killed?*

Yehuda continued to read the rest of the Hanuch scroll, to see if Shemuel had made any more notations. Nothing. *He did say, however, that he had left another message for me at his home in Paneas. Well, maybe his son Mikhael will know something.*

He heard a gentle knock on the door and Ioannis's voice.

"Yehuda, are you all right? The midday meal is nearly over. They said you're probably fasting, but that doesn't seem like you."

Yehuda arose and opened the door. "Yes, it's all fine, Ioannis. Please come in. I have some things to tell you."

"I have things to tell you, too, Yehuda. I have discovered a few more complications here."

Chapter 18

The Dance of Separation

The sun was halfway to setting by the time Ioannis and Yehuda had told each other all they had learned. There were sitting on the floor of their room, perched on pillows embroidered with grape vines and branches. Both fell silent. Yehuda closed his eyes and seemed to go somewhere else. Ioannis, as usual, waited patiently for his master to return to this world.

"It seems to me," said Yehuda, opening his eyes again, "that the reason for Shemuel's murder must hinge on how much he knew, both about the Natzara's secret wealth and about the stockpile of arms that you discovered. There is also the question of whether everyone in this community knows about the weapons, or only a few people. Then there is the possible treasure that he refers to in his letter.

"Finally, there is the matter of Yohanan and Yeshua. Their relation to the other part of their family that lives in Batanea beyond the Jordan may also be important. Batanea is a significant border area, between the Parthians and the Romans, and people would kill to get intelligence from there, not to mention control it. What is going on there, and did Shemuel know about it? Some Israelite families who lived in Babylon for a few generations and then returned may be friendlier to the Parthians than to the Romans. The Parthians at least have one God, Ahura Mazda, 'indestructible wisdom,' which some see as a male-female unity, at least somewhat similar to ideas found in our scriptures. The Romans have a whole family tree of gods and goddesses, which they don't take that seriously, anyway."

Ioannis asked, "So it boils down to one thing: whom do we trust?"

The two looked at each other, and the answer immediately appeared in both glances: no one.

"We still need more information," said Yehuda, shaking his head.

"More? It seems as if we have too much already!" exclaimed Ioannis. "Weren't we just going to leave for Syria, sell a certain object and get out of this mess completely?"

"Yes. But that's no longer possible. We've become part of this story. Anyway, Ioannis, did you really want to become a merchant?"

"Better a live merchant..." Ioannis muttered. "Are you sure there's nothing else in that inlaid box of Shemuel's?" he continued.

"I think I looked through it all," said Yehuda. "Here, have a look for yourself."

Ioannis reached over to take the box, and as Yehuda looked on, he began to rustle through the writing utensils that were left after the letter and the scroll of Hanuch had been removed. After removing various objects, Ioannis lost patience and shook the box back and forth. He noticed an odd rattle that didn't seem to come from anything inside the box. Turning it upside down, he emptied it, but still noticed the rattle.

"Must be some other compartment inside, Yehuda."

"Let me have another look," said Yehuda. He began to push on various edges and sections of inlay. When he pressed one of the pearl engravings of a hand, a small drawer on one side popped open. Yehuda reached inside and took out something small. Between his first two fingers he held up another pearl, almost identical to the one he had found in the temple.

"So."

"So."

"A good reason to travel on to Damascus and forget all this, Yehuda?" asked Ioannis, without much hope in his voice.

"A good reason to stay and try to unravel all this," replied Yehuda. "Now I'm wondering how the first pearl got into the temple just at the moment when I might find it."

So as Shabbat sundown arrived and the community gathered to wish it farewell, Yehuda and Ioannis only had more questions and even less clarity than they had at sundown the previous day.

While the community waited for three stars to appear in the sky, the sign Shabbat was officially over, some of the women began to play round hand drums and sing a song for the *havdalah,* the "separation." It not only celebrated separation from Shabbat, but also commemorated all of the separations, divisions and partings that life had brought, or would bring. The Natzara women sang:

> *My soul longs for the candle and the spices.*
> *If only you would pour me a cup of wine for the separation!*
> *O you angels, clear a way for me!*
> *Clear a path for the bewildered,*
> *and open the gates so I may enter.*
> *My heart yearning, I shall lift up my eyes to Yah…*

the breath inside the breath,
Who provides for my needs day and night!

After the stars appeared, Elishyba blessed another cup of wine and then branches of aromatic herbs, all of which were passed around to the family members. Ioannis thought that he could still discern the distinctive smell of balsam behind the more fragrant herbs used. Following that, Elishyba blessed a braided candle with several wicks, and everyone gazed at the reflection of its light in their fingernails. The community sang together a verse from the Psalms:

The blessed way of the Holy One is clear,
luminous, enlightening the eyes…

Then came a final blessing chanted by Zakarya and Elishyba together:

Blessed are you, Breath of our breath,
Life of our life, YYHHWWWWHHH,
who divides for us
what is sacred and part of our purpose,
from what is a distraction and we can ignore;
what is the light, clarifying our path,
from what is the dark, and we don't yet understand;
what is truly Israel, those who wrestle with the One,
from what are the nations, those who live as if only their
*   small self matters;*
what is the seventh day, when we turn and return to
*   emptiness,*
from the six other days, when we fill our lives with
*   activity.*

Blessed are you, O Holy One,
who makes clear and divides for us
what is sacred and part of our purpose,
from what is a distraction and we can ignore.

The two extinguished the candle in the wine and passed the cup around again so that community members could touch some of the wine to their eyelids. Ioannis felt the short ritual wake up all of his senses—taste, smell, sight, hearing, touch. Suddenly, the drums began to play, and the whole family broke into spontaneous dancing while singing:

Hiney anoki sholeach lakem et Eliyahu han-nabi…
See! I am sending you Eliyah the prophet!

"Why is Eliyah coming, Yehuda?" asked Ioannis.

"He is coming, according to the prophecy, to prepare for the 'awesome and dreadful day of the Holy One,'" replied Yehuda.

"And what is supposed to happen then?"

"No one knows exactly, of course, but things will get better. Enemies defeated. Everything good and according to the divine plan again."

"'Awesome and dreadful' doesn't sound very promising. Why is everyone dancing?"

"I asked Shemuel that once, Ioannis, and he told me, 'Simply for the joy of it. What else can we humans offer in the face of grief and separation but our joy?' I had forgotten all about that until this moment, when you asked. There wasn't much joy in the *havdalah* at the temple, you understand. Here they do it so differently."

The Dance of Separation

Ioannis looked around at everyone dancing and felt inhibited to join in. He was a stranger here. But he could still feel the urge to dance in his blood. He remembered his mother's lullabies at night and how she used to talk about her homeland with such longing. He had been in the midst of this land, her land, for so many years. Yet this was the first time he really felt his Israelite heritage. He was still a stranger, of course...Just at that moment, someone grabbed his hand and swung him into the dance. Zilpah.

Ioannis looked toward Yehuda, as if pleading for some help. But the scribe just winked and called out, "You are Yehohanan—in Aramaic, it means 'the heart is your way to Yah!'"

Then he saw Yehuda began to dance freely, spontaneously, transformed with a radiant smile, as he had never seen his master before.

"Hey, who are you dancing with?" said Zilpah. "Let your friend have his own joy; you have yours!"

Yes, thought Ioannis, *that's exactly what I will do.* "I'm not used to dancing, Zilpah," he shouted over the sound of the drums and voices.

"You don't have to be used to it, just let the spirit use *you.* There are no rules, just a rhythm, a melody and what you feel inside."

As he began to dance, he suddenly noticed that he wasn't really dancing with Zilpah, or she with him. They were dancing with everyone. The whole room danced. Separately, and then holding hands in a line that snaked through the room, and then separately again, but somehow all together. The whole world was dancing. He looked into Zilpah's eyes and saw that she was in love, but it wasn't with him, or at least not only with him. Ioannis felt more joy than he had at any time since he was a boy. As night fell and the candles were lit, the dancing continued. Young and old together, Ioannis noticed, no one tired in the least.

Suddenly, everything stopped. Everyone looked toward the door, where someone Yehuda recognized had entered: Mikhael, Shemuel's son. Tall, gaunt, with brown hair thinning around the temples, he looked much older than when Yehuda had last seen him. *Never did have much of a sunny disposition,* he thought. *And he looks displeased now, also a bit worse for wear from the journey.* Yehuda never really understood what Mikhael bought and sold, and he hadn't wanted to pry into Shemuel's family's business. Since it seemed that he was the only one who recognized the man, Yehuda stepped forward. Mikhael gasped and took a step back before regaining his composure.

"Shalama and welcome, Mikhael."

"Shalama, Yehuda. What are *you* doing here?"

"I was on my way north to see my brother in Sepphoris and heard of your father's death. I was led here to this community, where your father regularly taught. We arrived just before the Sabbath, and they have welcomed my friend Yehohanan and myself."

"On your way to see your brother?" he said, frowning and shaking his head in confusion.

"Yes, we haven't been there yet."

"I see."

"These are our hosts, the leaders of the community: Eliyuhena. Zakarya, who invited your father here originally. Yauseph, one of the elders. And this is Ya'aqub, one of Yauseph's sons." Yehuda noticed that when he was introduced to Ya'aqub, Mikhael averted his glance. The exchange was all very cordial—and very chilly. Perhaps it was because the dance had been interrupted. Or something else.

"We are all very sad at the passing of your father, Mikhael," said Zakarya, bowing and touching his heart. "We offer you our condolences and our service in any way. Your father's body has been buried for the first time in our family vault. We're sorry that you missed this. You can take his bones back home in some months for the second burial if that is your wish. We now place the bones of family members together in a stone box to honor them. Some still return them to their ancestors in a group burial, we know. Do you have a place in Panias?"

"Well, I am here alone," said Mikhael grudgingly. "I came as soon as I heard. Perhaps my father would want to be buried in your community rather than back in Paneas, since he spent so much time here."

That is an odd response, thought Yehuda. Mikhael isn't revealing anything. Just like him.

"Can you tell me who found my father and how and why he died?" asked Mikhael.

"He was found near Megiddo, stabbed," said Eliyuhena. "Some Roman soldiers garrisoned nearby found him, and through our contacts, we recovered his body. Your father visited here just last week and offered teaching to us. He said that he was heading south on an important mission. He didn't say what it was. Perhaps you can tell us more about that."

Eliyuhena doesn't miss a trick, either, thought Yehuda, *responding to questions with another question.*

"My father rarely told me much about his important missions," replied Mikhael bitterly. "Not that I would have understood much about them if he had."

As he spoke, Mikhael kept glancing aside, looking at Yehuda. *Clearly nervous,* thought the scribe, *and not hiding it very well.*

"His student here," said Mikhael, nodding to Yehuda, "would know more about my father's world, or worlds, than I would."

"Did he say how long he thought he might be away?" asked Yehuda as innocently as he could.

"As I recall, he said he might be back in a few weeks, sometime after the Festival of Weeks, maybe." Mikhael waved his hand in the air. "It was all very vague. He must have run into robbers on the road. I am, of course, devastated by his death."

If this is you devastated, reflected Ioannis, *I'd hate to see what you look like when your enemy dies. I thought only Pilatus could cool off a room this quickly.*

As if reading Ioannis's thoughts, Mikhael put his head in his hands and began shaking. When he raised his head again, there were tears in his eyes.

"What are we thinking of?" exclaimed Yauseph. "Let's welcome our guest properly and allow him to have some rest after his long journey. Are you hungry? We have just finished *havdalah,* and there will be food now."

Mikhael shook his head.

"Then, Ya'aqub, please show Mikhael to the guest room next to the one Yehuda and Yehohanan are sharing."

Mikhael left and everyone relaxed, but no one felt like dancing again. Dinner was served, and various family members fell to talking in small groups. Yehuda and Ioannis found themselves talking with Eliyuhena, Yauseph, Ya'aqub and Zakarya.

"Well?" asked Eliyuhena.

"Well," replied Zakarya.

"It could just be bad character," said Yauseph. "Or shock and his quick travel from Paneas."

"It could be," said Eliyuhena slowly. "But he didn't look as though he had traveled long, or fast, to me. And he wasn't hungry. Yehuda, you know him. What do you say?"

"As I said, I never knew him very well. And he was always difficult to read. He and Shemuel seemed to have a strained relationship. I always thought that was because Mikhael chose to become a merchant rather than a scribe and teacher like his father. Mikhael both tolerated and resented me, I think. Tolerated because I relieved him of a burden. Resented because he clearly felt what his father did was nonsense, not of the 'real world.'"

"Let's see what he can tell us in the morning, after a night's sleep and some food," said Ya'aqub. "I wonder how much Shemuel told him about our community."

"Whatever he told him," said Eliyuhena, "he doesn't act as if he knows who his friends are, or his family."

As the evening ended, Yehuda and Ioannis began to walk back to their room.

"Wait, I want to check something out, Yehuda," said Ioannis.

"I think I know what that is," replied Yehuda. "And I'll go with you."

They headed for the stables in the courtyard and asked Shallum, the family member acting as groom and guard on duty, to show them the mount Mikhael had ridden to Natzara.

"Mount? I would hardly call this donkey a mount," said Shallum, pointing dismissively to a gray beast in the corner. "He doesn't seem to have been in any hurry. I would have thought someone like a merchant could have done a bit better."

"Were you here when he arrived?" asked Ioannis. "Did you see from which direction he came?"

"Yes, I was just taking over from my cousin," said Shallum. "I remember thinking I would miss the havdalah dancing. But I suppose we still need someone to welcome visitors, or raise a possible alarm, even at times like that. He arrived shortly after. I'm sure he came via the path over the ridge through the flax fields," he said pointing to the northwest.

"That's the path I took this morning," said Ioannis, glancing sideways at Yehuda.

"And where does that path lead, most directly?" asked Yehuda.

"To Zippori," replied Shallum.

"That donkey didn't break any sweat today, Master," said Ioannis as he and Yehuda walked back to their room.

"And the road to Zippori is not the most direct way to Paneas, either," added Yehuda.

Just then they felt a breeze rise. Some storm clouds rolled overhead, and they heard thunder in the distance.

"Late-spring rain," said Yehuda. "Just in time for the Festival of Weeks, when Sinai rumbled with the Holy One's name."

Chapter 19
A Brotherly Meeting

Mikhael couldn't provide anyone with more answers the next morning, because Mikhael was dead.

Yehuda had been engaged in his morning meditation when Ioannis burst into the room, up early, as usual.

"He's gone, Master. They can't find him! I'm sorry to disturb your prayers, but it seemed important."

Yehuda was already standing and heading for the door. "Let's go, Yehohanan. I'm calling you Yehohanan now, so that I don't need to remember to switch. And anyway, after last night's somewhat abbreviated dancing, you are really Yehohanan now—'the grace of Yah,' the Ever-living One. My name Yehuda means 'Yah is guiding us.' My meditation told me that we are now committed, and we have left our past behind. You said it before, but now you really are my kinsman."

Ioannis looked a bit puzzled but nodded as he followed Yehuda into the courtyard. They went immediately to the stables and found Mikhael's donkey gone.

"How well can you track, Yehohanan?"

"Well enough, Yehuda. My father taught me when I was a boy, as we roamed the hills around Rome. There's a bit of mess of footprints here in the courtyard, but let's guess that he left the same way he came."

They walked quickly out of the rear entrance to the courtyard and up the hill toward the balsam field.

"Here they are," said Ioannis, pointing to some hoofprints. "That's about the right depth for a donkey carrying someone of Mikhael's weight. And we are lucky that it rained last night. He was the first person up this way, probably just before dawn."

They walked quickly uphill through the flax fields and found themselves higher on the hillside, passing the field of jumbled rocks, trees and shrubs that cleverly hid the balsam crop. The donkey's tracks left the path and headed into the tangled undergrowth. It was slow going, and they quickly lost any trace of the tracks.

"Shall we return to the path?" asked Ioannis. "Maybe Mikhael set the donkey free?"

"Not likely," said Yehuda grimly. "Look over there." He pointed a hundred *pedes* away, where just over the top of one of the bushes, they could see the head of a donkey sniffing one of the balsam plants contentedly.

As they rounded the corner of a thicket of trees, they saw feet, then splayed legs and then Mikhael's bloodstained torso, facedown and draped over one of the balsam bushes, as though he had dived headfirst into it to take the healing sap into his whole body. He wasn't breathing.

"All the healing herbs in the world wouldn't heal that," said Ioannis trenchantly, pointing to two small but deep wounds on either side of the merchant's rib cage. "Just like Shemuel, same type of knife, but two clean stabs this time, moved around inside for the most damage just to make sure. He, or she, is consistent if nothing else."

"Or they all learn the same technique," said Yehuda. "Maybe it has to do with the balsam crop?"

"Maybe, but then why kill him here? It would only draw attention to the field," said Ioannis. "Look, he was also hit in the head, so he could have been knocked out first and then killed and dragged here. What now, Yehuda? It seems that, like Mikhael, we've reached a dead end."

"We will go back and tell the family, notice their reactions and then take our leave. I'm not sure we can trust anyone here. Then we're going on to Sepphoris. If Mikhael was there, someone may have seen him. Anyway, I still need to see my brother. After that, we'll go on to Paneas and look for the message that Shemuel told me he left there."

"All right." Ioannis sighed, looking a bit downcast.

As they left the balsam field and rejoined the track downhill, Ioannis looked around quickly and then scurried uphill.

"Look, Yehuda!"

"I see. Tracks coming from Sepphoris."

"Yes, then the same tracks returning. One man, alone, from the looks of it," said Ioannis, squatting next to the trail. "Walking quickly, not a merchant. Someone in good shape."

Everyone in the Natzara compound seemed suitably shocked by Mikhael's murder. They dispatched family members to bring the body down from the balsam fields. Eliyuhena was convinced that Mikhael's murder was connected to Shemuel's. No one betrayed any reaction when Yehuda reported where they had found the body.

"What was he running away from?" wondered Yauseph.

"Or whom was he meeting, father?" asked Ya'aqub. "This is just the kind of attention we don't want right now."

"Let's keep calm. We don't need to report it to anyone," said Zakarya. "Mikhael may not deserve it, but there is another platform free in our family tomb. We will put him there. When the bones are ready, we will place him and his father together in the same ossuary and have one of our craftsmen carve special blessings and protections on it. We should say some extra prayers for them both. Would you like to stay for this?" he asked Yehuda.

"No," replied Yehuda. "I have already said my *qaddish* prayer for him. I think that Mikhael may have traveled here by way of Zippori and was heading back that way, or meeting someone from there. We're going to follow that trail before it goes cold. If we discover anything, we will let you know."

As they headed to their room to gather their things, Yehuda said quietly to Ioannis, "You say your own good-byes, too." He placed his hand on the younger man's shoulder. "Don't worry. If the Holy One intends it, you can always return."

"Yes, that's what I'm half afraid of, Yehuda."

Two hours later Yehuda and Ioannis were walking into Zippori. The rains had refreshed the whole countryside, and the many aromas of the hill plants filled the air. As they approached the city, Yehuda felt the urge to give a history lesson, whether his companion wanted it or not.

"*Sepphoris* in Greek, *Zippori* in Aramaic, from the word for a bird. See how it perches on the hillside. You can view the whole area from here. That made it a wonderful site to start a revolt after the death of old Herodes. His son Antipas reduced it to a pile of stones and then rebuilt it. Then he renamed it Autocratis, just in case anyone had doubts about who was in charge. I suppose Antipas never really felt safe there, since he built his new model city Tiberias on the shore of the lake, where he could always hop in a ship and escape to the other side. Or maybe it was just to impress his patrons and have a miniature Roman city for them to visit. He could also better control security and access in a town he built himself. No secret tunnels in, for instance."

"And what are we looking for here?" asked Ioannis in a disgruntled tone. He was still feeling low after taking leave of Zilpah, who had seemed indifferent to his going. *Did I botch the farewell entirely? Or maybe I just don't understand Israelite women. What do I really know about women, anyway?* he thought hopelessly.

"What did she say, Yehohanan?" asked Yehuda, reading his thoughts.

"She? Oh, well…*she* didn't seem to care whether I came or went. Kept her distance: 'We hope to see you again, if the Holy One wills. The family will miss you. Life is long, if the Holy One wills. Let us know if you discover what happened to Shemuel, or if you hear anything of Yeshua, if the Holy One wills.' All this talk about the 'Holy One' and 'we.' I just don't understand."

"It's a way of protecting herself, Yehohanan. Our culture is all about family ties. They go very deep, and strangers don't become family overnight. From what you've just said, she actually gave you several good excuses to come back. If that's what your heart tells you to do, that is."

"I suppose so."

"At some point, you will need to decide if you're Roman or Israelite, brother," said Yehuda, clasping his arm around the younger man's back. "That's nothing to do with me, you understand. You are as free as you choose to be. You could go back now."

"Sure, but I haven't found out anything she's asked, have I?"

"So let's put our minds to that, and we will both be free to move on. Agreed?" concluded Yehuda, as if sealing a contract in court.

"Agreed. *Ameyn*, you would say, right?"

"Correct. Ameyn!"

In that moment they found themselves in the main marketplace of Zippori, standing in front of a moneychanger's stall. A wrinkled Phoenician man with a faded orange beard and a bald head sat at the table, stooped over a pile of silver shekels from Tyre, some bronze coins minted by Antipas and another pile of Roman silver coins, denarii and tetradrachmae.

"Shalama, grandfather," said Yehuda in polite Aramaic. "We're coming from down south and are looking for a friend of ours who we believe is here in Zippori. He's a merchant from Paneas, name of Mikhael ben Yahayye. Have you, by any chance, seen him or happened to do some business with him?"

"You may be coming from down south, but I recognize you," said the old moneylender, looking at Yehuda with a sparkle in his eyes. "I was living here when your own father was alive. I moved here from Sidon just before the last revolt and got out just in time. Name is Sikarbaal—'Baal remembers.' And I remember you, even though you were a boy when you left. Seven years old, wasn't it?"

Yehuda was startled and then quickly regained his composure. "I'm sorry, Grandfather, but I don't remember *you*. I left a long time ago, and I have not been back since."

"Doesn't matter," Sikarbaal said and grinned. "I suppose you're here to see your brother. Oh, well, he's a big man here now. Lords it over all of us. Not like your father. But that doesn't matter, either. Maybe we need some big man to protect us from the Romans, or maybe along with the Romans from someone else. Or from Antipas or *with* Antipas. What do I know? I'm only a moneylender."

"I expect you know a lot and have seen even more," replied Yehuda evenly. "What about our friend? Have you seen him?"

"Friend?" asked Sikarbaal. "Oh, you mean the son of your uncle, the old scribe who adopted you! Yes, I remember that, too. Well, the son was here a few days ago. Went up to the big house; must have met your brother. Changed three hundred Tyrian-minted Roman silver denarii with a friend of mine after he left. I knew he was well off, but I didn't know he was that well off. That's a year's wages for most peasants here, working on the farm of some elite. He ate supper the same day with the fish broker around the corner. Can't remember what *he* looks like. New in town, doesn't look like a man interested in fish. Then Mikhael ben Yahayye left yesterday afternoon. Beyond that, I know very little, as I said. I keep myself to myself. Sorry I can't help you."

"Well, thank you, anyway," said Yehuda, suppressing a smile. "Until next time. It's good to meet a friend of my father's."

"Your father always did business with me," said Sikarbaal as though reciting a holy precept. "You should consider me a friend of the family. Stop by any time. Just for an informal chat, you understand. No obligation to do business."

"Yes, I understand. Shalama to you, Sikarbaal," said Yehuda as they walked away from the table.

"Do you think he's that talkative with everyone?" asked Ioannis, shaking his head.

"Let's hope not. In any case, I think it's time we went to see my brother. He knows I'm a scribe, so you're back to being my bodyguard."

"That could be helpful, anyway, if Mikhael was involved with him. Why would he come to see your brother?"

"That's what we need to find out. But without letting him know that we're interested."

"You don't trust your brother, do you?" asked Ioannis.

"As I said, we have a large family, and he is much older…"

"But there's more to it than that."

"Yes. As the oldest son, he inherited almost everything. So he should have taken care of my mother and my sisters, at least."

"But he didn't."

"No."

Ioannis didn't press him any further. *Families*, he thought. *That much is the same, Roman or Israelite.* At the same time, he noticed that they were being openly followed by two large-boned men, equipped with swords and the necessary expressionless faces for hired thugs.

"Yehuda, I think…"

"Yes, I know, Yehohanan. I half expected it. My brother has his own security force and spies, I'm sure."

Yehuda leading, they headed directly through the market and up a small hill to a grove of trees that shielded the largest private house in the city. It overlooked the Roman palace and surrounding buildings that Antipas had built after his father's death, mainly to stamp his

A Brotherly Meeting

seal on the rebellious town. After giving his name to the guards at the gate, Yehuda and Ioannis were ushered into a large room, designed to mimic a Roman throne room. Tapestries with Roman mythological themes festooned the walls, and at the far end, they saw a large wooden table, behind which sat Benyamin ben Yohanan.

Benyamin was writing in some ledger scrolls and hardly glanced up as they approached. He was already well past fifty years old, and his hair was graying. His face was fleshy from too much food and drink for too many years, but his mind was clearly focused and alert, at least when it came to the records of what he owned.

"I see you've finally made it here at last, Yehuda," he said, looking up briefly with a bored expression. "But you always were sloppy about being on time."

"I wasn't aware that I was expected, brother," replied Yehuda levelly. "And I missed you, also."

"Sarcasm will get you nowhere," said Benyamin. "There is no point in pretending any brotherly love between us. You left the family early and were always surplus to requirements, so to speak. Always a dreamer, not a practical boy."

"I didn't leave. I was sent away," retorted Yehuda. "And in any case, it was only due to Shemuel's generosity that I had a home at all."

"Oh, yes, yes. Shemuel, a good man. But let's not waste time, please. I had word from Yerushalaim that you were on your way here, so I had a watch out for you. I do have friends in many places, as you know. So what took you so long, and why are you here?"

"I was on my way here when my bodyguard and I encountered a corpse just below Megiddo," said Yehuda. "It was, in fact, Shemuel, who seems to have been on his way south to see me. Do you, or your friends, have any information about that?"

"I see, answering a question with a question. Perhaps you *have* learned a bit since you lived here. Perhaps Shemuel wasn't just a dotty old eccentric scribe, after all. Perhaps."

Controlling himself, Yehuda replied, "So do you know something or don't you? It seems from *my* friends that his son came to visit you recently. And now Mikhael is dead also."

"Mikhael dead, too?" said Benyamin, shrugging indifferently and fluttering a hand in the air. "I'm shocked. We're losing all of our best citizens. He was in perfect health when he came to see me on business a few days ago. He is, or shall I say was, a businessman like myself. We often had dealings concerning shipments from Damascus and even some from farther east at times. But of course trade is a dangerous business. That's why I stay at home as much as possible."

"And what kind of shipments did he discuss with you when he was here?"

"I'm really surprised, Yehuda. You know that I can't discuss trade secrets with you. I would only be placing you in the same kind of danger that apparently overtook our friend Mikhael. But I'm even more surprised that you would presume to interrogate me here in my own house. Of course, you know that you were followed here." At this point, Benyamin waved casually over the head of Yehuda, and the two men who had followed them walked quietly into the room, standing guard on either side of the door. "If I were you, I would really take care to cultivate the proper attitude toward your elder brother, who only wants what is best for you," he said, smiling thinly.

"So now you're my family again, are you?" spat out Yehuda, losing control. "If that's so, let me ask you the question I came here for. Why haven't you taken care of my mother and our sisters properly? They are, I've heard, living in complete destitution in a small village north of here. My sisters have no hope for anyone to provide a dowry and so can't escape that way either. And here you are in your large house in Zippori. I'm sure you can do better."

"Better? Oh yes, of course," replied Benyamin. "But you see, your dear mother prefers to live in the village. She likes the old ways. I hardly see her. As you know, she was never my mother, only yours. My father's young wife after my mother died," he said with disdain. "But my sisters are devoted to her, absolutely devoted. They wouldn't think of leaving her. She has, I assure you, everything she needs."

"That's not what I heard," said Yehuda. "And in this case, I'm sure that my sources are as good as yours. She wrote to me herself."

"Well, you know what mothers are like, brother. They do like to complain a bit when they get older. And your dear mother has, like me, lived to a ripe age, long past our father. That can't be an accident, can it? Rest assured that I have my eye out for her, as I do for all of our family. Even those like you who have shown no interest in being in touch over the years," he said, raising his hands as if he were helpless. Benyamin then took a look through his account scrolls in front of him on the table, and seemed to make some sort of decision.

"Brother," he said, looking up with a blank expression. "Let's try to settle our differences and begin again, shall we? I can see that we started off on the wrong foot here. Are you sure that there's nothing else you wanted to tell me?"

"Yes, on our way here, we stopped in Yaphia, on the day of their knesset. They didn't know that I knew you, but as a scribe, I was asked to speak for them about the high taxes you are collecting from them for Antipas. They are, I can tell you, close to revolt, or worse, strike. If they revolt, of course, Antipas has the troops to raze any small village. But if they strike, or simply aren't very diligent about planting, there will be nothing for Antipas to reap in tax. That sort of thing could easily spread through the region. Some people are speaking more openly, and even the headman there, who wants to please everyone, was accused of being a traitor. I heard that he was murdered shortly after we left the village.

"Yes, Yehuda. I'm well aware of that sort of thing. Our headman in Yaphia…you mean Felayah, that well-fed one?" he said, paternally. "Perhaps your sources are not as good as you think they are. Felayah was just here this morning with a small delegation, his cousin and son, Matthai and Yiremayhu, if I remember correctly. They made the same complaint you have. We came to an amicable agreement very easily. Felayah has always been a very reasonable man. Seemed in good health, too."

"I'm sorry, I must have been misinformed," said Yehuda, looking down and shifting his weight uncomfortably. "I'm glad that at least you were able to come to some agreement about the taxes in Yaphia."

"You know, brother," Benyamin said and sighed, sitting back in his chair and looking out the window over Yehuda and Ioannis's heads, "I only do what I do, suffer what I suffer, for the sake of our people. In particular, for our dear villagers who are the backbone of the Israelite land. Antipas, of course, is an Idumean, a foreigner at heart and a little too close to the Romans. But he does serve a purpose in keeping the general order. And as we know from our history, there can always be worse than him. He is, at least, a son of Noah, as we are." Benyamin glanced briefly at Yehuda, shaking his head.

"Yes, I know," said Yehuda, deflated. "And you don't know anything about the deaths of Shemuel or Mikhael?"

"Well...father and son. Could be some family matter, revenge between clans, perhaps? I try to stay out of all that. One needs to in order to do business successfully. I don't ask about my vendors' or customers' inter-family relations. It's simpler that way. I hope that, in any case, I've reassured you about our own family's welfare. I'm sorry that you had to come all this way for so little. Do you plan to return to Yerushalaim now?"

"Not quite yet," said Yehuda. "I have some business to attend to in Paneas, something Shemuel asked me to do before he died."

"Ah, I see," said Benyamin, scratching his chin, and standing up more quickly than they thought possible. "In that case, I wish you peace on your journey. I hope that you won't be such a stranger in the future."

"Shalama, brother."

Yehuda and Ioannis walked back through the house and courtyard onto the lane. Ioannis turned to Yehuda, who was shaking a bit and looked grim.

"You know, of course, he's lying, Yehuda. Excuse me. I know he is your brother, but it's my duty to say so, as your friend and adopted kinsman."

"Family isn't what it used to be, Yehohanan," said Yehuda disgustedly. "Let's get out of here."

CHAPTER 20

Fish Knives and a Big Fish

On their way out of Zippori, Yehuda asked Sikarbaal to show them to the house of the fish broker with whom Mikhael had dinner the night before he left the city.

"Yes, of course! It's just around the corner! Although I don't know if anyone is home, of course. He seems to go away quite often and has hired a village woman to mind his house when he's not there. Her sister told me that the broker often has visitors from the east, and they speak some language the housekeeper doesn't understand. Parthian maybe? Then he heads off east himself, sometimes for weeks on end. Most recently this morning, it seems. But I only know what I hear, you understand."

Sure enough, when they arrived at the door, the three were met by a middle-aged village woman in simple clothing and with a blank expression on her face.

"My master is away, and I'm supposed to say that I don't know when he'll be back or what he's doing," she said with her hands on her hips.

"Do you know *where* he went?" asked Yehuda.

"He never tells me. He only sends for me on the day he leaves. I don't know anything of his business. My job is only to clean and look after the house and tell people that I don't know anything. Which I don't!" she said with irritation, as if defying them to prove her wrong.

"Yes, of course, mother, we understand," said Sikarbaal soothingly. "But surely you know *me*? I know your sister, the seamstress, and do business with her. Everyone around here knows me, because I've lived here forever."

"Yes, and you'll be a foreigner forever, too," muttered the woman under her breath.

"Come, come, we're all children of Noah," said Sikarbaal, "even if not of Moshe. I know that your master is a fish broker, no doubt an honest man with nothing to hide. He told us that we could come by to collect some contracts from his home, so that I could help him with a business deal we're involved with. No doubt, he simply neglected to tell you."

"Oh, all right," said the woman, sighing loudly with exasperation. "Come in, get what you came for and leave!" She swung open the door and allowed them to enter. They went through the front of the house, which served as a shop, passing by barrels that smelled of smoked fish. In passing, Ioannis lifted a few lids and looked inside. Each contained only pickled fish of various types—herring, tilapia, lake fish and sea fish.

"Sikarbaal," whispered Yehuda as they passed through the shop. "How could you tell such a blatant lie? We have no right to be here!"

"My cousin," said the old man mildly, waving a hand, "you are family, and you want to find out about the death of your adopted brother, don't you? Yes, I heard about that, too. Which takes more precedence? The death of a family member, or a simple lie? If there's nothing to find, our nameless friend will be none the wiser. It is odd, in any case, that no one in Zippori knows his name, or at least no one I know, which is absolutely everyone. He moved here a year ago, after all. He should have introduced himself, told us where he was from and about his family."

"He has a point, Yehuda," said Ioannis. "We might as well see what we can find."

As they entered a room at the back of the house, they were faced with a large table covered with various papers. Shelves filled the three walls surrounding it. Yehuda began to slowly lift up and examine the papers on the table, taking care to replace each in exactly the same place where he found it.

"Most of these papers are maps," said Yehuda. "Some quite common, some with trade routes to and from the sea to the interior. The map on the top of the pile is the trail to Kochaba, in Batanea east of the Yarden River. Others are much more detailed. They show trails and caves in remote areas of the Galilean hills, small paths and passageways into and out of various villages. This one shows an underground network of tunnels into and out of Zippori. Here's a similar one for Tiberias, for Caesarea on the coast, several for Yerushalaim itself. I didn't know most of these existed."

"Why would a fish merchant need maps of secret tunnels into and out of the cities?" asked Ioannis over his shoulder. The younger man was looking at various items on a shelf to the rear of the table and came across a wooden box containing a tray of fish knives. "He does seem to have something to do with fish, though," he said, placing the box on a free corner of the table. Yehuda picked up several knives and smelled them.

"Yes, these have definitely been used on fish," he remarked. "This box seems a bit deeper than the number of knives here, however." Carefully picking up two of the wooden dividers of the tray, Yehuda pulled it away from the bottom of the box. Underneath was another tray with a different row of knives. They had carved bone handles and finely wrought, very thin silver blades.

"These knives never gutted a fish, Yehuda," said Ioannis, picking up one of the stilettos. "Not unless it was a human fish. Looks like the same type that killed Shemuel and Mikhael."

Sikarbaal looked on with wide eyes. "My friends," he said, "I have the distinct feeling that we should disturb nothing else and leave as soon as possible. Who knows when this fiend might return? More smells fishy here than at the front of the house. I will warn all of my relations in Zippori to be on their guard with this stranger."

"Yes, we've seen enough," said Yehuda.

As they walked back into the lane outside the house, Ioannis asked, "Isn't Batanea the area Yohanan and Yeshua may have disappeared to? The no-man's-land between the Romans and Parthians?"

"Yes, it is," replied Yehuda, closing his eyes and breathing slowly. A moment later, he opened them again. "That fits a pattern, at least, but I still don't see what the pattern means. Staying longer won't help, though. Thank you, Sikarbaal. I hope that Baal will remember you, and please remember to guard your back until we find out what all this is about."

"Don't worry, young man," said Sikarbaal to Yehuda. "I haven't lived this long away from Sidon without having friends of my own and knowing how to disappear when necessary."

Yehuda and Ioannis didn't waste any time walking south to Yaphia, where they immediately went to the house of Felayah, the headman. They were ushered into the large room that had served as the meeting place of the knesset the previous week. This time it was completely empty. Suddenly Felayah appeared from behind a curtain, walking toward Yehuda with open arms. He seemed in as good health as when they had last seen him.

"My friend! How wonderful to see you again! Don't worry; I do understand why you didn't tell us before that you were Benyamin ben Yohanan's brother. A man as wise as he is certainly needs to know who his friends are."

Yehuda grimaced, as he understood that Felayah thought he had been spying for his brother at the village meeting.

"Felayah, please accept my apologies. By my word of honor, I was only here on my own account. Before I saw him yesterday, I hadn't seen my brother in many years."

"Yes, yes, of course!" said Felayah with a fixed smile. "Families, families. What would we do without them?"

"We came today not on my brother's behalf," insisted Yehuda, "but because we heard that you had been attacked, possibly killed, just after the knesset last week."

"Attacked? No! I don't know who told you such a thing," replied Felayah, puzzled. "We may have our differences in Yaphia, but most people here understand that I'm trying to do my best for everyone. My best in a difficult situation, mind you," he said, his eyes narrowing. "One never knows whom one can trust, what with the Herodians and the Romans. We Israelites need to stick together, right? As I told you the last time we met…" His voice trailed away, as if he couldn't even convince himself of what he was saying.

"Yes, of course," said Yehuda. "Thankfully, I see that the rumor we heard was wrong. I did speak on your behalf when I saw my brother, by the way. I communicated the difficulty that he was imposing on your village's people with all of the taxes he was collecting."

"Oh, well, yes," said Felayah, looking down at his feet. And then as if repeating a script, "But we know that your brother is also trying to keep us as safe as he is able, pleading our cause to Antipas and his Roman masters. There is a price to pay for security, even if it does appear that the bill is a bit high."

"We won't take more of your time, Felayah. Shalama to you and your village."

"You are always welcome here, always welcome," said Felayah as they turned to go. "Any friend of your brother's…" His voice trailed away again as they left the house.

"Well, that was a bit embarrassing," said Yehuda. "He clearly thought I would report everything back to my brother."

"Don't worry, Yehuda," said Ioannis, placing a hand on the older man's shoulder as they walked. "Sometimes it pays to have people think you are more devious than you are. Especially if you don't know everything that's going on."

"That's certainly describes us," said Yehuda ruefully. "All that remains for us here is to find that thin man who told us that Felayah had been killed. He seemed so certain."

"Yes, looking back on his enthusiasm, perhaps a bit too certain," said Ioannis.

In a village that small, it didn't take them long to find the man's house. He met them at the door and invited them in.

"Excuse me, friend, but it seemed a small thing to do," he apologized. "You were strangers here. My family is very poor, and your friend offered me the equivalent of a month's earnings from my poor fields, just for a bit of a joke. I didn't see any real harm in it."

"Who offered the money to you?" demanded Yehuda.

"Why, that stranger with the ragged clothes. You must know him, since I saw you and your friend talking with him. I don't know who he is, but his silver denarii were good. They'll provide for my family for several weeks to come. Maybe I can make them stretch a bit further…I thought it was just a harmless joke on his part."

"You had never seen him before?"

"Never. But we often have strangers show up at the knesset. Most of them are traders in town for the day, wanting the latest news. Some are just nosy. Some are, of course, spies for someone else—a family, Antipas or the Romans. I don't pay much attention. I'm too worried about providing for my blood family to worry about intrigues."

"All right," said Yehuda, relaxing. "Thank you for your time," he added, turning to leave.

"You don't need to go," replied the thin man. "My family and I are just about to eat. We don't have much, but you are welcome to join us. Hospitality, taking care of each other—those are the old Israelite ways, aren't they?"

"Yes, friend," said Yehuda smiling sadly. "Of course they are. Thank you for your generosity, but we need to travel elsewhere by nightfall. Someone is waiting for us. Shalama to you…"

"Shalama, friend. You are always welcome here."

"Who is waiting for us, Yehuda?" asked Ioannis as they walked away from the house. "I thought we were going onto Paneas, or at least heading in that direction."

"We are. But ever since we left my brother's mansion in Zippori, I have had the feeling that Shemuel is trying to contact me. Yes, I know that you've seen me go into trances before. But this is different. Ever since I was a boy, I tended to go 'absent.' I found myself in other worlds, worlds of light and darkness, flames and wheels, and didn't know how to find my way back. I was terrified. Shemuel taught me how to deal with these attacks, how to find my own center during them. He said that visions were the same whether in dream or in waking. I had to learn how to test them, to take control of them and to make sure they were from the Holy One, rather than from somewhere else. Now I feel that he's trying to contact me directly."

"So what do we do?" asked Ioannis.

"We just need to find some quiet place where I can sit and close my eyes. My head is splitting. Let's head north out of the village back toward Zippori. We need to go that way anyway to reach the Roman road east toward the lake and then north."

A short distance outside of Yaphia, Yehuda paused and veered off the path toward the same ancient Tabor oak tree they had visited previously. Without speaking, he sat down underneath it. Ioannis understood that his job was to protect his friend and master while he went on another of his journeys. Ioannis sat down on a rock nearby, watching Yehuda, and prepared for an extended wait. Before the younger man had put down his shoulder bag and settled himself, however, Yehuda suddenly opened his eyes and stood up.

"Nothing, Yehuda?"

"No, little enough, but clear. I didn't travel into strange worlds as I usually do. I only saw Shemuel's feet, just in front of me. He turned around and began walking, and I followed him. Then I forced myself to raise my gaze and look over his shoulder into the distance. He was leading me toward the southern part of Lake Kinneret. So it must mean that we're to go to Paneas by traveling around the bottom, near where the Yarden River exits the lake, and then up along the eastern side through the Decapolis and north through Herodes Philipos's territory. I don't know why. The other way, along the western side of the lake, is much easier, with many villages where we could take food and shelter. The way he's showing me is dry, rugged territory with few villages. It's fairly hard going until we hit the Yarden again, north of the lake. Anyway, that's the way we're going. At this point, just gathering more information isn't helping. We need to follow some clear vision to unravel this mess. All right?"

"All right, Yehuda. I've followed you this far. Let's hope this vision helps us. How do we get there?"

"We'll head northeast, bypassing Zippori this time, and meet the Roman road heading east just north of Gath-Hepher. I know someone there who can give us lodging for the night. It's a bit of a walk after a long day, but we'll make it before nightfall. Then tomorrow we will go over the Adamai Neqeb, the 'red earth pass' that runs down through the hills south toward the bottom of the lake. We're unlikely to run into any trouble if we stay clear of Antipas's bunch in Tiberias."

Three hours later, just toward sunset and after a hard walk through the foothills east of Zippori, they entered Gath-Hepher. Yehuda led them toward a hut at the outskirts of the village and knocked on the door.

"What's here, Yehuda? An inn?"

"No, a hostel for visitors to the prophet Yonah's tomb. He was born in this village, and his grave is just in back of this hut. Shemuel sometimes brought me here to sit in the atmosphere of the prophet." An old man with white hair sticking our wildly around his head opened the door and immediately clapped his arms around Yehuda.

"Shalama, Master! We haven't seen you or your teacher for some months. How is Shemuel ben Yahayye? He and I always used to share the old Israelite stories together. He would teach me about Hanuch, who will come back to save us soon, God willing."

"Shalama, Aqqub. I'm sorry to say that my master Shemuel is dead. We've only just come from Natzara, where he spent much time recently. We're on our way to his home in Paneas, to see to his affairs. His son Mikhael is also dead. Peace to them both."

Aqqub gasped and put his head in his hands, shaking. After some moments, he embraced Yehuda again and then stepped back, grasping both of the scribe's elbows, as he looked up at him imploringly. "Terrible, terrible! We live in dark times," he moaned. "Who knows when deliverance will come? Peace to them both! I can only thank God that I won't be around much longer. I have heard that there is a baptizer calling everyone to repent and prepare for the coming doom. He's down south around the Yarden somewhere."

"Do you know where, grandfather?" interrupted Ioannis. "Is it near the lake?"

"Yes, yes, somewhere there, my son," said Aqqub, releasing Yehuda and looking at Ioannis. "Either in the rocky area where the Yarden exits or farther south. He moves around, I hear. I'm too old to go there myself. And anyway, I'm prepared for whatever happens. I have Yonah here. I suppose you would like to visit him first. Then I'll prepare some food for you and your master."

Aqqub shuffled through the hut into the rear courtyard with the other two following. They found themselves faced with a simple mound of packed earth. An odd thorny plant had been left to grow on the grave, offering some small shade during the day.

"The thorn is to remind us that sometimes the Holy One sends mercies, small mercies, that we don't deserve," Aqqub said to Ioannis when he noticed the young man looking at the plant. "He sent the thorn plant to shade Yonah, even as the prophet was arguing with the Holy One himself, if you can imagine. As your master has probably told you, Yonah wanted the Holy One to burn up the whole city of Nineveh. They were heathens, after all; who could blame him? But the Holy One showed that mercy extends to all, beyond tribe and nation. 'Dwelling on pride cuts us off from mercy,' Yonah said, even while in the belly of the whale. But he forgot quickly. So I keep his grave and remind those who visit—and they are few enough—that we can't judge the Holy One's ways, or dwell too much on the terrible things that happen around us." He turned to Yehuda and said, "Master, will you pray for us?"

Yehuda closed his eyes and raised his cupped palms before his heart. Aqqub and Ioannis did likewise.

"We are Yonah in the whale," said the scribe. "And we breathe with as much mercy and compassion as we can feel in our hearts. We are surrounded by pride, intrigue and dishonesty. We are all in the belly of the whale, traveling God knows where. But we allow the Holy One to breathe mercy through us, making our love stronger than the fear and uncertainty we feel."

They stood awhile in silence. With his eyes closed, Ioannis began to feel light around them emanating from the grave. He opened his eyes, and the light was still there, even pouring out of the small thorn plant. He closed them again and felt a burning in his heart, both pain and joy increasing until he could hardly bear it.

"Holy One! We continue to breathe your breath," said Yehuda. "That's the only way we can endure. Ameyn. Thank you, Nabiya Yonah!"

Chapter 21
Gratitude

Why doesn't anyone appreciate me?

High Priest Qayapha put his head in his hands and rubbed his forehead. He just had a visit from Prefect Pilatus's man, warning him that he wasn't doing enough to maintain Roman security, to protect Roman interests, to collect taxes for Rome, to fight terrorism and banditry against Rome and on and on. After the pompous ass had left, he had dismissed everyone and sunk into his chair in despair.

Was it always this hard being a high priest in Yerushalaim? It seemed to him that his predecessors had done well enough for themselves with minimal effort. Throughout the previous hundred years, the high-priest position had always been awarded on the basis of noble family connections or potential alliances with whoever controlled the kingship, even if they were clients of someone else. Even the Hasmoneans operated that way. *After all,* he thought, *how could a small land in the middle of every empire's path of conquest survive without powerful friends?*

The high priest helped keep the people's loyalty (and support, in the form of tax called "sacrifice") even as the political rulers came and went. Some of the rulers were actually totally mad, like the old Herodes. So it was no easy job to keep rulers from slaughtering every peasant they could find out of misplaced paranoia, or a deranged magician's reading of some star's position.

Yes, of course he had made compromises. All of his predecessors had done the same. If one didn't compromise, there would be no temple at all. Those fanatics out near the Dead Sea didn't understand this. They only thought in terms of "purity." *Hah! Purity is for those who don't bother to engage in the real world.*

Qayapha poured himself a cup of wine and continued to muse dejectedly. The Romans! Why couldn't they be satisfied with what he was doing, rather than what he wasn't? There had been no armed revolt since the old Herodes died, and he didn't see any on the horizon. Did they think this was because people loved the Romans so much? They only thought about money and how much they earned from each colony for the minimum effort expended. What could the Romans do to him? Replace him? They'd find it much harder to find his replacement without causing a revolt than they would to find a new prefect. Of course, some of his predecessors had been murdered on political grounds, some even inside the sacred precincts. Qayapha shuddered. Like most holders of his office, Qayapha was a member of the Zaduqya sect, so he didn't believe in an afterlife or worry about divine judgment there. The soul was not immortal, so God would send any reward or punishment in this life. Consequently, Qayapha was afraid of physical violence, and the Romans were good at torture.

They didn't understand the passion that some people in Israel wasted on their odd notions of "God." It wasn't like the Egyptians. They had dozens of gods and goddesses, so no one could get very upset by any one of them—who was the greatest and so forth. But here things were different.

Our one God is unseen, Qayapha reflected, *so some-one is always prone to hearing voices telling him that he, and he alone, knows the true way. Or that God is telling people to protest about this or that, rise up to free themselves from foreign yoke, or complain that their rulers are corrupt and are acting badly. The Romans need to understand the sort of fantasy this land seems to foster.*

Qayapha allowed himself to think the unthink-able. *What we really need here are a few dozen good idols to occupy people's religious fervor so that they don't spend it all on useless fanaticism. An idol is easy to break, a prophet with charisma and a vision not so easy.*

Qayapha picked up a bell on the table alongside his chair and rang for his personal secretary. The secre-tary, who had been one of Yehuda's assistants, entered with head bowed, waiting expectantly.

"Did we receive any message back from Sakaryut yet?" asked Qayapha.

"No, Sacred Father, nothing yet. But let me check and see if anything came today." The secretary left, and Qayapha indulged in a second cup of wine. *Decent vin-tages coming on this year,* he thought. *It must have been a very warm season when these grapes were grown…*As he looked into the cup, the wine, *dami,* seemed thicker than usual and a different color red, a bit like the other mean-ing of *dami.* Blood. He shivered again as his secretary returned.

"Holy Father, as the Holy One would wish it, Sakaryut has just returned from the north and will be here in a short while."

"Very good. You may leave me again. Just show him in when he arrives."

Qayapha didn't enjoy waiting for an inferior, especially not a spy, but in this case…He had a strange feeling of anxiety about the information the Levite would bring. To calm himself at moments like this, he kept a small bowl of sand from the Dead Sea area in a bowl next to his chair. He picked up a handful and watched it slip through his fingers. He had been raised in the arid hill country to the south and found the touch of sand somehow comforting. So much cleaner and simpler than the dirt of the city.

He did not have to wait long. Sakaryut strode into the room as though he owned the whole temple. *If only I didn't need the man so much,* Qayapha grumbled to himself.

"Sacred Father, Shalama. I pray every day for your good health and give thanks for all you do for the well-being of the nation of Israel."

"You can dispense with the formalities, Sakaryut. Somehow your gratitude is unconvincing. As you frequently remind me, we have a business arrangement, which has been beneficial to both of us. Both our livelihoods depend on the relative peace and well-being of the nation of Israel." *First game to me,* thought Qayapha. "Do you have something?"

"Ah, yes. I do. Yehuda Tauma and his bodyguard did travel north to Zippori to see his brother. However, what happened on the way seems important…"

"Yes?"

"Sacred Father, I admit that I am a bit tired from my travel south to you. I arrived here with the news as quickly as I could. Do you mind if I sit?"

Qayapha hid his disgust. Now the man wants to sit with me! Blackmail. But I refuse to drink with him.

These Levites, just because they think they're related to Moshe's brother, Aaron! Who knows if Moshe even lived? It could all be a story...

Qayapha nodded toward a chair in the corner of his audience room. Fortunately, only the two of them were present, so none of his servants or secretaries would see his humiliation. Sakaryut walked deliberately to the chair, picked it up and slowly walked back with it, setting it down a few paces away from the high priest. Then he sat and looked pointedly at the wine bowl near Qayapha's elbow. Qayapha simply stared back at him. *I still have my self-respect and will power,* he thought. A minute passed. Sakaryut blinked.

"Well," he said, "my sources tell me that Yehuda and his servant traveled quickly to the Jezreel Valley, near Megiddo. There they found the body of Shemuel ben Yahayye, the retired scribe, Yehuda's uncle and adopted father. It seems he had been stabbed to death."

Qayapha shuddered. Personal violence against a scribe reminded him how vulnerable his own position was. "Damnation!" he said disgustedly. "I knew ben Yahayye; he worked for me before he retired. Always seemed knowledgeable, kept his head down, did as I told him. He was getting old, so he retired back to his village up north. Perfectly sensible. Who would want to kill *him*?"

"My sources tell me that this Shemuel may have been at the center of a renegade scribal cult that is plotting against the Romans, the temple and yourself."

"Gehenna! Impossible. But I would have known. I would have heard something...wouldn't I?"

"I can't say, Holy Father," said Sakaryut, smiling slightly. "When did Shemuel ben Yahayye retire back north?"

"About three years ago. Why?" asked Qayapha angrily, banging the arm of his chair with his hand.

"And when did I begin to work for you providing intelligence, Sacred Father?"

"Let me see," replied Qayapha, rubbing his eyes. "I suppose…about two years ago?"

"And how efficient were your spies before that time?"

"Sakaryut, you're trying to provoke me!" yelled Qayapha, standing up and pointing at him accusingly. "Anyway, what did Tauma do next?"

"He seems to have traveled farther north, but not directly to Zippori. He went through Yaphia, where he stopped at the weekly knesset. Then he and his man traveled on, but made a side trip to Nazara. They stayed there two nights."

"Nazara? Do I know it?"

"One of the new towns, Holy Father. Founded by a group returning from Babylon."

"Well, those people are not usually a problem," said Qayapha, sitting down again and relaxing. "They're well adjusted to living under empires. Prophets and rabble-rousers don't come from these new towns, since the old Galileans think they are just as much incomers as we are here at the temple."

"It turns out, however, that a prophet *has* arisen from that town. It's this Yohanan whom you asked me to investigate, the one who is preaching against Antipas down by the bottom of the lake."

"And what does this have to do with Yehuda Tauma, Sakaryut? Are you wasting my time again?"

"Sacred Father, they both had the same teacher: Shemuel ben Yahayye," said Sakaryut with his face like a stone wall.

Qayapha put his head in his hands. "I have a bad feeling about how this is developing," he said.

"It gets a bit worse, my Father. Before Tauma and his man left Nazara, ben Yahayye's son Mikhael arrived, a successful trader in Paneas, apparently."

"Yes, I suppose they were all arranging for the body of his father to be returned home."

"You might think so. But the morning after he arrived, Mikhael was also found murdered, just outside Nazara."

"And what did Tauma do then? Don't make me pull it out of you!"

"He went to visit his brother in Zippori, stayed for a half hour and then left. They headed farther into the Galilean hills the last I heard."

Qayapha sighed. *Why do these things happen to me?* He straightened in his chair and tried to take command of the situation, or at least of the interview with his spy, which had gone from bad to worse.

"Sakaryut," he said levelly, looking at the spy accusingly. "You've given me facts or supposed facts, but I'm no wiser than I was before. I want you to find out for me what's really going on up there! Has Tauma gone over to some sect that is a threat to the temple? I mean, my God, he knows secrets, my personal secrets! What could a group of renegade scribes do with that? This whole country is awash with bandits, prophets and messiahs, all claiming to have the answer for Roman domination. Don't these people understand that there is no answer? An empire is an empire is an empire. And always has been. Live with it!"

"That may be easier for some to say than others, my Father," said Sakaryut wryly, looking at the opulent hall around him.

"Oh, we all have our lot in life to endure, Sakaryut. My life is no garden of bliss, you know!"

"Of course, Sacred Father."

"Still one tries to be grateful that one's troubles are not worse. Life can be short." Qayapha ran his hand through the bowl of desert sand morosely.

⌒

"This is outrageous, impossible! Why didn't anyone tell me!" thundered Antipas to his chief minister Gaius Metallus. He had a splitting headache that morning and was in a mood to be upset about everything.

"What is outrageous, my liege?"

"Well…this whole situation with the prophet—what's his name?—spreading lies about me and my personal relations! I heard about it from someone…maybe yesterday."

"But I told you about that days ago, my liege," said Metallus, a bit bored. He was used to Antipas's forgetfulness, the product of frequent hard drinking at his numerous feasts. "The prophet's name is Yohanan. He has set up camp down south on the lake where the Yarden exits. He is mainly drawing local peasants, and I would say he's providing some harmless entertainment."

"But, but—what he's saying!"

"He's saying only the usual things, vague gener-
alities about corruption in high places—meaning you.
People expect their rulers to be powerful and a bit corrupt. Makes them respect you more. He tells them they
have no hope, which is true, and they need to be baptized so they can reach a better place in heaven, or within themselves, or whatever. In my view, it just occupies
the crowd's energy in metaphysical speculation, which
another person could turn to armed revolt."

"But, about my, err, personal relations! Surely
that's treasonous."

"He's only saying that you have married a divorced woman, your brother Philipos's wife. And, well,
that *is* true, my liege. Happens all the time in the best
kingdoms, if you read the reports I present to you about
news in minor royal families in Roman territory."

"Minor! What are you implying, Metallus?
Anyway, we need to do something about him! Yesterday,
if possible. By the way, what did I do yesterday?"

"Yesterday you had a feast, sire. Similar to the previous three days before that."

"I see. That must be why my head hurts. Did I get
anyone pregnant?"

"We don't know yet, sire."

"No close relative, hopefully…"

"The gods willing, no."

Antipas sighed. "I'm bored with Tiberias, Metallus.
Let's leave for Machaerus down in my eastern territory
Perea tomorrow. I need a change of scenery. I'm missing
the peace and quiet of the *Araba,* the Sea of Salt. I need
the waters there to help purge me of these awful head-
aches that I keep getting for some reason. It will also get
us away from all these people petitioning me for relief

from this or that. I mean, what do I have to do with their state of wealth or poverty? Really!"

"Some would say quite a bit, my liege. But that *is* your privilege. You are the friend of Rome, as was your father."

"Rome, Rome—I am my own man!" shouted Antipas, waving his arms wildly. "I know you report to them, Metallus. I hope you tell them that I take care of my people so that they're not hoodwinked by false prophets dunking them in water and hypnotizing them into believing that I am an evil ruler! I have history to think about, Metallus! I want you to send troops to bring this so-called prophet Yohanan to me in Machaerus. We deal with him down there, far enough away from any supporters he may have up here in Galilee. Galilee—what a Gehenna-hole! Why couldn't our friends in Rome have given me Yerushalaim instead? It was all due to that forged will my younger brother Archelaos produced after my father died. How could Rome believe such a blatant lie? I wouldn't have made the mess of Judea that he did. Imagine, killing thousands during a Passover riot—a good way to get yourself deposed. Anyway, my younger brother always had the luck…"

"You do remember what happened to your younger brother, sire?"

"Well, yes."

"Rome exiled him to Gaul after he made too many mistakes."

"Yes, well…" Antipas shivered at the thought of winter in Gaul. Not to mention living among barbarians…

Gratitude

"And your younger brother Archelaos *is* dead now, sire."

"All right! I suppose I should be grateful to our friends in Rome, but…"

"Exactly, my liege!"

Chapter 22

The Baptizer

Just after dawn, Yehuda and Ioannis thanked Aqqub and headed straight north, scrambling slowly overland through the foothills and meadows of mid-Galilee. By midmorning, they reached the Roman road leading east toward the lake. From there, they were able to make better time. Many travelers were on the road heading toward Tiberias, but just before midday Yehuda and Ioannis came to a crossroad and veered right, toward the southern end of Lake Kinneret, avoiding the city. As they followed a small tributary feeding into the Yarden River, they entered a valley where villagers were pasturing sheep. The road wound through a region of low, forested mountains about six hundred Roman pedes high on either side. As they reached a wider pass, they saw a village nestled within the rich red earth surrounding it.

"It's called Adami Nekeb. This region traditionally belonged to the tribe of Napthali," explained Yehuda. "During the time of the judges, they were famous for their military leaders, including Barak, the general whom the judge Deborah commanded. But after the Assyrians went through, I doubt there has been much of that kind of activity, with it being so close to Tiberias and Antipas's garrison."

As they walked through the village, however, Yehuda noticed the incongruous appearance of the male villagers they passed. All of the men wore the clothing of shepherds, but were built and walked as though they were in an army.

"Shalama, friend," said Yehuda, stopping a tall, muscular, bald-headed man. "We are strangers passing through from Natzara to the lake. Are we on the right road?"

"Yes, of course," said the man, stiffening as though to attention. "Strangers? From *Natzara*? Whom do you know there, may I ask?" he said with an air of authority.

Touching his ear and pretending to rub one eye as he closed it, Yehuda replied vaguely, "Oh, we have many friends there. Eliyuhena is a business partner, and of course we know Zakarya ben Abiya, who was a friend of my teacher."

"I see," said the man, displaying no emotion. "And where, may I ask, are you headed?"

"I was a student of the late Shemuel ben Yahayye, a scribe," continued Yehuda, causing the man to blink. "We are heading north to his village near Paneas to tie up some affairs for the family. We are going this way because we promised Zakarya that we would try to obtain some word of his son Yohanan. We heard that he was baptizing people somewhere near Sennabris, where the Yarden exits the lake."

"Look, friend," said the man, touching his right ear, and then looking down briefly and pretending to remove some dust from his eye, "we have friends in common. But I would stay away from that area right now. Yes, Yohanan is down there, with a crowd. But he is not doing anyone any good, taunting Antipas within a stone's throw of Tiberias."

"What would Antipas care about a harmless preacher?" asked Yehuda. "Surely baptizing people and asking them to lead a better life is no threat to him."

"Of course. If that's all he were doing, he would just be another one of those dreamy ones who come out of the hills every so often. The Herodes family—grandfather, father and sons—always loved them, since they made people believe things would be better in some other world. But Yohanan is preaching against Antipas, his morals—as if he had any—taking his brother's wife, all that. Antipas's old wife, the one he got rid of, is not very pleased," he said, wrinkling his weather-beaten face in what passed for a smile. "Since she is the daughter of the Nabatean king, we could have a war here soon." He paused and looked meaningfully at Yehuda and then at Ioannis.

"That could be good, or it could be bad," the man said, "depending on whether one is ready or not. But the more Yohanan draws attention to himself, the more Antipas's spies will try to find out where he comes from. Yohanan may think he's working with a force from another world, but he may spoil things for those of us who would like to see a better world here."

"Thank you," said Yehuda. "We have made a promise to his father, and we will be careful."

"Shalama. Go well," said the man, almost saluting. "We knew your teacher and were sorry to hear of his murder. If you ask me, that wasn't the Herodes, it was the Romans, or some of the temple criminals. Shemuel ben Yahayye was a friend of all true Israelites, and his murder was a blow for us here. I don't suppose we will ever know who did it."

"Maybe. Maybe not," said Yehuda. "Shalama, friend."

It was midafternoon when they descended from the foothills near the lake and saw the village of Sennabris nestled next to it. From a distance, nothing seemed to be happening in the village, but people were streaming out of it to an encampment just to the south on the shore of the lake. As they neared the lake, they entered a crowd of hundreds of people, clustered around the Yarden on both sides. Many had Yohanan's name on their lips.

"Looks like the place," said Ioannis. "Shall we find the man?"

"Yes. It shouldn't be too hard," replied Yehuda. They followed the buzzing of the crowd toward its most intense point and found a large group perched around an open space on the shore, where fresh Yarden water cascaded down through stepped rocks. Everyone seemed to be waiting for something, and most were looking in one direction. Groups of women and children sat along the shore, while separately a group of men clustered around one spot.

"Over there, Yehuda," said Ioannis, pointing left a hundred paces toward a short, burly, bushy-headed man with long brown hair and wild eyes. He looked like he had been in the sun and the wilderness for a long time. "That must be him. He looks the part of a prophet."

"Probably more than looks, judging from the crowd," said Yehuda. "This many don't come out for just anyone. So many people have claimed to be a special son of Moshe or some other messiah—an anointed one of some sort—that most folks are a bit jaded. Let's go meet him now. It appears he may soon be occupied."

The two walked straight up to Yohanan, and Yehuda introduced himself immediately as Shemuel's student.

"How I have longed to meet you!" Yohanan exclaimed, immediately embracing Yehuda vigorously and then looking into his eyes as he continued to hold his elbows. "That I have lived to see this day!" he said with tears in his eyes. "Shemuel spoke frequently of you and said that if anything happened to him, you would know what to do."

"And something has happened to him," said Yehuda. "You must have heard."

"Yes, of course. But I knew even before I received word through my students. Shemuel appeared to me in a dream the night he was killed and told me to continue what I am doing to bring a new Israel."

Yehuda noticed in the man's eyes the same mixture of fire and light that he remembered from Shemuel's, the result of communication with other worlds. In fact, for an instant, it seemed to be Shemuel looking out through the younger man's eyes.

"But your family in Natzara doesn't seem to understand what you are doing. They don't believe it is helpful," said Yehuda softly. "Your father asked us to try to find where you are and what you are doing. And to try to stop you."

"My family. Yes," said Yohanan, looking down and losing some of his emotion. "I have compassion for them. I understand that they think they know the right way to bring the new Israel. But they have their own information, and at least some of them know exactly what I am doing and where. They have only sent you to try to talk me out of it. Or," he said, turning his gaze within a bit, "perhaps to divert attention away from them and toward you…

"Brother," Yohanan continued, holding the scribe's arms firmly, "anyone around me must be ready to reveal himself and his inmost thoughts. All is clear before the Holy One, and only complete honesty and harmony between the outer and inner worlds, complete righteousness, will bring the new Israel."

"That may be, Yohanan," said Yehuda. "I know that Shemuel might say so, too. But in the few days after his death, I discovered that Shemuel himself had many secrets. He was my teacher, and I loved him, but I believed him to be a simple retired scribe, living in Paneas. Now it turns out he had other lives."

"Other lives, other worlds, other truths…" mused Yohanan. "Who of us can judge a prophet like Shemuel? You may be one part of him. I may be another. My cousin may be the third. He is wandering somewhere in the wilderness near Lake Merom, communing with the lions that I often see in my visions. If you put us all together, we might see the vision clearly. Apart, we are stumbling in the dark. We continue anyway. What else can we do when we get the inner sign, eh? Excuse me, Yehuda, but my people are waiting. The *malkuta*—the new reign—cannot wait. We will talk later, and I can tell you more." Yohanan gathered his robe around himself and moved slowly toward a level, rocky place slightly higher than the waiting crowd.

"But do you know why Shemuel was killed and who did it?" asked Yehuda urgently, walking alongside him.

"You yourself said that Shemuel had many secrets. How can we know if the blow came from the enemies within or the enemies outside? Shemuel was fighting our battle in both worlds, or perhaps in many worlds."

"And your cousin," broke in Ioannis, walking behind them. "You said he was wandering. Is he all right? Is he healthy?"

Yohanan stopped and turned around. Ioannis felt the prophet's eyes looking straight through him, into the void. At the same time, he felt his heart exposed and burning.

"My friend, I don't know you in this world, but maybe I do in another. You accompany my master's chief student. I see that your heart has been wounded, but it is strong. Your love is strong. Follow that love. Who can say who is 'all right' and who is 'healthy,' when the land and all of our people are ailing? *We* must be the healers, all of us together, not waiting for one person to do it for us. I can tell you that my cousin may be worth all of us together in his power in the inner world, the power to bring the *malkuta*. I have the power to move people with words. He has that, plus the touch of the healer and something more, something I don't understand: the power to heal all the worlds. Who knows what that would look like if it came to pass?"

They had reached the level rock overlooking both sides of the Yarden, which was very narrow at that point. Yohanan stepped to middle of the bluff, and those around him fell back, as the prophet closed his eyes and gathered himself. Yehuda looked around and saw mostly poor people, probably from neighboring villages, but also several dozen men on horseback on the opposite side of the Yarden in the Decapolis region.

Ioannis caught the direction of Yehuda's gaze and also looked at the group of horsemen more closely. "Those riders…" he said.

"Yes, they look to me like Israelites," said Yehuda. "From their demeanor, they seem to be devotees of Yohanan…"

"But I've not seen a group of Israelites handle horses in that way," replied Ioannis.

"You mean, in such an experienced way, Yehohanan? Yes, you're right. They must be the relatives of the Natzara who live in Batanea farther east."

Yohanan suddenly opened his eyes and began to speak. The instant he began, Yehuda found himself shaking. Yohanan's voice became like Shemuel's had been when he was speaking to large groups—from the heart, forceful, inspiring. And much louder than could possibly come from that small body, thought Yehuda. Yohanan's tone, his breathing, even his face became like that of Shemuel. Yehuda felt like he was seeing his teacher alive again, except that the words were new:

> In the name and light of the most powerful Life!
> Worlds combined to form our first flesh—
> head, neck, limbs, liver, spleen, stomach, genitals.
> All—all, my friends—were originally their own world!
> Now they talk together in us, and when they are not
>   united,
> we have trouble. We are ill.
> So we are ill as a people, because we should be united.
>
> Now listen!
> The soul is the light in us.
> The soul brought the separate worlds together.

A Murder at Armageddon

And when the soul is trapped and sick, everything is ill.
So Adam fell, like our souls, and he was trapped.
But then he was raised up to the House of Life,
washed in the heavenly Yarden by the messengers of
    light.

Yarden means "go down," my friends,
so Adam went down into the waters,
let go of his old self, his small self.
He left the illness, the trouble, the evil behind,
so that he could enter the House of Life.

So, my friends, I rise out of the waters to help you.
We will rise together like the Great Fisher Hani
rising from the waters at the beginning,
and every year dying and returning, dying and
    returning,
bringing life, health, wisdom, joy,
and a good world for us and our children!

Let what is unripe—out of place, time—the evil, die
    within you.
Rise again from the waters of life in this baptism!
Return, return—stop what you're doing.
Stop the lives you are leading!
Turn around and go the other way!

Reject the evil of the rulers around you.
Do not submit to Antipas, who steals his own brother's
    wife,
or to the false prophets living in that
gilded nest of vipers in Yerushalaim, the temple,

or to any of those who stand over you, keeping you
    captive,
demanding that you call them "father."
There is only one Father and one Mother.

Wisdom speaks! Hear her voice!
Free yourselves from error and bondage!
Start here and now by washing in this little Yarden,
dying to the little self you thought you were.
Then you can be free,
and your children can be free
and the land can be free,
from this gathering until the next
and the next and the next!

When Yohanan paused, the crowd exhaled together, as though hundreds of people had been holding their breath. Then they breathed in together and began to move imperceptibly toward Yohanan, ready to accept his offer.

"Stop!" An arrow fell at Yohanan's feet.

Yehuda looked around. While everyone had been entranced by Yohanan's preaching, a group of soldiers and horsemen had come over the rise from the north. They were dressed in the livery of Herodes Antipas's service, a cheap parody of the Roman costume. Their captain dismounted, pushed through the crowd and planted himself in front of Yohanan, placing his hands on his hips.

"Stop in the name of Tetrarch Antipas, whose name you are dishonoring!" shouted the captain.

"My friend," replied Yohanan calmly, "you are an Israelite. My message is for you also. Free yourself from these delusions of false power. We are all Israelites in the name of the most powerful Light and Life."

"I don't know what you're talking about," said the captain, "but you cannot continue to gather all of these people here. I have been ordered to take you in for questioning by Herodes Antipas himself."

"Ordered? Questioning?" replied Yohanan, somewhat bemused. "Who gave the orders for Antipas to exist, for any of us to exist?" Then he gathered his full energy and shouted at the man, "And the only question worth asking is: *Who are you?*"

Chapter 23

Straddling the Rift

"Take him!" cried out the Herodian captain, and a small group of his foot soldiers rushed through the crowd toward Yohanan. A group of Yohanan's male students moved quickly between them and the prophet.

"We are prepared to die to defend our prophet!" cried one of them, who stood directly in front of the captain.

"All right then. Die," he replied, snapping his fingers. One of his soldiers ran the man through the heart with his sword, and he fell instantly, his blood spilling at the prophet's feet. A woman cried out sharply, and the crowd fell silent. In the next instant, an arrow struck the soldier directly through the heart, dropping him on the spot next to the student. The horsemen from Batanea, Yohanan's kinsmen, had crossed the Yarden and outflanked Antipas's soldiers from the side.

"We are not defenseless peasants," called one of them to Antipas's captain. "We serve our prophet and the Unnamable Light and Life. We are free Israelites who live beyond the reach of Antipas or any earthly power. Join us! Do not force us to kill more of you, who are our Israelite cousins. Even if you do not die, you will be dishonored, which is as good as death in Antipas's service."

The captain paused for a moment, considering. He looked at Yohanan, who gazed at him with a strange combination of righteous anger and pity.

"Alternate plan!" he called to his troops. The crowd began to relax a bit and then noticed that Antipas's cavalry was not moving. Instead, the tetrarch's horsemen had aimed their bows at the clustered groups of women and children, and foot soldiers had moved to surround them.

"I think that is the end of this little game," said the captain to Yohanan. "Your move. Do you come with us willingly, or after the deaths of all these women and children?"

"Your soul will have much to purify itself from in the next world, friend," said Yohanan sadly. "I feel the pain already." Turning to his kinsmen and the crowd, Yohanan called out, "Friends, I am going with these men willingly! Perhaps the Great Life and Light wants me to preach to Antipas, to appeal to his soul to return and repent. Remember the real power, and you will be able to do as I have done! If I do not return, follow the one with the dove, my kinsman who was here last week. He will help you complete your purification and show you how to fulfill your soul's purpose. Freedom to Israel!"

"Let's go," said the captain, pushing Yohanan ahead of him and then bundling him onto the back of a horse behind one of his men. They all disappeared quickly over the rise, the horsemen first, the foot soldiers protecting the rear.

"We could follow them, pick them off, rescue the prophet," said Ioannis to the leader of the horsemen from Batanea, who had ridden up to Yehuda and dismounted.

"Yes, we could, friend," the well-built man replied soberly. He was middle-aged, with rugged features and long hair; a Babylonian nose made it hard to place his family background. "But they will slit the prophet's throat if we come close to doing so. Also, our reinforcements are far behind us, east in our fortress in Bathyra. We do not, in any case, have the troops to storm Antipas in Tiberias. We will need to trust that the prophet's vision is true. Perhaps he can turn Antipas's heart. If anyone can, he can."

He turned to Yehuda. "Shalama. My name is Shemei ben Yair. I saw our prophet embracing you as a brother. Can you tell me where you are from and who your people are? Excuse my directness, but we have not much time. We need to return to the other side of the Yarden."

"I am Yehuda Tauma ben Yahayye, the adopted son and student of Shemuel ben Yahayye," replied Yehuda. "And this is my friend, Ioannis Vivis, who is also known by his Israelite name, Yehohanan. His mother was Israelite."

"Then so is he, and he is our brother also," said Shemei. "Your teacher spoke of you. We will avenge his death if we can find out who murdered him. Like some of our kinfolk, Shemuel believed that it was important to purify that den of vipers in Yerushalaim, and he told us that you were a key to that cleansing."

"I am finished with the temple," countered Yehuda. "Yehohanan and I left Yerushalaim two days before Shemuel was killed. We found his body on the road below Megiddo, just before Roman soldiers appeared. I was on my way to meet with him at his home in Paneas about some instructions he had sent me. Now we are still going to Paneas to tie up his affairs. His son is dead also. Perhaps you've heard?"

"No, we didn't know that," said Shemei, frowning. "We never met the son. According to Shemuel, he was only interested in business, not in the great work of his father. You were Shemuel's real son, he always said. Both the father and son dead. Very strange. Do you have any clue who has done this?"

"No," said Yehuda. "We were hoping that Yohanan had some idea. But in the short time we had together, he only referred to Shemuel's many secrets…"

"'What the eye has not seen and what the ear has not heard'…to accomplish anything worthwhile, one needs to hold the vision inside, in the heart, and not speak it aloud to every person," said Shemei, nodding. "This is what Yohanan taught us, or what was taught through him, really. His ordinary personality and what came through him from the other world were very different, as you've seen."

"Yes. It was very extreme," agreed Yehuda. "Other than Shemuel, I have never experienced anyone else able to hold so great a split between the different parts of themselves. My teacher seemed to move easily between these worlds. Inner, outer. Wisdom, power. Light, shadow."

"He is gone—may he rest with prophet Moshe! And we don't know what will happen to Yohanan. We will carry on as before, I suppose."

"The one with the dove, Yohanan said…"

"That's his cousin, Yeshua. He was here last week. There were fewer people then, of course, but those of us here clearly saw a dove fly down and perch on Yeshua's head as he came out of the Yarden after being baptized by Yohanan. Then the bird hopped down onto his shoulder and stayed near him the whole time he was here, as though it were whispering something in his ear. He and Yohanan were inseparable for those days. Yeshua went into the Yarden with each new group that came to be baptized, and he came out each time with less of *him* there, it seemed to me. It was as if he had no self remaining, and only his breath held his flesh together. When he wandered away finally, heading north, the dove was again on his shoulder. It seemed to me he was so insubstantial that his feet barely touched the earth. I don't see how he could lead us anywhere, except into the heavens."

"Yohanan said that Yeshua was somewhere in the wilderness around Lake Merom," said Yehuda. "I know that place well, and we would also like to talk to him. Shemuel appeared to me in a vision and is sending us along that way to Paneas. Perhaps Yeshua knows something about Shemuel's death. If there were a conspiracy against him, or against what he had planned, then Yeshua might know."

"Yes, perhaps. We would also like to know. My brothers and I can accompany you through the Decapolis to the border of Gaulanitis before heading home. Technically, it all belongs to Herodes Philipos, but he doesn't send patrols there. Most of the Decapolis is rough country. It's helpful to go with some protection, as no one is really in charge there, and loyalties change without warning. The Romans have few outposts there also, and they only use it as another buffer zone with the Parthians. We in Batanea are just next door, another buffer. Philipos likes to play both sides, or all sides, if he can."

"Thank you, Shemei. We accept."

"Can either of you ride?"

"I can," replied Ioannis.

"I have ridden a bit," said Yehuda, "but mostly donkeys, I'm afraid."

"No problem. We will give you an easy mount and place you toward the middle, where my men can keep an eye on you."

Shemei eyed Ioannis carefully and then selected a faster mount for him. They all set off east without delay. A short time later, Ioannis found himself toward the front of the procession, next to Shemei. He was reveling in being on a good horse again. After he had been sold into slavery, it had been a long time.

"I see that you are no novice to horsemanship," said Shemei.

"I learned early. My father taught me as a boy, and we used to go riding in the hills above Rome. They were wonderful times," said Ioannis wistfully. Then he explained. "He was a Roman officer here during the old Herodes's time."

"Fell out of favor, did he?" asked Shemei with a knowing smile. "I suppose marrying an Israelite woman didn't help."

"Neither did plotting against the emperor."

"Ah. So you've had a bit of hard life, I imagine. Lucky to be alive, really. But you clearly know how to ride, and you carry your sword as if you know what to do with it."

"I was a bodyguard for the old Roman prefect before being assigned to guard one of the temple scribes. That's how I met Yehuda."

"Rediscovered your roots then, did you?" replied Shemei, laughing. "I see that he trusts you. So that's good enough for me."

"Shemei, can you help me understand what all this is about? Who are you, and how do you relate to the family of Yohanan and Yeshua in Natzara and…well, to what they say they're planning?"

"They let you in on that, did they?" asked Shemei, shaking his head. "All right. We are really from the same family, as they may have told you. We all returned from Babylon after the Persians kicked out the Babylonians some centuries ago. Damn the Persians. Some saw them as rescuers, but I found the Babylonians better chiefs, at least for those of us who could provide them with some useful service.

"Some of us journeyed only as far as Batanea, and the rest went farther and reestablished the 'branch' in Natzara. We stayed on the border, because our part of the family has always been good with horses. Horsemanship is in our blood, and we have always served whichever group was willing to pay for our services—Babylonians, Persians, Hasmoneans or Parthians. It doesn't make much difference, as far as I can see. If you're a client to a patron, you might as well be as high up the ladder as possible. Since we were the best at what we did, we could name our price, and we did. We raised everyone's horses and trained their cavalry. Frankly, I think we had it better in Babylon than our brothers and sisters who ended up under the Roman heel here. The Romans have always been too proud to think they could learn from anyone who wasn't Roman blood. Sorry, I know…"

"Don't worry; I have no love for the Roman state, and I know what you mean about the pride. Not our best feature."

"Anyway, some of the family in Batanea think that the temple reestablished in Yerushalaim by the Persians under Cyrus was just a fraud, an imperial trick, to keep the masses there happy and keep taxes flowing. It's been corrupt since the beginning. That group of us spends all of its time fasting and cursing the temple and blessing themselves. They have another settlement down near the Sea of Salt, in the hills above the western shore.

"My part of the family prefers action to prayer. Of course the temple is corrupt, but why fight over something that small? If you want to build an empire, get together with empire builders, not villagers. So we have made ourselves indispensible to the empire builders: in our case, the Parthians. For the moment, at least..." he said, smiling.

"From what Yehuda told me, Shemuel felt that the true temple was never in Yerushalaim. It was the portable one carried by Moshe, which real Israelites carry in their hearts."

"Right. That's why we agreed with our family in Natzara that Shemuel might be the prophet we have been waiting for. You understand—an empire is never built only with armies. People need a charismatic figure to bring them together and, more importantly, to *keep* them together. Shemuel could have been that figure. It could be Yohanan, too. He has the fire. But now he's gone, too."

"What do you think will happen to him?"

"Who knows? Probably Antipas will take him south to his fortress in Perea on the west shore of the Salt Sea. We might be able to raid that better than Tiberias. We could reach it faster since our territory lays just to the east. Difficult, but possible. We have spies inside his fortress, of course."

"And this Yeshua? I met his sister in Natzara..."

"Ah, you did, did you? Well, good luck to you! She's more than enough for any two men. Yeshua? As I said, hardly a person at all. Can't build a revolution, or an empire, around someone like that. As I said, that's our main difference with the family in Natzara. They're thinking of an independent Israel. That's hopeless. I would rather see a semi-independent Israel, self-governing as an honored client to the Parthians. We already have people in the Parthian elite, so we can get a favored position—less tax, more independence—in exchange for our help in their military and keeping the border lands quiet. But we would still need a prophet-king who can hold the people here together. Someone who has the words, the strength and the fire that people respect. Yeshua has one foot in each world, or maybe more than one on the other side. We need someone who can stand with two feet here. And…" Shemei hesitated, giving Ioannis a long look.

"And?" asked Ioannis, giving him the same look back.

"It has to do with your master, or friend, Yehuda. Please understand, I don't wish to be offensive in any way—we respect him because of Shemuel. Let me say this cantering in a circle a bit. I know that our part of the family, those of us who are masters of the cavalry, have had a privileged life for generations. Because of our skill, which has been passed down from father to son, we have not been in want or poverty. Actually, for us, things got better when we came to Babylon, since the lines of the old Israelite kings, north and south, had completely run out of sap by the time they showed up. We disagree with our Natzara cousins about this, of course. Our cousins say that the poor can be just as happy as the rich, if they have their own country, but I don't know what poor they're talking about. The type of poverty we've seen when we've traveled secretly into Israel…it's like the rulers there—the Romans, the Herodes and the Yerushalaim priests—are just trying to grind people's faces into the dirt. Except for a few rich retainers in Yerushalaim, life under the Romans and the Herodes family has been devastating, especially for the villagers." Shemei shook himself and patted his horse's flank gently.

"Yes, I've seen that, too," said Ioannis. "The poor in Rome don't have an easy life, but at least the emperors realized that they don't want a popular revolution in the capital every year. So they tend to share the wealth some—just a little, of course."

"So you understand. Well, in these small villages, there's grinding poverty, with no work—or all the work you do just goes to the rich. And you're already in debt, and so are your sons and their sons, if they should be foolish enough to have any children. No hope. So things go on inside families, things that should not be mentioned. Just because human beings can only take so much without…without opening the doors of their souls to demons and spirits that should have no place in this world."

"Demons, spirits? What do you mean?" asked Ioannis. "We have demons in Roman stories, of course. But they usually stay outside of human beings and torture them that way. Not from inside of them."

"OK, well. Here it seems to be different. The earth often trembles and shakes. Large gashes and rifts open up suddenly, as though the whole land—east, west, north and south—met in battle right here eons ago. The other world and this world meet and sometimes mix. And it's usually not for the better. Sometimes a person simply goes mad, and they go wandering around the village, raving. But other times it's more hidden. Life in some families becomes its own Gehenna, a rubbish heap of violence or strange mating or other ways the madness shows itself."

"I see. But what does this have to do with Yeshua? Or Yehuda?" asked Ioannis.

"You understand, it's only my opinion," replied Shemei apologetically. "I was trained by my father to look a man in the eye and assess him clearly but compassionately. All men are brothers. But one has to look clearly to know whether to trust someone or try to help him. It's just like looking a new horse in the eye, feeling its character, what it *is* now, not what I may need or want it to be. I have noticed that people who come from families where…strange things happen…usually have a certain look in their eyes. It's like they have learned how not to be *here*, how to fly away and escape somewhere else. Yeshua has that look. So does Yehuda. Of course, some are born that way—born with vision, you could say. Others have it forced on them. I have seen it destroy a man, or save him. It all depends…"

"Depends on what?"

"On how they go to that other world. Do they go willingly or unwillingly? With a purpose or to escape? And only the Holy One can know that, really. So it's hard to trust a man who has that gift, or cross, to carry."

Chapter 24

Into the Wilderness

The small troop continued to travel quickly through the rough country to the west of the lake, which Shemei called Yam Kinneret. "Yam is a Canaanite water spirit," he explained. "When traveling through wild country, it's wise to invoke as many spirits as you can, I think. They were all here before Moshe came, and certainly before us. I am keeping us away from the coast, where the few villages are. It's harder going out here, but we can pass unnoticed, and that will save more time than it loses."

By sundown, they had quickly covered the eleven Roman millia from one end of the lake to another, even with rest stops along the way.

"The horses can't keep up this pace for more than a few days," Shemei announced to Yehuda and Ioannis around the campfire that night. "But I've decided that we will take you on into Gaulanitis, Philipos's territory. It's nearly ten more millia to Lake Merom, and that's mostly uphill. We can take you there much faster than if you proceed on foot. Half a day at best, since we know the quickest paths and can stay close to the Yarden. From here on, there are no settlements to avoid. We will leave you near where the road to Damascus branches east from the track that continues north into the Merom wetlands. From there it's all level to the lake and best done on foot, anyway. Then we'll double back and head home, probably making it to our first safe camp by nightfall."

The next morning they were up at dawn, moving quickly north up the Yarden river basin. The spring waters came cascading down toward them through the winding gulches. By midmorning they viewed cormorants and other birds flying north toward the valley ahead, which lay sandwiched between steep slopes, the Naphtali Mountains in Galilee to the west and the heights of Gaulanitis in the east. They stopped at the sight of a huge wall of black basalt, perhaps six hundred Roman pedes high, looming ahead of them.

"This is a very ancient valley, a deep crack in the earth that some say runs all the way south into the land of the *Afri*, who may be connected to our tribe of Ephraim." said Yehuda. "Usually I've entered the Merom wetlands from the west, through Galilee. This way is new for me. You can feel the energy of different worlds colliding here, like flat dishes crashing together. Maybe that's why this land has always been fought over by empires. Or why it's been the scene of inner battles of spirits and eruptions of visions received by prophets like Shemuel. It's comforting to see the birds return from the south each spring, as they are now. Somehow it reminds me that creation and nature will continue, no matter whether our human ambitions succeed or fail."

"Look ahead there," said Shemei, pointing a few millia away to the base of the basalt cliffs ahead. "That's where the Yarden flows out of Lake Merom, and you will find a pass-through. Then you'll come to the lake itself. On the north side, you'll find a huge swamp—reeds, wetlands, thousands of nesting birds this time of year. Watch out for the wild pigs, lions, bears, leopards and Alaha knows what else. It's a jungle. You will likely find Yeshua in there somewhere, as that's where people like him usually go not to be found, or to talk to the spirits or demons. I don't like the place, myself, since you can never see what's around the next stand of papyrus or thicket of trees. A horse is no good in there—too easily spooked."

"Yes, don't worry, Shemei," said Yehuda. "From here, I know the way well. Shemuel used to take me to Merom for my own retreats as a boy. He would send me out into the *madbara*, the wilderness, to seek a vision or to test my faith in the Holy One. With trust, one only receives what one is meant to. Or meets whom one is meant to meet…"

"I understand, Yehuda," said Shemei. "Sorry, I forgot whom I was speaking to."

"Once we're out of the wilderness," said Yehuda to Ioannis, "we will continue uphill all the way to Paneas and the headwaters of the Yarden near Mount Hermon. That's a different world again…difficult to describe, so I won't try. You'll see."

"After the swamp of Merom, you will think you died and went to the heaven of the Persians at the springs of Paneas," said Shemei, smiling. "At least I did after spending my life riding through dust most of the time. I'll bid you both Shalama for now. If you'd like, I can send one of my men with you for protection, but…"

"That won't be necessary," replied Ioannis. "Whatever's not from the spirit world, I can handle."

"In there, that isn't very much, in my experience, son," said Shemei. "If you discover something useful to us, send a messenger from Paneas."

"I will," promised Yehuda, "*if* we can find someone we trust." The two dismounted with their knapsacks and continued on foot toward the basalt cliffs.

As Shemei had promised, they found their way easily through the pass, and a short while later they stopped on the eastern side of the small lake for a meal. Shemei had given them enough bread and dried fish to last them for a few days. Birds were nesting around the lake—pelicans, herons, storks, cormorants and cranes. Thousands of them seemed to cover its surface, which was about six square Roman millia in area. Water lilies edged some of the banks, as the lake blended into pools and increasingly dense marshland farther north. A flock of gazelles arrived fifty feet away, seemingly unconcerned about the men's presence.

"Aren't they afraid of hunters?" asked Ioannis.

"No, the animals and birds here don't worry about that," said Yehuda. "It's as if they also feel they are only travelers here, like the people who pass through. Mind you, unless you know your way, or are willing to be led, it can be a bit dangerous. I have never seen many hunters here, although I have seen human bones picked clean by lions or other big cats."

Ioannis shuddered. "I'm like Shemei, Yehuda. Give a military man open spaces, or a good hill to defend, and he's happy. Swamps are not for me. Anyway, I'm glad I'm with you."

They continued on around the east side of the lake, until they reached the northern edge. Facing them was a dense growth of tall papyrus, a veritable forest of stalks, up to twice Ioannis's height, topped by large balls of threadlike stems, which stuck out horizontally. Ioannis looked back toward the relative safety of the lake a bit longingly.

"I suppose there is only one way to go on from here, right Yehuda?"

"Yes, that's right. There doesn't seem to be a path here, but actually there are many. We need to go this way anyway to get to Paneas directly. And as Shemei said, if Yeshua is here, we're likely to find him in this jungle."

"And how will we do that?"

"Don't worry. If we're meant to find him, we will."

"I'm glad you're so trusting, Yehuda. By the way," Ioannis said, stalling a bit for time, "what does the name of this lake—Merom—mean?"

"Flow piling on flow. It's a reminder to float, not fight, in here. The Egyptians used to call this lake *Semachuna*, which means something similar—the flowing force for good or evil brought to earth. The Greeks turned that into *Semachonitis*, which is the name the Romans use too."

"Very helpful, although not reassuring."

"People don't come here to be reassured, but to face something they need to face. We had better be going. We need to make it at least halfway through by nightfall."

"Halfway?" asked Ioannis bleakly.

"Yes, the whole area is about ten times that of the lake."

"Do you know of a campsite?"

"It's all about equally comfortable, or safe. Don't worry."

Ioannis remembered Shemei's words about people who live their lives in two worlds, without feet firmly in this one. In this light, Yehuda's words were not reassuring. As he followed the scribe into the papyrus jungle, he tried not to think about the fact that even he, an experienced tracker normally, could barely see any path ahead of them. After what seemed like an hour to him, it all still looked like a sea of green—damp earth underfoot, with a cacophony of birdcalls around them. Then he noticed that the growth above them was so dense that he couldn't tell the direction of the sun.

"Which way is north, Yehuda? I can't find the sun."

"In this world, we don't use the sun out there, Yehohanan. We use the sun in here," he said, pointing to his heart.

As they continued on, the light began to fade. Occasionally, Ioannis heard a screech to his left, a growl or grunt to his right, a rustling behind him. He thought that he saw a large tail slither into the underbrush. His imagination began to conjure up lions, leopards, snakes and boars everywhere. The constant din of different living sounds, coupled with the complete lack of wind, made him break out in a sweat, and his breath became labored. Forcing fear out of his mind, he focused on the middle of Yehuda's back ahead of him as he trudged on. Finally, as the light faded further, Yehuda stopped and began to look around him. It was the same confused nowhere.

"We're going to camp here?" asked Ioannis incredulously. Yehuda put his finger to his lips and continued to gaze around and listen. To Ioannis, there seemed to be nothing more to look at or listen to than the stifling, chaotic jungle they had wandered through for half the day. Nothing here seemed better than anywhere else.

"Yes," said Yehuda slowly. "It seems so." He continued to stand, now with his eyes closed, listening. Suddenly, he opened his eyes. "Ah!" he said, looking quickly off to his right ahead of them.

Ioannis followed his gaze and listened intently. Finally, through all the din of the wetlands, he heard something else. Human voices. One of them was very high. A woman? Yehuda dashed swiftly into the jungle, between papyrus plants, ignoring any semblance of a path. He took off so quickly that if Ioannis hadn't had eyes fixed on him, the younger man might have lost him in the twilight. Although Ioannis usually walked faster than his master, in this case it was reversed. Yehuda was walking fast on his toes, his heels barely touching the ground. Ioannis followed suit, just to keep up. Shortly, they came to a small pool in the clearing of the jungle. In the dusk, Ioannis could make out a man and a woman sitting side by side quietly at the edge of the pool.

"You made it, I see," said the man, who at least to Ioannis's exhausted eyes looked remarkably like Yehuda himself. Brown hair, about the same medium build and olive complexion. His eyes looked closely at but also through Yehuda. The woman on his left had her eyes closed. She also had brown hair and a face very similar to the man's.

"Yes," said Yehuda. "We have been looking for you...You know who I am, then?"

"Yes," said Yeshua. "And I know why you're looking for me. Please join us for the night. We were just about to start a fire. Let's start one together." Without another word, he stood up. The woman opened her eyes and began to move around, collecting any brushwood she could find. Yehuda put down his knapsack and began to do the same. Ioannis looked a question at him, and Yehuda stopped for a moment.

"Just breathe and do what we're doing as best you can. The object is to start a fire."

Start a fire in a wetland jungle, thought Ioannis. *Sure.* He looked around, but everything seemed damp. As he moved around more, his eyes began to focus on details, and he found some fronds of dead papyrus. Then he noticed that Yeshua was digging into the side of a bank with his hands and brought out some chunks of dry peat. His woman companion came back out of the brush with an armload of dried lake algae. Using his fingers as a rake, Yehuda had gathered long, dry, dead grasses from the previous season that were covered under the new growth. Just as the sunlight was about to disappear completely, they found themselves standing around a pile that Yeshua had carefully laid next to the pond.

"Need some spark here, I think," said Yehuda.

"Yes," said Yeshua. "I have some flint. Do you have anything for starter?"

Yehuda rummaged through his knapsack. "Here," he said, handing Yeshua a couple of pages of an old manuscript.

"Nothing too sacred, I hope?" said Yeshua.

"No. Some jottings from the temple. But not the part that Shemuel…"

"Yes. We'll talk later. Fire first."

Not much of a talker, thought Ioannis. Yet he found something strangely magnetic about the man. He was a bit like Yehuda but with more energy, as though a whirlwind had picked him up, spun him around in the air for a day and landed him on his feet here a moment ago.

Somehow the fire caught easily, and small flames gradually rose through the layers. Yeshua and Yehuda kneeled on opposite sides and blew in rhythm into specific pockets of the pile. That helped the flames develop without being put out, each layer drying the next one with more heat until, somehow, they were soon sitting around a very substantial fire. Not that much flame, but a lot of heat, which would go on for some time. As Ioannis watched, the other three opened their knapsacks and brought out food—bread, dates, boiled eggs. The woman began to roast some fresh fish that looked as though it had been caught that day.

It must be some sort of silent code I don't know, thought Ioannis, grumbling. *Either that, or they're really hungry. I suppose I am, too.* He brought some bread and dried lamb that Shemei had given them out of his knapsack and shared it around the small circle. After they had eaten and put the remainder of the food away, they sat and stared into the flames. Or at least Ioannis did. He noticed that the woman had half closed her eyes and seemed to be gazing at something she saw in the fire. Yehuda and Yeshua had glanced at each other and closed their eyes together. After what seemed like a year to Ioannis, they both opened them again simultaneously.

Yehuda said, "This is my friend, Ioannis, or Yehohanan. His mother was Israelite; his father was Roman. He has a good heart."

"Welcome," said Yeshua, looking Ioannis straight in the eyes for the first time. The younger man felt his heart skip a beat and suppressed a gulp.

Nodding to the woman, Yeshua said, "This is my companion, Maryam. All Israelite. Ran a business. Formerly suffered from devils. Like most of us here, I think," he said, smiling broadly and looking first at Yehuda and then Ioannis.

chapter 25

Deeper Waters

"All right," said Yeshua. "Let's talk about why you're both here. You want to know about Shemuel," he said, turning to Yehuda.

"Yes," said Yehuda. "Although on one level, we know all we need to. He's dead. The dead can bury the dead. What I really want to know is what to do now. That involves finding out what happened to him and why. He asked me to do something in the temple."

"I know. He told me when I last saw him, maybe two months ago. Do you understand what that was about?"

"No, not exactly. I think it was to do with a coded message, a *pesher*, in the scrolls he directed me to. Something to do with the old Herodes's treasure buried under the temple."

"Do you have the manuscript with you?"

"Yes," said Yehuda, pulling it from his bag. He handed it to Yeshua, along with both the short summary that Shemuel had inserted in it and the letter his teacher had sent him earlier. Yeshua looked at the letter and the summary. Then he unrolled the scroll from left to right, holding it near the fire to see it better. "You think that the 'eye has not seen' part is a key to a coded message, a key to treasure?" he asked.

"If old Herodes hid his treasure in the underground vaults of the temple," said Yehuda, "somewhere only he knew about after it was remodeled, then it would be worth killing for. Romans, priests, rebels, anyone. You know what your kinsmen are planning. We found the same words as initials on a talisman that Shemuel was wearing. Korah in Taanach has one, too. It's certainly the watchword of the Natzara, but Shemuel could have discovered that it's more—a substitution code for a hidden message in the old manuscript."

"Of course, Yehuda." Yeshua sighed. "Plans are many and devious; there is no end to them. But Alaha—the Holy One—is a better planner. Did you find anything else in the temple before you left?"

Yehuda pulled the pearl from his pocket and held it out in the palm of his hand. "This is what really forced me to leave so quickly. I found it in the inner temple."

"And you left because…?" asked Yeshua. "You could have sold it secretly, kept the money and remained in Yerushalaim, doing what Shemuel asked of you."

Yehuda started. *Why did I really leave?* he wondered. *I could have just stayed and kept the pearl until someone claimed it. I could have waited safely in Yerushalaim to see what Shemuel intended.*

"I don't really know," he replied. "All of a sudden, I heard a voice in my head saying, 'Get out of here!' We left that night, and the next morning we found Shemuel's body in the ruins above the plain of Megiddo."

Yeshua nodded and looked sympathetically at the scribe. As if in slow motion, he removed Shemuel's letter from the manuscript and handed it to Yehuda. "A keepsake for you," he said. Then he threw the scrolls and the summary into the fire. "The pearl is the key, Yehuda. Not the manuscript."

"Wait! But! The pearl? What about the pearl?"

"Well, you said that was what pushed you out of the city. You wouldn't have found Shemuel otherwise. And you wouldn't be here, would you?"

"Yes, but I don't understand. There is no treasure?"

"There may or may not be treasure. Who knows what crazy old Herodes was capable of hoarding and hiding? He was a master of greed. Do *you* want to possess the treasure? What would you do with it? Who would you give it to? Do you want to lead an armed rebellion against the Romans?"

"But our people have been suffering for years, centuries…"

"Yes, suffering. And the solution to suffering is… kicking out one group of armed bandits in favor of another?"

"But…"

Yeshua held up his palm. "Follow me, Yehuda," he said, closing his eyes.

Before, when he and Yeshua had closed their eyes together, there had been only peace and space, the sort of communion with Alaha that Shemuel used to share with him. He had immediately trusted Yeshua, and this had confirmed it. Now, he closed his eyes again and felt a flash of intense heat and light tear open his chest. In front of him, framed by daylight, appeared a scene from his childhood. A boy of seven years, he wandered one afternoon over the hills of Galilee with his father, who led him to a small clearing in the woods.

Yehuda had completely forgotten about this until now. He felt intense grief and longing, as though it had been bottled up inside him all these years. He actually felt that he was there with his father, that it was not just a picture or a vision but absolutely real. His father sat down beside him in the grass and seemed to be saying good-bye.

"Son, I will be going soon. You are very special to me. People will tell you all sorts of things about me, or you, after I am gone. Don't believe any of them. You are my son. Never forget it. I'm making provision to send you to my brother Shemuel. He will be your father now. Don't worry about your mother. She will be fine. But stay away from the rest of your brothers. I'm sorry I have to tell you this, but…"

At that point, the light exploded again in Yehuda's heart, and he was pulled upward into the sky. Then he found himself again flying over the surface of Lake Kinneret, just as he had in his vision on the way to Taanach. This time, halfway across, he dived into the water. The cold shocked him awake, and he opened his eyes, but he was still inside the vision, under the water, looking at the tilapia fish swimming around him. They were all swimming very fast underwater in the same direction that he was. Then he looked to his right and saw Yeshua swimming along beside him. They were being propelled effortlessly through the water, without moving their arms or legs. Yeshua smiled at him and pointed straight ahead with his right hand. Then they shot out of the water and landed standing on its surface. Together they walked on the water the rest of the way to the shore. When they stepped on land again, Yeshua turned to him and said, "Remember, Yehuda. If you don't bring out what is within you, it will kill you. If you do, it will save you. Learn to dive, to swim, to come back to the surface and to keep walking."

Yehuda opened his eyes and shook his head. He was still sitting around the glowing fire with Yeshua, Ioannis and Maryam. It was night now, and out of the shadows, Yeshua's eyes searched him with a look of curiosity mixed with compassion, as though he were wondering who, or what, was hidden inside.

"The pearl reminded you of who you are," he said. "And that you don't belong in the temple anymore. Also that you should go home and find Shemuel. He was coming to meet you, but didn't quite make it."

"But who put the pearl there?" asked Yehuda. "And what did Shemuel want to tell me?"

"Shemuel had many friends, as you know. As to what he wanted to tell you, I can't say exactly. He didn't tell me. The answer is for you to find. Maybe it was something simple, like 'You're free.'"

"All right," said Yehuda, frowning. "But if it wasn't all part of some larger plan, who killed him and his son, and why?"

"That answer must also be inside of you. Make sure you find it before it kills you, too."

Yehuda turned to Maryam, who spoke for the first time.

"We all have our demons," she said. "Trying to shut them away just makes them stronger. Maybe it's best to bring them out where we can deal with them, or get help to do it. That's what he taught me," she said, nodding toward Yeshua. "We don't have to go into another world to escape the pain, and we don't need to leave our flesh behind. We can use the same ability to travel within ourselves to join hands with Holy Wisdom. She's always there, teaching us to love."

"Holy Wisdom, of course, from Shelomoh's book. Yohanan also talked about her. But she's just a metaphor, isn't she?" asked Yehuda. "A character in a story?"

"Maybe," said Maryam. "But if she's just a character in a story, so are we."

Ioannis turned his head in confusion from Yehuda to Yeshua to Maryam. *They seem to be sane,* he thought. *But what are they going on about? Outside of the word "love," I don't understand a word they're talking about.*

As though he heard Ioannis's thoughts, Yeshua looked directly at him but spoke to Maryam.

"Yes, my beloved Maryam. For some of us, love is the simplest way. It solves all the riddles without needing to know everything. And as Shelomoh said, it's stronger than death. If we have enough love, it doesn't matter when, or how, whatever hides within us emerges. It can't kill us. Love makes a person *yihidaya*—united inside. That's the best gift you can give yourself, or another, or Alaha, for that matter. Outside of love, why would the Holy One have created the worlds in the first place? Love helps us endure from one *ahlam*, one level or world, to the next."

As Yeshua was speaking, Ioannis only half heard him, although he remembered every word later. The sound of the other man's voice became like a river roaring in his ears, and he imagined that he saw his mother and father standing behind Yeshua, smiling at him. They radiated light from the inside but seemed very solid, just as solid as the other three sitting around the fire. His father was in his best dress uniform, holding a short Roman sword in his hand. He looked at his son and then slowly and deliberately placed the sword back in its scabbard. Then he unbuckled his belt and let it fall to the earth. Ioannis heard the clunk of metal. His mother just watched her husband lovingly and clapped her hands with joy. Then she looked at her son, stepped forward and placed her hands on Yeshua's shoulders. He seemed not to notice but kept on speaking:

"...*l'ahlam almin*...from one world to the next, from one gathering to the next."

When Ioannis looked at Yeshua again, the vision of his mother and father vanished.

"You see, my friends," Yeshua said, looking around at them all. "There is another way. Not escaping into other worlds because this one is so bad. Not fighting the phantoms we have given flesh to outside us—a world governed by rulers who embody our collective feelings of separation. There is a middle way: we all travel together—those of us here together with our ancestors traveling in the unseen, in the caravan ahead of us."

"And what of those coming behind us?" asked Ioannis. "If this is a caravan, there must be children coming later. Shouldn't we worry about them?"

"The children move easily between worlds, at least until the age of seven," said Yeshua. "But if you mean those children we don't yet see, then yes, we must do all we can to make it possible for them to walk the way of the prophets, the ones who have tried to bring both worlds together for the benefit of the community. But that journey starts here," he said, pointing to his heart. "There are always more questions, otherwise life wouldn't be interesting. Here's my question: now that you found me, what will you do?"

"We will still travel on to Shemuel's house tomorrow," answered Yehuda, noticing the forced conviction in his own voice. "In a letter to me I found in Natzara, Shemuel wrote that he left something else for me there.

And as you say, your family's fate may be tied up with mine."

Yeshua smiled. "That's not exactly what I said, but anyway, keep searching. When you've finished searching, you'll be confused and then amazed, and then maybe you'll feel free to rule your own destiny, or let Alaha do it. I'm going to meet some of my new students in Paneas, near the old temple dedicated to Pan, after which the city is named. They weren't strong enough to come in here, so I didn't ask them to. Only Maryam, and she's more than my student. She and you," he said, glancing at Yehuda, "may be the only ones who can really understand what I'm saying between the words. Let's sleep. Each day completes itself with is own unripeness. That leaves room for tomorrow to grow further."

Yehuda nodded, smiled weakly at Ioannis and then began to clear a space near the fire, putting his knapsack on a rock for a pillow. Yeshua seemed not to have a bag, so he just laid his head on a flat stone. Maryam curled up in his arms, and soon they were fast asleep.

Ioannis lay on his back, awake for some time. First, all the sounds of the jungle kept him awake. The night animals began to come out, and there seemed to be a lot of activity in the brush. Then at various times, a growl would be followed by a screech and the sound of flesh ripping and bone being broken between teeth. In the back of his mind, Ioannis knew, or hoped, the fire would keep them safe. But after some time, his thoughts faded into a gray cloud above him that paled in comparison to the feeling of warmth in his chest. He looked into the sky; the moon was not yet up, and the stars shone brilliantly. He saw the hunter constellation turn toward him and launch an arrow in his direction. He followed the arrow on its way to earth, unable to move a muscle, but not caring. The arrow entered his heart, and sparks shot up and down his spine. Instead of falling apart or dying, he felt all of the stars outside now inside him, too. It didn't matter whether his eyes were open or closed. It was the same sky.

Yehuda had fallen asleep quickly, although he had intended to invite a dream vision first. When he woke in the middle of the night, he began breathing in his heart as Shemuel had taught him to do. He was more confused than ever, and he really wanted a clearer message. He said a protection prayer, felt his breathing rhythm connect with what he remembered of Shemuel's and then imagined his heart like the pond they were camped beside. There were ripples. He calmed them with his breath. Then he breathed and waited for an image to appear. Nothing. He breathed a question into his heart: what now? The pond, instead of remaining a mirror in which he could see the future, whirled wildly and became a waterspout and then quickly a storm-tossed sea. He was drowning in the sea. Awake inside the dream, he said to himself, *This is not an answer! I do not accept it!* He drew the Secret Name on the waves, and they parted in the middle to reveal a narrow path. Yeshua was walking on the watery path, with high waves on either side, and gestured for him to follow. *All right, better,* he thought, and stood up again on the sea. He was just about to take a step toward Yeshua when a hand from underneath surfaced, grabbed his foot and began to pull him under. He struggled, but the arm was stronger, and he began to go down. As his head was disappearing below the water, he awoke in a cold sweat.

O Alaha, he thought, *what in Gehenna is going on?* He tossed around on the hard earth all night.

Chapter 26

The Thread Leads Home

The next morning they were all up at dawn, which was brisk but damp in the late spring around Lake Merom. After breakfast, Yeshua and Yehuda went a little way into the bush for a private talk, leaving Ioannis with Maryam beside the campfire. Just as Ioannis was about to start feeling uncomfortable, Maryam began to speak.

"It's clear why Yehuda is here, Yehohanan," she said, glancing toward him and raising an eyebrow. "But what does all this have to do with you? You weren't Shemuel's student, and you don't seem to me to have the same sort of inner demons that some of us do, or did."

"Yes, it's true," he replied, looking down. "I'm a straightforward person. I like action, and I don't really have time for these vision things that seem to happen for you or Yeshua or Yehuda when you close your eyes. But I feel a loyalty to Yehuda. You see, I was a slave and he freed me. Since he is on the run from the temple, it's not clear how free that really is. But anyway, I have nowhere else to go…"

"Is that so?" She looked at him more closely.

"Yes," he said, turning up both palms. "You see, although I was a Roman soldier, I was a slave. My father was a general who rebelled against the emperor. Which one doesn't really matter; rulers of Rome come thick and fast."

"Loyalty is a good thing, Yehohanan," Maryam said slowly. "Friendship is the first step in loving. But you're avoiding my question. I see something or someone else around you, someone with whom you have a bond. Parents?"

"My father was executed, my mother sold into slavery. I don't know where she is."

"Someone younger. Don't make me pull it out of you!" she said, laughing.

"Well, there is someone in Natzara. Yeshua's sister, Zilpah, actually."

"All right. I thought I sensed her around you, but I wanted to hear you say her name. You know, my friend, the only thing that blocks the heart is a secret that we keep from ourselves." She sighed. "You heard the master last night. Something like that can kill you. But more than that, if your way is love, then you need to cleanse your heart from anything that makes it smaller, or threatens to." She left the statement hanging, like a question.

Ioannis paused and then looked up at her. "There *is* something else. I do have somewhere else I could go. With what I know now, I could go back to Yerushalaim and report it all to my old Roman master. He would probably free me and then give me a regular commission in the army again. The army is full of sons of executed former officers. The Romans probably think the 'family dishonor' will keep these sons on the straight and narrow."

"And what would that do to your relationship with Yehuda, not to mention Zilpah?"

"Probably destroy both," he said softly.

Maryam raised both hands in front of her, as though pretending to weigh two things, and continued to look gently at Ioannis. "So...honor or love, status or... something insubstantial, something you can't decorate a uniform with?"

"Yes," he said after a long pause. "How did you make the choice...I mean, to follow, or be with, Yeshua? Sorry, this is a bit awkward, as I was taught that Israelite women rarely talked to strangers without their husbands present."

"They do tell you strange things in the Roman army, don't they?" She smiled sadly and took a breath. "All right. My story is not noble or beautiful. I was the widow of one of the few wealthy merchants that Galilee has, or had. He died. Before he died, he used to beat me regularly, torture me and offer me as a plaything for his friends." She shuddered, breathed more deeply and then continued. "So in short, I poisoned him. He had so many enemies, no one suspected me. I thought I would feel free, but I was tortured by voices, demons, devils—whatever you call them. First they appeared in my dreams. Then I would wake each morning paralyzed; I couldn't move a muscle. In front of me was my husband, as real as you or I, blood streaming out of all the pores of his skin, his mouth, nose and ears. His eyes were dead, staring accusingly like the prince of flies himself. I was afraid to sleep, afraid to wake up. By the time I met Yeshua, I was most of the way to madness. I had lost so much sense of any 'me' that all sorts of voices of abuse were pouring out of me. I had become a river of filth from the other side. I couldn't find anything to tune me to a better reality."

"I thought the 'other world' was all good, all blessing, all Alaha, as you say."

"It's all of everything, Yehohanan. *Alaha* means all in everything. *Al* and *La*—all yes, all no. It's not a person; it's the reality we really come from and exist in from the beginning. Everything is there, every potential for everything. We can choose to become more human, to fulfill the music that Alaha wants to play through us, or not. We choose what we make real—what we see and experience in our lives. My choices had tuned me to so many wrong notes, and that's what resonated. That's the music I was playing. Yeshua retuned me. He knows more of the beautiful music of the other world than anyone I've ever met."

"There *is* something different about him," said Ioannis. "And in the last week, I have met many strange people. What is it about the people who live here? So many of them seem cracked open, divided, as though they were split between this world and another."

"Maybe it's history; this area has always been a place on the way to somewhere else, east or west. There's been so much bloodshed, so many ghosts here. Maybe it is the land pushing itself and us together in a way we can't manage in our normal, unconscious way of living. When I come here to Merom with Yeshua, we just offer ourselves to this intense feeling, a sacred *between-ness.* Rather than feel split, we let our love grow until it glues us together with each other, with the land, with the Holy One."

"But when you leave here, then it's a different world—emperors, priests, bandits, prophets, messiahs, wealth, poverty. What then? How do you live with all that? How do you *live*?"

"We, Yeshua and I, we live in each breath. And then we ask, what's next? His new students whom we're meeting in Paneas, they always want a plan—let's kick out the Romans, let's head east away from the Romans, let's try to find the 'lost' Israelite tribes. Or they want some rules to live by—how should we fast, how should we pray, what diet should we follow? I want to tear my hair out sometimes. He and I can't live that way. But Yeshua has so much patience with them…I really don't know what the next day will bring, but as he said last night, maybe none of us really knows. So?" She raised a palm.

"So?"

"What will you do now?"

Ioannis looked up hopefully. "I promised Zilpah that if I found Yeshua, I would let her know whether he was all right. Now I can, I suppose."

"And then?"

"Then I don't know. I have to help Yehuda finish his search, if that's possible."

"You and Zilpah could both join us, you know. If you're willing to follow Yehuda on the crazy search he's on, then you're crazy enough to come with us."

"But do you think it's crazy for him to want to find out who killed his teacher, his uncle?" Ioannis glanced at her sharply, feeling protective of his friend. "From what Yehuda said, Shemuel was really his second father."

"Of course," she said, touching his arm lightly. "Sorry, my friend, I didn't mean any disrespect. Shemuel, from what I knew of him, lived in many worlds at the same time. Who was he? A scribe, a prophet, a hermit, a spy, the head of a revolutionary conspiracy? Who really knew? Anyone could have killed him. I have the feeling that, as Yeshua says, if Yehuda keeps searching in that direction, he will really find a lot of trouble for himself. Maybe that's *his* way, though. He needs to *know*. You, my friend, need to *love*."

At that moment, Yehuda and Yeshua came out of the papyrus jungle again, arms around each other, looking even more like twin brothers.

"You see?" Yeshua was saying. "You really *do* already know, Yehuda. Why not come along with us? It would be good, thank Alaha, to have someone who understands besides Maryam."

"It's tempting," replied Yehuda. "I see now why both Shemuel and your cousin Yohanan thought you might be the one to keep it all alive. Living day by day, breath by breath, taking care of each other as best we can, traveling freely like the birds migrating around us. That's fine when you're camping in the middle of a jungle. But what about…"

"What about? What about!" Yeshua put his right palm on Yehuda's heart. "Let's find *what* first, brother, and the *about* comes later. Look first for the big What, the *malkuta,* the ruling force behind the cosmos, and the rest comes much more easily. Then you'll know what is yours to do and what is someone else's. My half brother, Ya'aqub, believes that outer action is the only way, and then the inner will follow the outer. He believes it so strongly that he may make it happen. But he is not me— or you."

"Yes, you're right, of course. But it's clear to me that finding what happened to Shemuel *is* mine, not someone else's."

"All right," he sighed. "You've found us once. You can always do it again, I'm sure. Go with Alaha. And you also, Yehohanan," he said, clapping the younger man on the middle of his back. "Keep your heart strong and your love simple. I expect we will see you again as well."

They broke camp and traveled the rest of the way northeast out of the jungle in silence. As they emerged from the sea of papyrus, they saw Mount Hermon looming to the northeast, the tallest mountain in the land and the source of the Yarden's water. Snow covered some of its peaks, making it a stunning sight in the clear spring morning. *It must be more than a league high,* thought Ioannis, transfixed, who had never seen it before.

Around midday, they had joined the road coming up from Seleucia to the east of the lake. Just outside of Paneas, near the entrance to a small valley, a group of men seemed to be waiting for them.

"Yeshua's students. Alaha help us," whispered Maryam to Ioannis.

The group looked on curiously as Yeshua and Maryam embraced Yehuda and Ioannis. Some suspicious glances were directed at Ioannis's sword.

"We're going down into the gorge and will camp along the springs by the old temple to Pan," said Yeshua. "After you've found what you're looking for and before you leave the city, why not stop by?"

Yehuda nodded, and he and Ioannis walked west away from the gorge. Shemuel's house was a short distance outside of the town in an isolated area near a small grove of oak trees. For Yehuda, it was like coming home. In his youth, he used to sit with Shemuel on the porch of his small house, gazing eastward toward the snowcapped peaks of Hermon, a holy mountain for those who remembered the old Israel. As they entered the house, it was clear that someone had already been there. The few pieces of furniture Shemuel owned were broken and strewn everywhere, and when they came to the teacher's room, his bed and writing desk had been turned over, and papyrus scrolls were all over the floor.

"Someone wanted to find something, that's for certain," said Ioannis.

"Yes," Yehuda replied, looking sadly around the room. "But they didn't know all of Shemuel's secrets, including where he hid things. Follow me. They went out of the house and around the back, where they found a large rubbish pile. Yehuda began removing some of the rubbish, Ioannis helping, and underneath they found a rough platform of loose boards. Tipping up one side of the boards, Yehuda revealed a shallow hole in the ground. Inside of it was a tin box.

"Good Israelites wouldn't dare look in a rubbish dump for fear of polluting themselves," he said. "Good Romans probably wouldn't bother. I don't think, anyway, that we're dealing with Romans here. Their style would have been to burn the house down. Even Mikhael wouldn't have known about this, as Shemuel only used it when he was away."

They took the box back into the house and opened it. Yehuda found a letter and two scrolls. The scrolls were the regular size, not like the small ones he had found in Natzara, but both appeared to be very short. He read the letter first, aloud:

My dear Yehuda,

One can never plan for all eventualities. If you found my letter in Natzara, then you have probably figured out that I went to the hill near Megiddo, the valley that has seen our greatest triumphs and defeats. According to Hanuch, the place may see an even greater battle to come. It also means that I didn't come back. I had hoped to meet you there or in Yerushalaim, but someone else may have found me first. That was a possibility once I had set some events in motion.

Don't limit yourself to my mistakes. I can make clear one path for you in all this. The other path is up to you and depends on the will of Alaha. The two scrolls buried with this letter are the two ways.

The first scroll purports to be an inventory of King Herodes's hidden treasure. I found the scroll in the bowels of the temple on my last visit there, when I saw you six months ago. Does the treasure really exist or not? I don't know, but the inventory seems genuine. Of course, Herodes was more mad than sane, so perhaps the inventory was his delusion, or part of some elaborate trick. Perhaps he had nothing hidden when he died, or he hid it all somewhere else. What's certain is that the scroll bears his signature and personal seal. It is not a forgery.

"What eye has not seen and what ear has not heard…" With these words repeated in my letter and summary of the manuscript, you have likely guessed that I sent you in search of that old Aramaic commentary in the temple to point you in the direction of the Natzara. The manuscript was meaningless, only a veil over the search itself. My summary notes contained a coded version I made of this inventory, which I hoped you would retrieve, just in case.

The inventory may only be a veil, an illusion. It could, nevertheless, be a useful illusion.

Many people believe that this treasure exists, and they will reveal their true souls (and loyalties) when confronted with the document, or a copy of it. Some may kill to try to get the document, believing that the key to the treasure's location is somewhere in it. If I'm dead now, this might be one reason. Others may see in this list, real or fanciful, an encouragement to revolt against the Romans, take Yerushalaim and find the treasure. Maybe the encouragement is more important than the actual treasure. Sometimes an illusion is more powerful than an army. Other times an illusion may be fatal. From one standpoint, we are all illusions in the mind of Alaha. So you could take this scroll with you and use it. It could save you or kill you.

The other scroll has to do with you, and it is my last teaching for you. Use it as an inner guide, and it will tell you about your origins. If you stand at the beginning, you will know where you are now and where you need to go next.

The pearl you found in the temple was left for you by one of my other associates. Your father, who was worried that your other brothers would deprive you of your legacy, gave two of them to me. The other you probably found in Natzara. Before your father left on his last journey, on which he expected to be killed, he asked that I give them to you in your moment of greatest need. I hoped that when you found the first, you would feel the messages I breathed into it: free yourself, meet me in Megiddo, follow where your heart leads, rather than simply follow patterns dictated by who you think you are, or have been.

You have been a real son to me. My love goes with you.

Shemuel ben Yahayye

"Your father was killed?" asked Ioannis. "You only said he died."

"Yes, that's what I was told," said Yehuda softly, looking away from the younger man. "As a young boy, he seemed very old to me, and so they probably reckoned I wouldn't think anything of it."

Yehuda looked at the first scroll. As Shemuel's letter said, it was a list of incredible treasure, mostly gold and silver, also some valuable goblets and jewelry. Calculating quickly, Yehuda reckoned that it would exceed the entire wealth of Israel for ten years. The last lines of the scroll were cryptic but clumsy. They could, as Shemuel said, be either a trick or a key to some location. Yehuda presumed that Herodes himself had tried his hand at poetry:

> *Better that this scroll be engraved*
> *on copper, bright as the sun,*
> *hard as a sword.*
> *Better yet that it be engraved on the*
> *sun of the heart of a righteous man.*
> *In the ruin that is within the sacred precincts,*
> *the sacred mountain of war,*
> *near the steps, at the entrance to*
> *the old place of blood,*
> *below the bones of our ancestors,*
> *find this sun at the beginning*

of its longest day,
the first day of creation,
it will be like a festival for you.

"The sacred mountain of war, Yehohanan," said Yehuda, nodding. "The old place of blood. Where is the oldest place of blood in the land? It can't be the Yerushalaim Temple. With the other clues Shemuel left, it must be Megiddo. His corpse was the biggest clue. That's why he was there!"

"It still doesn't tell us who killed him, Yehuda."

"No, but it tells us a way to find out."

"Wait a moment, Yehuda." Ioannis put a hand on his friend's shoulder. "That would mean setting ourselves up as a target, wouldn't it? But what's in the other scroll?"

Chapter 27

The Pearl

Yehuda took up the second scroll, which was in Shemuel's own distinctive script, and began to read:

In the name and light of the most powerful Life, hear this story, all you who feel caught in the prison of life's confusion.

Once upon a time there was a young prince in Parthia. His father, the king, and his mother, the queen, saw in him a special nature and purpose—the inner urge for a quest of accomplishment. They told him of a very special pearl, the key to all wisdom, which had once been the possession of the ancient Magi in Parthia. But the Magi lost the pearl, and it now lay far away in Egypt at the bottom of the sea, encircled by a deadly serpent. Did the prince wish to go on a quest to recover the pearl? It was, they said, his destiny to complete this quest and then to rule together with his brother as their successor when the king and queen died.

"Yes, I'm willing," he said. "What do I need to do to prepare?"

"We will give you supplies for the journey," they said, "and enough gold and gems to give away as tribute and bribes as you go down through Babylon and then all the way across the plains of the sacred valley into Egypt. Only one thing: you need to give up any tokens of your status or your royal birth. That means giving up the golden tunic you like to wear and the purple robe that gives you comfort. You must go in disguise, but not forget who you are."

"That doesn't sound so difficult," he said. "It will be safer and allow me to live among the Egyptians undetected until I can fulfill my mission."

And so he traveled down through Babylon, down past the sacred mountain, through the valley of crossing and down into Egypt. There he found lodging near the northern sea where the serpent resided. A proficient swimmer, he easily found the sea serpent and treasure. True enough, the serpent when awake was all fangs and claws, a veritable dragon of the ocean. But it often fell asleep. The young prince saw many try to wrest the pearl from under the serpent's grasp and fail. They either made too much noise or couldn't hold their breath long enough. The prince was very patient. He made note of all the regular times that the snake fell asleep and for how long. He trained himself for years to be able to hold his breath long enough and to dive deeply enough, quickly enough, to steal the pearl.

Finally, he felt he was ready. The next day would be the day. He rested that night at his lodgings and, as it just so happened, was befriended by a young Egyptian man. The young prince mentioned that he would be leaving Egypt the next day, and his new friend offered to take him to a special inn, where the food was remarkable, as going-away celebration. He accepted. However, unknown to him, his new friend was an agent of the Egyptian king, who had been watching the prince make his preparations to steal the pearl. Even though the king couldn't use the pearl, just keeping it in Egypt allowed him the status and credit he needed to borrow whatever wealth he wanted from abroad. So he didn't want anyone else to steal it.

At the inn, the young prince ate the food provided, which was delicious but also heavily drugged. When he awoke days later, he couldn't remember who he was, where he was from or what he was doing there. His young friend, sitting by his bedside, told him that he was the son of a dead nobleman who had served the Egyptian king all of his life. The king's spy told him he had just awoken from a long delirium during an illness. The Egyptian king was waiting for him, eager to have one of his favorite retainers back with him. They returned to the palace together, and the young prince spent seven years in service to the king of Egypt.

Meanwhile, back in Parthia, his father and mother had become worried and sent their own spies down to Egypt. Most of these also failed to return, since the Egyptian king possessed advanced intelligence and security forces. Finally, one spy was able to slip through all the nets and returned to Parthia to report the prince's predicament.

"This is terrible!" the queen said to the king. "We must send our son a special letter, reminding him of who he really is."

"But how will we get it to him?" asked the king. "It seems that he is unreachable, buried beneath heavy layers of Egyptian luxury, guarded by a palace of mirrors that tells him he is someone else and that everyone is not who they really are but only what they possess."

"We will send a letter, but not one on parchment or leather," said the queen. "For that we need three of us—you, the prince's twin brother and I. Together we will weave a spell and a spirit into a living soul that will remind our son who he really is."

And so the three of them did. They called on the help of the king of the birds, who sent one of his eagle messengers to assist them. They wrapped their message into the eagle's heart-cloth, who learned it and carried it away on the wind, all the way down to Egypt.

Days later, the eagle landed beside the young prince as he sat resting near a canal by the palace. The eagle began to speak, and as it did so, a scroll of silk written in blood-red ink in his brother's handwriting appeared before the eyes of the prince.

"Brother! Wake up! Remember who you are! Remember the pearl. Remember the tunic and robe waiting for you at home. Return again!"

In that moment, the young prince immediately awoke from the spell of drugged hynosis and amnesia he had been under. He went directly to the sea and without hesitation dived in and stole the pearl from the serpent. Within the hour he was on his way back to Parthia, with the eagle guiding him along secret ways that allowed him to elude any pursuers. Traveling day and night, he quickly arrived home at dawn on the seventh day.

As the sun was rising and he neared the palace, he saw the eagle fly ahead and bring back in its claws a tunic and a robe. The tunic was his old one, but instead of appearing gold, it now reflected all the colors of the rainbow. The robe that had been purple had turned to silken crystal, so that when he put it on over the tunic, it allowed the colors to shine even more brilliantly and to change as he moved.

His father, mother and brother embraced him at the gate. "Welcome home, son!" they said. "We have been waiting so long for you! We are ready to retire, and now you and your beloved brother can continue in our place."

"What about the pearl?" asked the young prince. "Why was it so important? Why did I have to forget?"

"So that what was hidden could be revealed," replied his brother. "So that what was forgotten could be remembered, and so that everything—the hiding and the revealing, the forgetting and remembering—would make your soul whole."

"Does it mean anything to you, Yehuda?" asked Ioannis, who noticed that his friend had turned a bit ashen.

"There are several levels of meaning to a story like this, Yehohanan," the scribe replied slowly. "But I think Shemuel meant one in particular. And that's very disturbing. It suggests a possible course of action. Before I tell you, I suggest that we spend a bit more time here, looking for anything else Shemuel may have left us, and then go to the grotto where Yeshua is. We will need his help."

Having found nothing else, by late afternoon they were descending into the gorge that held the temple of Pan, yet another of the "green men" who die and are reborn each season. Making their way through the small, winding canyon, they found cascades and waterfalls at every turn, the spray refreshing them after a day spent in the heat. One of the first tributaries of the Yarden River, the canyon's water was fed by winter runoff from Mount Hermon. The sound of living water pervaded the whole area, which was laced with a network of paths. Water plants that only existed in the gorge hung from every crevice, creating a green paradise. It was a stark contrast to the dusty, arid tablelands of the Gaulanitis heights that spread around the gorge above them. Unlike the still waters of Merom, the rushing cascades and springs here were exhilarating. The two found Yeshua and his group at the far end of the canyon, directly in front of the ruins of the old temple.

As they approached, Yehuda quickly scanned the crowd in front of the teacher. He whispered in Ioannis's ear, "That plain-looking man over there in the blue cloak, brown hair. That's a spy from the temple, one of Qayapha's informants. They're keeping an eye on Yeshua, although they can't do anything to him while he's in Philipos's territory. He seems to be standing with Yeshua's other students, though...strange."

"And don't we know that one as well?" asked Ioannis, pointing to a tall man with a scar, wearing ragged clothing.

"Yes, we do."

At that point, Yeshua noticed them and called out, "Welcome, friends! We were just discussing a question I put to my students here: Who do people say I am? Some apparently think I'm Moshe come again. Some Eliyah. Some even Pan. Some think I've come to overthrow the Romans, or the temple in Yerushalaim. So I put it to you: Who do *you* think I am?"

"Master," said Yehuda, "my tongue cannot say the words aloud! But if you allow us a brief word in private, I can tell you."

The crowd murmured at the impertinence of the newcomer, whom few of the other students or followers recognized, except the temple spy and the man with the scar. Yeshua smiled and walked toward them. They went around a corner of the gorge, while the rest of the crowd stared after them in stunned silence.

"Ah, I see you've found something," said Yeshua, looking from one to the other.

"Yes. And we need your help. Do you have a student we can trust who knows Batanea?"

"Yes, that one there in the cream robe, brown hair," said Yeshua, glancing briefly over this shoulder. "He's one of our cousins from there. Anything else?"

"You know that there is a spy from the temple here?"

"Of course, name similar to your own. Qayapha thinks he's spying for them, but he's really spying on

The Pearl

the temple for me. He is from Korah ben Izhar's family. His name is Yahuda Sakaryut, and I'd trust him to do anything. You see, I'm not as otherworldly as they say," he said and smiled. "I just don't care about that world most of the time. I care about the One who controls it."

"That's what I care about, too," said Yehuda, "and that's where my instructions come from."

Turning to Ioannis, Yeshua put his hand on the younger man's shoulder and looked him in the eyes. "As I said, you, my friend, are a lover. It's time to purge your heart of all secrets, so you can love properly." He turned abruptly from the two of them and then returned to the front of the crowd as they followed.

"This one," called out Yeshua, pointing to Yehuda, "he's the only one who really knows who I am! The other doesn't need to know, because he knows how to love. You here are all so concerned with diet and fasting and the right ways to pray. My only law is: don't lie and don't do what you hate! You ask me: what will the next world be like? I ask you: have you discovered where you came from, how you were born? First, find the beginning, and then you will find the end! My friends here," he said, pointing emphatically to Yehuda and Ioannis, "they've been searching for their beginnings, the mystery of their birth. Now they've been rebirthed from the first, cosmic Beginning! It's possible, my friends!" Various members of the crowd mumbled disgruntledly and gave Yehuda and Ioannis dirty looks over their shoulders. But Yeshua was forging ahead.

"Listen to me," he continued. "There once was a man who happened upon a field under which was buried hidden treasure, a pearl of great price. What did he do? He sold everything he had and bought the field.

My friends here have done this. They know where their treasure lies, and the location is here!" He pointed emphatically to his heart.

From the back, Ioannis noticed that both Yahuda Sakaryut and the scar-faced man from Yaphia shifted simultaneously at the mention of the word *treasure*.

Yeshua went on. "Listen, friends! Ripe, blessedly ripe, is the one who stands at the beginning. He will be the one who can rule over everything in this world, who will reign over all and from the All. She understands," he said, pointing to Maryam. "My friends who just joined us understand. Please let someone else here understand me! Some of you are as hard as a rock," he said, walking over to a tall man and patting him affectionately on the head. "Isn't that right, Kepha? Does anyone here have ears? So listen!" He suddenly closed his eyes and remained that way for some minutes, while the crowd shuffled uncomfortably, waiting for clarification. Yehuda and Ioannis looked at each other, nodded and both closed their eyes.

Just as he had in the Merom wilderness, Yehuda again felt his face and features becoming more like those of Yeshua. His breathing also seemed to change and became more like that of the other man. Suddenly, he found himself standing facing Yeshua on a hillside. It seemed to him he was looking in a mirror. The face of Yeshua, his own face, beamed with love. He looked around and saw that they were standing with two other men, whom Yehuda knew somehow to be Moshe and Eliyah. He looked around and found the whole hillside flooded by light. He felt for the first time in his life that anything was possible. He could go anywhere and do anything; he was free. He looked back toward Yeshua, who had taken on his own appearance again. "Yes, it would be good to stay here," he said. "But we both have work to do. When you first looked at me, you just saw me mirroring back your own potential to you, your sacred image, your *tzalem*, which was there from the first beginning. It's what the old stories talk about when Alaha created the human in the divine image. When you find this real image, your family history in this life doesn't matter. Remember that!"

Ioannis meanwhile was having a different vision. He was standing with Yeshua on a hill looking over a large city. *Maybe Rome?* he thought. Yeshua pointed to the city and said, "Suppose you had a choice. I could give you all this—all the power and honor you wanted. Or I could give you your father and mother back. Which would you choose?" Looking at the teacher, Ioannis didn't hesitate. "My father and mother, of course!" he exclaimed. Yeshua gazed at him for what seemed an eternity, and Ioannis saw the loving glance of first his father and then his mother gazing through the teacher's eyes. "Yes, they're always as close as this," said Yeshua, placing his hand gently on Ioannis's heart. "That's why you will always be the student of love itself, the beloved disciple. There's nothing I can teach you that you don't already know. I can only remind you of the same thing until finally loving another as you have experienced me loving you, with the eyes of your deepest desire, becomes the way you live your life."

Yehuda and Ioannis opened their eyes again simultaneously, only to find that Yeshua had already gone back to the front of the crowd. They heard him say:

"Friends! I have come to give you what eye has not seen and what ear has not heard—and what has never appeared previously in the mind of us humans!"

"I know what I need to do now, Yehohanan," whispered Yehuda.

"So do I, master," said Ioannis, "and I'm using the word *master* in a different way now. You've helped show me something I didn't know existed and the way there. I'm not who I thought I was."

"Neither am I, Yehohanan, and that could be either the beginning or the end of me. I think I know who killed Shemuel, but I have a plan. First, I need to ask that trusted student of Yeshua's to take a message to Shemei ben Yair in Batanea."

"No need, Yehuda. I can do it. I have a plan also. I think I've guessed yours and can improve on it. We need that other Yahuda, that man of Korah's also. First, I need to tell you something I've hidden that might save us both."

Chapter 28
Invitations to the Solstice

A week later, Ioannis was back in Yerushalaim, two days before the summer solstice. The midafternoon winds from the west, arriving from what the Romans somewhat possessively called "our sea," were sweeping over the already hot and dry city. Ioannis was waiting in the antechamber of the Roman fortress for an audience with the prefect. He had gone the long way around getting to the city, traveling through Perea and then stopping first in Batanea to deliver a message to Shemei ben Yair.

Although he was wearing slave's clothing, Ioannis gave Pilatus a smart salute as he was ushered into the prefect's presence. Pilatus, slightly startled, looked him up and down more closely and then smiled.

"Ah, yes. Ioannis, isn't it? Well, it has been a while. I thought you had gone so far into that priestly den of snakes that you would never make it out with anything useful. So, don't waste my time. What do you have for me?"

"Prefect, I will tell you all. I trust in your honor as a noble Roman to provide whatever reward you think my information merits."

"Yes, yes," said Pilatus, already a bit bored. He had full-time, part-time and amateur spies reporting to him constantly. They usually brought little more than hearsay or useless gossip. However, as soon as Ioannis mentioned old Herodes's hidden treasure, he immediately sat up. When he heard about a list, an actual inventory with Herodes's seal, and what the inventory contained, and some possible clues to the treasure's location, his eyes widened and took on a fixed concentration, a bit like a hungry snake faced with a slow, fat mouse. Then when he heard that Ioannis knew who had the list and where that person would be found on the particular morning mentioned in a clue to the treasure, he stood up quickly and called for his aide, Aristeaus. They made immediate plans to leave on a journey, first to Caesarea and then to northern Samaria.

"You've been very helpful, young man," said Pilatus smoothly to Ioannis, trying to conceal his excitement. "I knew that Roman blood would prevail, eh? I suppose you can't go back to the temple, so you can resume your position here, a free man, as I promised. I will have the paper drawn up immediately. And what position are you fit for? You can ride, can't you? Your Roman general father trained you, of course. So let's say a decurion, with your own squad of cavalry. That should do nicely. Return to the barracks, and I'll give the immediate order for you to receive a proper uniform and a good horse. Aristeaus, see to it all! Rome honors its own, as I told you. Hail, Caesar!"

A few hours later, after he was sure that Pilatus had left the city, Ioannis was seated on a fine Spanish horse from the Roman garrison, wearing the uniform of a decurion. The pocket of his tunic contained a document confirming that he was now a free man and a Roman citizen. He told the stable master that he was just going to take a short ride to get to know his new mount. Then he rode straight out of the city northeast to Jericho. He rode all night and continued into Perea, around the top of the Sea of Salt and then south along its eastern shore. By dawn of

the next day, he was waiting in the antechamber of the palace of Machaerus for an audience with Herodes Antipas.
Since he said he had a message from the Roman prefect
in Yerushalaim, he was ushered straight into the king's
presence.

⁓

Just before he left Yerushalaim, Prefect Pilatus
made a quick stop at the temple with a squad of his personal security force. When he left an hour later, he wiped
his hands on his tunic in disgust and turned to Aristeaus,
who walked beside him.

"Well, what do you think?"

"Prefect, we gave Qayapha a good working over.
Mind you, as you commanded, we didn't leave any
marks. But we didn't use that much force anyway. He's
not used to any sort of physical punishment, or physical
work either, for that matter. I'm sure he doesn't know
anything about the treasure, or about this scribe of his
who is supposed to have an inventory and the clue to
its whereabouts. Qayapha still thought that the scribe
was just away visiting family. He did reveal, however,
that the same man collects bribes for him from a whole
network of clients he never reports to you. He came
clean about all that pretty quickly. So I'd still say that
he doesn't know anything about this treasure business."

"All right. Then let's have a small squad bring
him up to Samaria before dawn on the solstice. We'll
meet them after I gather a few more trusted people from
Caesarea, where we will spend the night. If it turns out
that Qayapha is involved in trying to defraud us, we
can deal with him there, or on the way back. People

are always getting attacked in Samaria, aren't they? Dangerous place, that," he said, grinning at his secretary. "If he's not being honest with us, we can lose him on the way back and replace him with someone else. By the way, I'm relying on your integrity to keep all of this to yourself. There will be something in it for you, of course. I take care of my own, eh?"

⁓

The shadow on Qayapha's imported Greek sundial had moved only one tick further after Pilatus and Aristeaus had left the temple, when Yahuda Sakaryut entered it and asked to report to the high priest.

"Master, I'm sorry to tell you that Yehuda Tauma, your personal scribe, seems to have betrayed you."

"You're telling me!" Qayapha raised both hands in frustration. "The Romans were just here. I have bruises everywhere!"

"He gave me this letter to give to you."

Qayapha opened the letter, which bore Yehuda's handwriting:

> Dear Qayapha,
> I no longer call you "holy father." There is only one Father of us all. You may have wondered why I have been gone so long. Perhaps you thought that I was collecting some debts of my own. In some ways, that is true.
> In short, I resign. I can no longer be part of the fraud you perpetrate on the Israelite people solely for the sake of enriching yourself. The temple, if it means anything, should be a house

of prayer for all people, not just the rich. That's what the prophet Malachi says.

I am finding my own treasure, in a place that you will never find. May you find peace someday!

Yehuda Tauma ben Yahayye

"Treasure, what's all this about treasure, Sakaryut? The Romans seem to know something I don't."

"Master, while I was away, I heard from one of my sources that Shemuel ben Yahayye, Yehuda Tauma's uncle, may have discovered where old Herodes's hidden treasure is buried. And that's why he was murdered a couple of weeks ago."

"Herodes's treasure, you say? My God! We can't let the Romans have it! Where do the rumors say it is?"

"Ruins at Megiddo, the location will be revealed at dawn on the longest day. That's the day after tomorrow."

"All right. The Romans said they're taking me somewhere with them tomorrow night; it must be there. You know all the Levites in my guard. Go with my secretary and tell the most trusted ones to disguise themselves as bandits and arm themselves to the teeth. They will follow at a safe distance when the Romans take me north. Give instructions for them to circle around from the southwest to arrive near the site at dawn. They need to rescue me—first things first—and then secure the treasure. We'll say that bandits took it, and we can use it in secret for my work here. For God's work, of course! That's without the Romans knowing. I leave it all in your competent hands!"

In Taanach, the morning before the solstice, Korah ben Izhar and Yahuda Sakaryut were looking over a detailed map of Megiddo.

"Good work, Yahuda. I knew it would pay off to have you track that prophet from Nazara. He was a student of Shemuel's, and I suspected that Yehuda Tauma would end up there. Anyway, that prophet Yeshua attracts all sorts of people we need to keep our eye on. Including, it seems…"

"Yes, *that* one. We now know at least one of the people he is working for. But I think he has other fish to fry, so to speak."

At that moment Korah's portly bodyguard Shimeon ben Itzak entered the room.

"Shimeon, we need your help and that of your cousins. Some members of our extended family are in trouble. It's trouble of their own making, but there is some advantage in it for us as well. How well can you pretend to be someone you're not?"

"I can act whatever way you tell me, Master. Just as my father did before me."

"Excellent man. Now listen. First, you're going immediately to the money changer Sikarbaal in Zippori with an important cargo…"

After Shimeon had left, Korah turned back to Yahuda Sakaryut.

"Yahuda, let me get this straight. The high priest thinks you're spying on Yehuda and Yeshua for him. Yeshua thinks you are one of his most loyal students, spying on Qayapha for him. I think that you're working for me. We are cousins, after all. Betraying any one of us could be very dangerous for you, either in this world or the next. So whom do you really work for?"

"Korah, don't be so boring. Life is an adventure, isn't it?"

"Sakaryut, you must love playing with fire. That will get you in trouble some day. The other thing I can't understand is why you often smell of fish."

"Many people around Yeshua smell of fish, Korah."

⁓

Later that afternoon, Benyamin ben Yohanan sat in the audience room of his mansion in Zippori. He slouched in his armchair, his head resting on his hand, as he listened to a tall man with a long scar on his left cheek, who seemed curiously well fed and muscular for someone with ragged clothing. Benyamin nodded and smiled, although only with his mouth, not his eyes. *Such a good spy,* he thought, *he would do anything for the right payment.*

"My poor brother Yehuda," he said, shaking his head sadly. "It was always like him to get involved with something way over his head. With your prompting, I knew that he would somehow find his way into that nest at Nazara and the various prophets it seems to spawn. They are, of course, harmless, but all that mystical nonsense would fascinate Yehuda, make him show his true colors, and he might lead us to what we were looking for. And you had to be in Paneas anyway, didn't you? There are bandits, prophets and messiahs everywhere in this land. None of them are worth *this*," he said, snapping his fingers with disdain. "Only wealth protects a man or gives him any power in the world today. I suppose my brother finally came to that conclusion too. But he's out of his depth and needs our help. Fortunately, I've just gotten a message from him, confirming the report you gave me."

"Oh, it did, did it?" said the tall man, his eyes taking on a wolfish look.

"Yes, except it seems that he's figured out something you didn't."

"He did, did he?"

"Yes, you know, you've been a very good spy and provocateur, my friend. I don't really understand how you can be doing everything yourself. Granted, your ragged disguise is a bit too calculated. You could use more versatility in it, of course. That supposed fish merchant who has a new shop here, the one who seems to come and go. Who is he? He's no more a fish merchant than I am. I wonder whom he's working for. But, never mind, you can easily act like a revolutionary in order to flush out the real revolutionaries, the ones who resist paying the very reasonable taxes I impose for my services. You have even succeeded in pretending to be a religious seeker interested in the sort of nonsense that prophet from Nazara is peddling. And you're not afraid to get your hands dirty, right? That's why I pay you so well."

"Exactly." The tall man nodded, expressionless.

"All right, then. You have another little trip to make, and this time I will go with you."

"Where to?"

"Not that far; we'll take horses. There's a good Roman road south to Megiddo—bless the Romans! We only need to be there by dawn tomorrow."

At midnight that same night, the gates of Antipas's palace in Machaerus opened, and the tetrarch led a large company of his cavalry on the road that ran north around the Dead Sea to Jericho and then on to Beth Shean. They had a long way to go to reach the Jezreel Valley before dawn.

An hour after they left, a bird squawked from one of the hills overlooking Machaerus. Shemei ben Yair peered out from behind a boulder.

"That's it," he told Ioannis, who stood beside him. "Praise Alaha, they took even more men than I anticipated. This shouldn't be too difficult. One of our people inside will open the gates, and we'll be in and out with Yohanan before they know it. When they discover he's gone, they won't dare follow us, because it would leave the palace undefended. Antipas would rather lose a troublesome rabble-rouser than risk any of his wealth or family."

"Yes, he bought the story I gave him about me being a half-Israelite defecting from Pilatus's guard."

"That, of course, is true, Yehohanan," Shemei said and chuckled softly.

"Then I told him about the treasure hunt at Megiddo. Any doubts he had vanished. The promise of more riches for the rich does that, I guess. But won't he lose face with his Roman masters for making such an obvious blunder?" asked Ioannis.

"Not at all, my friend," replied Shemei. "I'm sure you were very convincing. He will be fully engaged in the wild chase on which you sent him. In any case, if I know Antipas, he'll make up some sort of outlandish story to explain the prophet's disappearance. He might spread the story, for instance, that he had Yohanan

beheaded as part of a drunken party game he was playing. That would be in character. Anyway, no one around
here will see our prophet again."

"Where will you go with Yohanan now?"

"We're taking him farther east to live in Batanea,
closer to Parthia, where he will be safe. He's finished
in this land, what with the Romans, the dense-headed
Israelites here and rulers like Antipas. He can find a
better audience for his message where we come from.
His message from the Indestructible Life and Light is
universal, and everyone can use a good baptism to start
the day. Also, since he's the enemy of the Parthians'
enemy…"

"He's a friend of the Parthians. Right!"

"Of course. Anyway, Antipas will get what's
coming to him, without Yohanan lifting a finger. Once
Antipas divorced his old wife, the daughter of King
Aretas of Nabatea, to marry his brother Philipos's wife,
Aretas began preparing for war against him. Antipas
doesn't know it yet, but his days are numbered." Shemei
turned to the rest of his men and whispered as forcefully
as one can whisper, "Men, it's time! In the Name and
Light of the Indestructible Life!"

⌐━━⌐

It was the middle of the night before the solstice,
and the elders of the Natzara—Yauseph, Mariam,
Elishyba, Zakarya and Eliyuhena—were sitting with
closed eyes around a lighted candle on a table in a darkened room, as Yauseph's son, Ya'aqub, guarded the
door from the inside. On the table in front of them lay
a small open scroll that Yehuda had sent them. He had

marked a particular passage from the book of Hanuch with notations from Shemuel in the margin. After a few minutes, they opened their eyes.

"All clear to everyone?" asked Zakarya.

"Yes, from the message that Yehuda Tauma sent, Yeshua is safe," said Yauseph.

"Or as safe as he chooses to be," said Mariam.

"And Yohanan soon will be, if the will of the Holy One be done," said Elishyba.

"Only one thing remains hidden, and it seems that Yehuda Tauma is determined to take a risk to bring it into the light," said Zakarya. "As long as he doesn't bring us into the light as well…"

"The time is ripe," said Eliyuhena. "If we are to play any part, Ya'aqub and I need to leave with the other brothers now."

"Before you go," said Yauseph, turning to Ya'aqub. "Son, keep an eye out for that other man, the one with the scar who seems to know our sign. Yehuda said he has been traveling with Yeshua. He could be dangerous. He's the type who can work for many groups or masters, maybe another family not part of our plan." Ya'aqub nodded silently.

"Go well, but be careful," said Elishyba. "We don't want attention pointed this way. Remember, the Holy One can be darkness as well as light, as the old creation story says. Before light, there must be darkness, before the new creation, a veil and a shadow. So remain in the shadow until it's time to 'let there be light.'"

Chapter 29
Megiddo Again

The following morning, the first glimmer of dawn was just beginning to creep into the sky, illuminating the Jezreel Valley below the hill of Megiddo. Both the bottom of the hill and the valley were covered in a thick, early morning fog that would soon burn off sometime after sunrise.

Yehuda sat with his back against a tree on the hillside facing the ruins of an old pagan temple a short distance away. Behind him were the foothills separating Megiddo from Samaria to the south. He could see in front of him the remnants of ancient stone stairs ascending to the crude altar. This was the place of the blood, where the old human sacrifices were performed. Who knew how many cultures and how many bones were buried here? *Probably the early people who lived here were not bloodthirsty,* he speculated. *But if they had previously been wandering nomads, without knowledge of farming, and came here for annual rituals, there might not be enough food for the tribe if there had been many births that year. So perhaps each season some of the old ones gave up their lives willingly for the tribe.*

He shivered and shook himself more awake. *Your mind is wandering,* he thought. *Remember Shemuel. Eliminate all unnecessary thoughts and focus your mind on what is ahead. Or better yet, focus your heart on the unseen and the unknown world. You aren't different from the old ones. You are nothing more than a nomad, just passing through. Let go of who you think you are, so you can meet this moment as it is.*

A short time later, he heard the crunch of stones as the sound of two pairs of footsteps echoed from down the hill to his right. Two figures slowly came into view through the fog, both of whom he recognized.

"Good morning, brother," said Benyamin cheerily. "As you can see, I've trudged up this demon of a hill and come as you requested, before dawn. I brought one of my retainers along to help…in case there really is anything here, of course."

"I recognize your retainer, brother," replied Yehuda. "He posed as a poor villager in Yaphia a few weeks ago. He told my brother Yehohanan and me that he was part of a rebellion that was gradually eliminating the rich elites like you from Galilee. He implied that he was part of a secret network dedicated to rebellion."

"Oh, yes, that," replied Benyamin impatiently. "Well, you understand, I'm sure, that a person in my position cannot exist without his own sources of intelligence. There are so many bandits and rebels around these days. You can only flush them out by pretending to be one of them. Isn't that right?" he said, nodding to the man with the scar. He looked around him and then past Yehuda toward the jumbled rocks and cliffs behind him. "I don't see your 'brother' or bodyguard. Did he abandon you? Or did you send him away, wanting to keep this secret for yourself?"

"I sent him away."

"Quite right, too," said Benyamin contentedly. "You've finally come to your senses. Blood needs to stick together, doesn't it?"

"Yes, but it seems that your blood needs to shed other blood of ours."

"What do you mean?"

"I mean Shemuel, and his son, too. Didn't you dispatch your 'retainer' here to eliminate both of them and to try to find the map to old Herodes's treasure? I'm sitting just near where it seems you killed Shemuel. There are still a few bloodstains here."

"What if I did?" Benyamin said petulantly. "There was no reason to share those sort of riches with my uncle. He wouldn't have known what to do with them, anyway. He came to me asking inappropriate questions about our family history and tried to blackmail me to get money for some charity project he was involved in. I had to kill him. Then I talked with his son, who said that the old man had dropped hints that he knew something about Herodes's treasure. But the son was worse than the father, totally incompetent, and a liar, too. I hired Mikhael to search Shemuel's house, and he said he found nothing. Then I had him followed and found he was giving information to someone else in Sepphoris, some fish merchant I haven't been able to trace. I concluded that Mikhael was holding out on me and wanted the treasure for himself, so I eliminated him, too. What else could I think? Imagine, his own father's house, not very large, and he told me he couldn't find a simple list with the key to the treasure's location! Unbelievable. He made me kill him. Oh well, no matter. You've done much better. I suppose the foolish old scribe actually did consider you his real son. Let's get on with it…where is this supposed list, and what does it tell us about the treasure? We know that the old Herodes hid a lot of his wealth. I met him once as a young man, and he told me so himself in a drunken moment. I've been waiting more than twenty years for a clue."

"You've killed my uncle and his son," said Yehuda evenly, restraining his fury. "If I tell you what I know, what guarantee do I have that you won't kill me as well?"

"Kill you? Why would I do that?" replied Benyamin, opening his arms helplessly. "You're much younger and stronger than I am. Why, I'm old enough to be your father, you know. You could take over for me in Zippori when I'm gone, which won't be too many more years now. Your other brothers are simply useless at business."

At that moment, Shimeon ben Itzak and his two cousins came out of the hills behind Yehuda.

"Oh, I see," said Benyamin. "A clever trick. I never thought you had it in you, brother. Now I'm more convinced than ever that you are the right man to inherit the small bit of wealth I've accumulated. Surely you know that I don't have any children. Didn't you ever wonder why that is?"

"Perhaps guilt dried up your seed," spat out Yehuda.

"Now, now, let's not take things so personally. Or rather, perhaps you should. I didn't want to tell you this yet, but...Didn't you ever wonder why our father sent you away to live with his uncle?"

"He was providing for me in the event of his death, he said. He was worried that you and the rest of my brothers would leave me nothing after he was gone. Which was true."

"Our father was a fool...to make up such a wild story! No, Yehuda, he sent you away because he was ashamed of you. You were, of course, too young to understand. Not that it was your fault, anyway. I mean, for an old man like him, so late in life, to take such a young, beautiful wife. And then keep her under the same roof with a handsome young man. What could he expect?"

"It's not true!" Yehuda rushed toward Benyamin, but the older man stood his ground.

"Now, now. Isn't it better this way? It could have been some stranger, just a passing merchant. But instead, it kept the blood pure. So my brother, you wouldn't kill your own father, would you?"

Yehuda stopped and stood still, stunned. No one else moved either. The sun began to rise, creeping across the valley toward the small hill on which they stood. At that moment, everyone heard the sound of horses galloping up the valley, but from two different directions. One group came from the west, on the fast road along the coast from the Roman fortress at Caesarea. The other group came into the valley from the east up the Jordan Valley from Decapolis and Perea. As the five men at the altar site watched, the Roman troop with Pilatus at its head came storming up the hill from one direction and came face-to-face with Herodes Antipas's cavalry arriving at the same moment from the other.

Pilatus and Antipas came to the front, looking first curiously and then disdainfully at each other.

"My dear Antipas, I carry the Roman eagle here. I'm sure we can handle any difficulties that arise," said Pilatus.

"Oh no, Prefect," responded Antipas. "In the case of local problems—evidence of banditry, rebels and such—we prefer to deal with them ourselves."

Megiddo Again

"But we're not in Galilee or Perea here," countered Pilatus. "Aren't you a little far from your territory?"

"Not very far, Prefect. Galilee is just over there," replied Antipas, pointing across the valley. "We have a legitimate interest in all terrorist activity threatening the security of our border. I'm sure that your superiors in Rome's royal family would agree. I have many close personal friends there, you know."

"Let's not quibble, my good man," said Pilatus, with some steel in his voice. "You know you shouldn't play these games with me. Anyway, this is probably just some hoax perpetrated to set us at odds with one another." He turned to Benyamin, who was the best-dressed person present.

"I know you, don't I, Israelite?" Pilatus asked.

"Yes, of course, Prefect. I'm Benyamin ben Yohanan of Zippori. I collect taxes for both the honorable Caesar and King Herodes Antipas here. This young man is my son, Yehuda, with some of his retainers."

"That's a lie!" said Yehuda. "This man is not my father!"

"I'm sure the parentage of Israelites is not of interest to you, Prefect," continued Benyamin smoothly. "This person, who has been a scribe at the temple in Yerushalaim, told me something about a list of treasure, perhaps buried here, and asked me to help him investigate. Of course, we planned to report it to the proper authorities…if there were anything to find, that is. I only wished to ascertain the validity of his report."

"Of course," replied Pilatus with barely disguised sarcasm. He turned to the high priest, who was on a horse flanked by two Roman cavalrymen.

"Qayapha, is this your scribe, the one who went missing a few weeks ago?"

"It is, Prefect," replied the high priest, cowering on his horse. "But as I told you yesterday, I knew nothing about this, and…"

"Of course, of course," said Pilatus, cutting him off. Then turning to Benyamin, he said, "And by the way, my friend Herodes Antipas here is a tetrarch, a far cry from a king, at least in the eyes of Caesar. It is just these sorts of presumptions that got his brother Archelaos removed some years ago," he said, shooting a glance of warning at Antipas. "So what have you found here?"

"Nothing so far, Prefect," replied Benyamin innocently. "We were still discussing our family relations. Yehuda here has not yet shown me any evidence of a list, much less of any treasure. I am as much in the dark as you are."

"Well?" asked Pilatus, turning his most commanding gaze on Yehuda. "Have you wasted everyone's time coming here? If so, you'll see what reward Rome offers to those who upset the public order. Two long beams of wood, fastened crosswise."

Yehuda pulled the inventory out of his tunic and handed it to Pilatus.

"Examine it for yourself, Prefect. I found it in the home of my uncle, who was also a scribe in the temple for many years. After old Herodes's death, he found it in an area of the sacred precincts that the old king had remodeled and enlarged."

Pilatus looked the list over, examining carefully the seal at the bottom. He handed it to Antipas, who also peered at it closely.

"Is it your father's signature and seal, man?" asked Pilatus.

"It seems to be so, Prefect," replied Antipas slowly. "But I am not able to make anything of the postscript at the bottom. 'At the old place of blood…below the bones of our ancestors…sacred mountain…beginning of the longest day…' We have many of those types of places. It could be anywhere in Israel."

"You're either thick or think I am!" said Pilatus, disdainfully. "What about it, scribe?"

"Shemuel left other clues pointing to this valley," said Yehuda. "This place saw some of the Israelites' greatest battles. And more importantly, there is a prophecy from the prophet Hanuch that a great victory would be fought and won here in the future. My uncle and teacher Shemuel ben Yahayye, whom this man murdered," he said, pointing at Benyamin, "trusted this prophecy. 'At the old place of blood'— there was an ancient temple here from pagan times. This altar before us is where human blood sacrifices were performed."

"Such barbarians," said Pilatus, growing bored again. "It's a wonder that there is any civilization in a land like this. I'm really not interested in prophecies or the details of a possible murder. I'll leave that part to Antipas here, since it's a disturbance to the public order near his territory. But what about this rising sun part? The sun is rising now, isn't it?" he said, looking around casually.

At that moment, the sun shone through two large dolmens that stood close together at the end of the ritual path just below the ruins of the altar. The rays illuminated a spot about halfway up the small hill, where the steps would have been continued.

"There, Prefect!" exclaimed Benyamin.

"All right," said Pilatus, continuing to take charge. "Mark that spot! I still doubt that this is anything more than another product of the overactive Israelite religious imagination. But if there is something here, at least I won't arrest you and this scribe person for wasting Roman time and resources. I will, however, arrest you for not informing me ahead of time and attempting to steal wealth that belongs to Caesar. You're finished as our tax collector in Zippori either way."

"That's not just, Prefect!" cried Benyamin.

"Maybe not," said Pilatus, "but on the frontier we Romans practice frontier justice. It's the only type you Israelites understand. As for you, Antipas, I would have expected you to report this to me first, not try to fill your own coffers. I will report the whole incident to Rome."

Antipas stiffened, and his men looked around tensely, not used to seeing their chief humiliated. They began to finger their weapons nervously, which caused the Roman detachment to do the same.

"Here, let's not get too excited," said Pilatus soothingly. "You there," he said, pointing to Benyamin. "Start digging."

"I'm an old man," whimpered Benyamin. "My servant here…" He pointed to the tall man.

"No matter," snapped Pilatus. "Just do it!"

Benyamin gestured weakly to the scar-faced assassin, who moved toward the spot that the sun had touched a few moments before. He had brought a hand hoe and soon dug several feet into the hillside.

"There is something here, Master!" said the scar-faced man to Benyamin. "It's a wooden chest. And there seem to be others around it."

"Bring it to me!" ordered Pilatus. With some effort, Benyamin's man brought the box and laid it at Pilatus's feet. Antipas dismounted and came closer for a look. The chest, about three handwidths all around, carried an engraved image of a seven-branched candlestick. Three brass clasps welded it shut. Kneeling in front of the chest, Pilatus used his short sword to knock the clasps off. Then he opened the box. It was filled to the top with gold and silver coins, which flashed in the rays of the now fully risen sun. Both groups of horsemen released audible gasps. The wind rose and began to swirl the remnants of the morning fog around the area.

As everyone's attention was distracted by the treasure, an arrow flashed through the air and pierced the scar-faced assassin through the shoulder. Before anyone could see where it came from, two other arrows struck the Roman and Herodian captains in the shoulder in quick succession, knocking them both off their horses. With a confused and angry roar, the two groups of cavalry fell to fighting one another. Then a third group dressed as bandits came riding over the hill from the southwest and joined in. One of them separated Qayapha from his Roman captors and dragged him off. The battle intensified as various men tried to take possession of the wooden chest. Soon the whole area swelled with armed men, all fighting each other. Pilatus and Antipas both remounted their horses and tried to regain some control over their troops. But they were caught up in the melee, in which each group felt it was defending itself from the attack of the other.

Amid the chaos, Yehuda saw Benyamin stooped over the box, trying to pick it up. He raised it to his chest, walked a step, and then groaned loudly and fell forward on top of it. Yehuda pulled him off the box and turned him over. The older man was clutching his chest, his eyes bulging.

"Too heavy..." he gasped, clutching his heart, his breath failing quickly.

"That's your conscience, brother—or father—or whoever you are!" yelled Yehuda over the din around them. "Perhaps the Holy One can have more compassion for you than I have," he said, pulling from his belt a knife Ioannis had given him.

"Just like your supposed father," grunted Benyamin disdainfully. "So moral, but a coward at heart. What good did his goodness do him? He begged for mercy before I killed him on that last buying trip of his. Admit it, you know you carry my blood."

"If I had it, I rid myself of it long ago" said Yehuda, "Physical blood changes. My real *dami*, my essence, comes from Shemuel. Your only family is the Watcher Azrael, who brought greed to the earth. Return to him and see what judgment he gives you!" he said, raising the knife.

But Benyamin had already died by the time Yehuda finished his sentence. He dropped the knife and placed one hand on Benyamin's chest to check for a heartbeat; the other he placed on Benyamin's side to feel for breathing. The man had died very quickly. When Yehuda raised his hands, one of them was covered in blood. From Benyamin's side, Yehuda saw a slow trickle of blood, another red crescent produced with a fine, sharp blade.

Megiddo Again

At that moment, Shimeon ben Itzak, together with Korah's men, appeared out of the confusion and carried away the wooden box. The Levites disguised as bandits rode away with Qayapha, who kept shouting at them to go back for the treasure.

"It's time to go, brother," said Ya'aqub, who also appeared and put his hand heavily on Yehuda's shoulder. Yeshua's brother was dressed in a Roman uniform with a helmet to hide his red hair and had ridden over the hills with a small group from Natzara, some dressed in Antipas's livery and some in Roman uniforms like himself. They blended in perfectly with the other soldiers, who were too busy fighting each other to notice them.

"It seems we came just in time to start a little trouble." Ya'aqub grinned, shaking his bow. "Anyway, at least Shemuel is avenged," he said, spitting on Benyamin's body. "I shot that tall one with the scar in the shoulder, but he seems to have fled. We will deal with him later, if we can find out whom he's working for. Now, we need to get out of here before the Romans and Antipas's men get tired of fighting."

The sun had risen enough to burn the fog away entirely before Pilatus and Antipas finally brought their men under control. Both leaders turned back to the altar steps, where they discovered that the wooden chest had disappeared. Each looked at the other suspiciously, but then quickly turned his attention to the rest of the dusty hillside. The soldiers, both sides working together now, brought up another ten wooden chests.

Upon opening them, they discovered that each was filled with nothing but sand.

Chapter 30

The End and the Beginning

A month later, Yehuda and Ioannis were sitting next to one another on a hillside overlooking the western shore of Lake Kinneret. In the distance, they could see the village of Kephar Nahum, which Yeshua had begun to use as his temporary home when he was in that part of Galilee. Kepha and some of the new students had family there. The warm summer wind from the Great Sea behind them rippled the surface of the lake. It also made it a bit difficult to hear all that Yeshua was saying to the crowd of Galilean poor around them. However, they caught most of it.

Yeshua was talking about *malkuta d'Alaha*, the reign of the Holy One. It would come, he was saying, like a thief in the night, like a mustard plant that grows wildly, like a weed in the midst of cultivated soil. It would be like a man who thought he planted wheat and found that, as the new sprouts came up, both cultivated edible wheat and wild inedible wheat were mixed together. What to do? Should he try to tear out the inedible stuff? No, when young, the plants are too similar to one another. Better to wait. At harvest the difference would be more obvious, and the wild plants could then be burned and used to compost the soil, returning *hayye*—life energy—to the earth. Like the inedible plants, one can't always digest the divine plan immediately. One can't always expect a harvest in the usual way. Kicking out one group of tyrants by force usually just results in creating another tyranny ruled by force.

"I'm not sure they're getting all this," whispered Yehuda to his friend. "It's all a bit abstract for the poor Galileans. They're mostly here for the bread and fishes."

"You're probably right," replied Ioannis. "I'm not sure I'm getting it all either. But it's wonderful to be in his presence. I feel like I'm in love with life again."

"Yes, well. You're in love with Zilpah, Yeshua's sister," said the ex-scribe wryly, nodding at a clump of people just down the hill from them, where the young woman sat with her mother. "I suppose that's a good thing. But I think Yeshua is teaching something much more subtle than just how to love. It's about diving into yourself, knowing your real self, touching your soul power, coming to stand at the beginning before the creation of everything. That's where the real power is."

"Maybe you're right, Yehuda," said Ioannis, smiling peacefully. "I'm sure there's a message for each of us. You remember what you remember. I remember what I remember."

"That's the way with prophets, I suppose, Yehohanan," said Yehuda, sighing. "One thing I'm certain of, though: you could never build an empire around what he's teaching."

"No," replied Ioannis. "That would mean killing the teaching."

The two men sat without speaking and listened to the teacher. A short while later, he stopped and gestured to some of his students that it was time to eat. Food appeared from somewhere and was shared around the crowd, which murmured gratefully.

"There are a few things I still don't understand, Yehuda," said Ioannis, turning to Yehuda. "Not about Yeshua, but about Shemuel. So he left the pearl for you to find, to push you out of the temple. He must have known you very well—how impatient you had become there. Or he really did breathe a strong message into it. I understand about the treasure inventory. But was it a real document or not?"

"It seemed real at the time. That's why I made a copy while we were at Shemuel's house and sent it with you to Shemei in Batanea. I thought he would be better equipped to do something with it."

"He told me that he was going to have it engraved on copper, as the ending verses suggest," said Ioannis. "He planned to keep the copy you sent and send the copper version to some of his family that live in caves near Qumran around the Sea of Salt. Apparently, they're good at hiding things, and no one would ever think to look for it among a group of religious hermits living in the middle of nowhere. You didn't trust the Natzara group, then?"

"Well, I trust Yohanan, from the short time I had with him, but he's gone east to Batanea," said Yehuda. "I trust Yeshua. I'm not sure that their family in Natzara really understands what either of them is doing. The Natzara seem too enchanted with an outward solution to our problems, albeit a very devious and complicated one. As Yeshua just said, the problem is deeper. We won't have a new Israel here until we have built one in the unseen world first—one that doesn't depend on the use of force or oppressing other people, even if they have oppressed us."

"So the treasure, if it exists, wasn't at Megiddo, obviously. But how did that chest of gold and silver get there? And the other chests?"

"That was Korah's men, particularly your friend Shimeon. I sent Korah the two pearls from Shemuel along with a report via Yahuda Sakaryut. At Korah's direction, Shimeon took the pearls to Zippori, where Sikarbaal helped turn them into a chest of coins and a few other empty chests, of course. They buried it all the previous day and set up those stones where I told them, estimating where the sun would shine. Scribes are taught how to do these things with the heavenly bodies. It was only important that Pilatus and Antipas find the right box first. Really, if anyone had looked closely at the coins, they would have noticed that many of them were not from the time of old Herodes. I was also afraid that someone would recognize the seven-stick candelabra on the chest. That's a symbol made famous by the Maccabees and their rebellion against the Greeks. Herodes was an enemy of the Maccabees, so he would never have used that on a chest. Remember, he was an Idumean, not an Israelite. He also probably had very little knowledge of old Israelite history, much less the early history of Megiddo. So why would he bury a treasure near an old pagan altar there?"

"You took some chances."

"Not really. I understand the greed that makes men like Pilatus and Antipas blind and a bit crazy. They wanted to believe in a fabulous treasure that one or both could claim, tax-free, you might say."

"But how did you figure out that your brother, or…"

Yehuda cut him off. "I don't want to talk about him, Yehohanan. When we were in the wetlands at Lake Merom with Yeshua and Maryam, I had a vision of my father just before he left on his last trip. Probably it wasn't a vision but a memory I had forced down inside myself. He warned me about Benyamin. Combined with the story that Shemuel left for me, the one about the pearl, it was clear that I had forgotten who my real parents were."

"But in your case, that was a good thing, wasn't it?"

"It depends on what you mean by *real*. Shemuel was my real father, in any way I can define *real* or *father*. Now that he's gone, I agree with what Yeshua has been telling everyone: forget about your physical blood relations—call only Alaha your father. Or mother for that matter. I have burnt the scrolls of my own family drama. I don't have any more time for it, and I certainly don't want to start a family myself. Given my own blood family, that would probably turn out to be a disaster."

"From what you said, it seems that the tall man with the scar killed Benyamin. So whom was he really working for? It's a shame that you didn't let me go to Megiddo. I could have tracked him down."

"It was too risky, Yehohanan. If Pilatus had caught sight of you, the whole performance would have been ruined. As to the man with the scar, Benyamin thought he was working for him. But ultimately he may have been working for himself or for another group that our friends don't know about. I'm going to keep my eye out for him. What about your plans? Zilpah?"

"Well, I don't know," said Ioannis, blushing. "I clearly can't go back to Yerushalaim again. I've grown a beard, so it's unlikely that anyone would recognize me, even if Pilatus sent someone to look, which I doubt he will. He's probably inwardly amused that someone pulled the wool over his eyes. For now, I'm just going to stay around Yeshua and see where that leads."

"You could go anywhere. Remember, I gave you half of what was left in that wooden box, after Korah had taken a bit for himself, for services rendered."

"Oh, that. I already gave it to Yahuda Sakaryut to help fund Yeshua's work. He acts as his treasurer, you know. Where do you think the bread and fish came from?"

"You really are a romantic soul, Yehohanan," said Yehuda, laughing. "But at least you're happy. I see clouds gathering over Yeshua. He's relatively safe here in Galilee only because Antipas is busy trying to calm down King Aretas of Nabatea. Probably Aretas sees a chance to get back some of the territory of Perea that borders his own kingdom. Shemei ben Yair guessed right when he told you how Antipas might cover up Yohanan's escape. The tetrarch did spread a story about how he beheaded Yohanan over some foolish request by his daughter at a drunken party. That helped hide the fact that he had gone on a fishing trip to Megiddo only to be humiliated by Pilatus."

"What about you, Yehuda? Aren't you worried that someone will come after you?"

"Not really. They don't know that it was our trick. They probably think it was one played by old Herodes. Anyway, even if Qayapha sent someone, they wouldn't recognize me. As you see, I've grown a longer beard and let my hair go a bit. I now look like many other Galilean men my age. I'd be more worried that someone might mistake me for Yeshua."

"Yes, you do look very similar now, like twin brothers. So what will you do?"

"I've hidden my half of the money the pearl bought near Shemuel's house in Paneas, which I've made my home. I have enough to travel east to Parthia and be-yond. I've heard that some of the old Israelites left this area after the Assyrians and Babylonians conquered us and headed all the way east to the Indus River Valley, where they settled among a sympathetic race. I might just travel there. But first, I'm going to stay around here with Yeshua for a while. I'm curious to see how things turn out for him. I'm also grateful for what he's shown me. Without him, I would always consider these vision-ary seizures a curse rather than a blessing. He's taught me how to use them to help myself and others. He's shown me a different form of light, you could say. As long as it's something that makes practical sense to me, that I can experience here and now, I'm with him."

Later that night, as the two slept in a crowd of Yeshua's followers on the Galilean hillside, Yehuda woke with a start. At first, he thought it was already daylight because the sun was shining. But then he no-ticed that he was not on the same hillside where he and Ioannis had gone to sleep. Also, there was no crowd around them and no Yeshua anywhere in sight.

Ah, I've awoken in a dream vision, he thought. *So where am I, and when am I?* Using the methods that Yeshua had taught him, he drew the sacred name in light in front of him and looked around. He was back at Megiddo, and the sun was at the horizon in front of him. *But was it sunrise or sunset?*

At that moment he awoke again, sat up and found Ioannis sleeping beside him. The sky in the east was just beginning to brighten. Yehuda sat up and breathed with his eyes closed for a few seconds. Then he gently shook his friend beside him.

"Yehohanan!" he whispered in the young man's ear. "Wake up!"

"Yehuda—what is it? Another bad dream, or a good dream, or a bad vision or…"

"Quiet, my friend. I need your help once again."

"Of course," said the other man sleepily. He smiled and continued, "But can't it wait until after breakfast?"

"All right. But we need to leave just after daybreak."

"Leave?"

Chapter 31
The Owls

After an early breakfast, the two walked inland from Lake Kinneret westward through the Valley of the Doves, into the foothills of Galilee and then southward through Cana, Zippori and Yaphia. Rather than take the quicker way along the lake, Yehuda wanted to avoid Tiberias and other places where Antipas might have soldiers or spies. Toward the end of the day, they descended into the Jezreel Valley and climbed the hill at Megiddo.

"Why are we here again, Yehuda?" asked Ioannis. "You've barely said a word all day."

"It was safer that way—safer for you, Yehohanan—in case we were stopped."

"All right, so we're here. What now?"

"Do you remember the inscription at the end of that treasure inventory?"

"Vaguely. That's really more your strength than mine, Yehuda. Manuscripts, codes and so forth."

"I've been an idiot. The inscription said, *'…find this sun at the beginning of its longest day, the first day of creation.'* But at creation, the day begins at sunset, not sunrise. *'And it was setting and dawning, one day.'* The whole creation begins with darkness. We also begin the Sabbath and our festivals in the evening, not the morning. *'It will be like a festival for you.'* Now we mostly look at time the Greek and Roman way, and our day begins with morning. I was so focused on sunrise of the day of

The Owls

the solstice that I forgot about that. Also, given when we found Shemuel's body, he must have also been here at sunset, not sunrise."

"But it wasn't solstice when he was murdered."

"No, and it isn't now. But as I said, a scribe knows how to estimate accurately where the sun will shine at ritual sites, especially at important moments."

The two went around to the opposite side of the small hill from where they had played the trick on Pilatus and Antipas a month before. As the sun went below the horizon to the west, it struck to the left side of two boulders. Yehuda ran over to the gap between the rocks, quickly estimated the line and began to dig. After a few minutes, he found evidence that someone had dug a little into the hillside relatively recently.

"It looks like Shemuel *was* interrupted. It would have been hard labor for him alone, anyway," said Yehuda. "His heart was not up to it, so he covered up what he had dug." From his shoulder bag Yehuda took some short hoes that he had purchased in a village on the way. He and Ioannis began to work quickly as the light faded.

The twilight still glowed on the horizon when they unearthed the first of what seemed to be several wooden boxes buried on the hillside. It was full of gold and silver coins as well as jewels. So was the next.

"But you said that old Herodes wouldn't have known about ancient pagan temples and blood sacrifices," said Ioannis, wiping some sweat from his forehead.

"I was wrong again," Yehuda said and shrugged. "He had a touch of genius to his madness, it seems."

"So what now?"

— 301 —

"I don't know, except that we need to keep this to ourselves. Let's bury the boxes again, moving them away from the solstice line."

"Then what?" asked the younger man. "Shouldn't we tell someone?"

"Same old question: whom do we trust? Do you want to lead a revolution?"

"Well, no, not really."

"I don't, either. Sometimes it's more dangerous for something to come into the light too soon than for it to remain in the darkness. Let's leave it here for now and see what develops back in Galilee."

"So back to Yeshua?" asked Ioannis.

"Back to Yeshua. There are still various spies around him, some from the temple, some from…I don't know where."

"How can we know whom to trust, then?"

"Follow the fish."

"I don't understand."

"Many of Yeshua's students smell of fish. They're fishermen, of course. But some smell of the wrong kind of fish."

Ioannis shook his head. He wasn't that sensitive to fish. He did, however, suddenly remember the cave full of weapons in Natzara and shivered a bit. Then he remembered Zilpah and felt a bit warmer.

As night fell, the two men sat on the hill overlooking the valley. The moon was almost full now, illuminating many of the caves and crevices in the hills as well as the expanse of wheat fields, ready for harvest.

Yehuda took the moonlight into his heart and again connected with the sun as its source. His breath-spirit was flying high in the sky, but his heart felt heavy. There was trouble ahead, and he was torn between leaving it behind and heading straight into it. He determined to go higher in his meditation, looking for a sign.

He was startled out of his trance when he thought he saw, or felt, a shadow move behind him. But it was only two owls, which hooted in unison as they swooped downhill on either side of the men.

"Only owls, Yehuda. I thought I saw someone watching us."

"So did I, Yehohanan. Yes, only owls. Maybe they're flying from their home on Mount Carmel, from prophet Eliyah's cave, looking for likely prey," he mused.

"Is it one of your vision-signs? You know, in Roman religion, the owl reminds us of Minerva, goddess of wisdom."

"Perhaps. Maybe she's telling us to stay awake so that we don't get eaten. Holy Wisdom says: Be aware, this moment. Be the owl, not the prey."

Characters
(in order of appearance)

Shemuel ben Yahayye: a retired scribe living near Paneas in Gaulanitis.

Dawid: David.

Yoshiah: Josiah.

Moshe: Moses.

Eliyah: Elijah.

Shelomoh: Solomon.

Hanuch: The prophet Enoch, who "walked with God" and was taken without suffering physical death.

Herodes: King Herod "the Great." The "old Herodes" ruled as the Roman's client king 73–4 BCE. After his death, the Romans divided his territory among his sons Herodes Antipater, Herodes Philipos and Herodes Archelaos, whose status they reduced to "tetrarchs." At the time of the story, Rome had already removed Archelaos for incompetence.

Ioannis Vivis: a.k.a. **Yehohanan,** a.k.a. John. A Roman-Israelite slave, Yehuda Tauma's bodyguard, formerly attached to the Roman prefect's detail in Jerusalem.

Yehuda Tauma ben Yahayye: a.k.a. **Yehuda Tauma ben Yohanan,** a.k.a. Ioudas Didymus, a.k.a. Judas Thomas. A scribe escaping from work at the Jerusalem Temple, Shemuel ben Yahayye's adopted son.

Lewi, Lewiyyim: Levi, Levites—ancestors of Levi, son of Jacob by his wife Leah. Moses and his brother Aaron were part of the Levite clan.

Korah ben Izhar: a Levite, retired from the security force at the Jerusalem Temple, head of a "family" based in the Samaritan village of Taanach.

Shimeon ben Itzak: former farmer; now a bodyguard, spy, soldier and general factotum for Korah ben Izhar.

Yauseph Qayapha (a.k.a. Caiaphas or Kaiapas in Latin): high priest in Jerusalem at the time of the story, appointed by the previous Roman prefect Valerius Gratus.

Yahuda Sakaryut: Judas Iscariot, a freelance spy and informer working for various "families."

Pontius Pilatus: Roman prefect in the Roman province of *Iudaea*. He had succeeded Valerius Gratus in 26 CE.

Herodes Antipas: Tetrarch of Galilee, one of the sons of the old Herodes.

Gaius Metallus: chief minister of Antipas, appointed by Rome to keep an eye on him.

Felayah ben Abitub: the village headman of Yaphia.

Eliyuhena ben She'atiyel: outward leader of the Natzara clan or family in Nazara.

Yauseph ben Ya'aqub: Joseph. Yeshua and Ya'aqub's father, an elderly leader of the Natzara clan.

Ya'aqub ben Yauseph: James. Yeshua's half brother and another son of Yauseph.

Yoezer: one of the wealthy members of the Natzara community.

Zakarya ben Abiya: Zachariah. The former head as well as *kahna*, priest, of the Natzara community, Yohanan ben Zakarya's father.

Elishyba: Elizabeth. Yohanan's mother, wife of Zakarya and ritual leader in Natzara.

Zilpah: younger sister of Yeshua and Ya'aqub.

Mariam bat Hannah: Mary. Wife of Yauseph, mother of Yeshua, Zilpah and Ya'aqub.

Aristeaus: personal secretary to Pontius Pilatus.

Mikhael ben Yahayye: Shemuel's son, a merchant from Paneas.

Shallum: member of the Natzara clan, a groom and guard.

Sikarbaal: a Phoenician moneychanger living in Zippori.

Benyamin ben Yohanan: Yehuda's brother, an elite resident and tax collector in Zippori.

Aqqub: guardian of the small shrine at the tomb of the prophet Yonah (Jonah) in the village of Gath-Hepher in Galilee.

Yohanan ben Zakarya: John the Baptist. Member of the Natzara clan, another student of Shemuel ben Yahayye, Yeshua's cousin, and a prophet baptizing people near the village of Sennabris at the south end of Lake Kinneret (the Sea of Galilee).

Shemei ben Yair: kinsman of Yohanan ben Zakarya and the Natzarans, a leader of the Batanea horsemen, living near Kochaba in Batanea, the borderlands east of Lake Kinneret.

Yeshua ben Yauseph: a student of Shemuel, Yohanan's cousin, son of Yauseph and Mariam.

Maryam: Yeshua's companion and close student, formerly a businesswoman from Galilee.

Places and Regions in the Story (in alphabetical order)

(**Note:** All distances in the story are given in Roman feet (*pedes*), paces (*passus*) and miles (*millia*). These were slightly shorter than the English equivalent: one Roman foot (*pes*) was approximately .971 feet or 296 millimeters; one Roman pace (*passus*) was 4.854 Western feet or 1.48 meters; one Roman mile (*mille*, a thousand paces) was 4854 feet or 1.48 kilometers.)

Batanea: A border country just south of Gaulanitis and east of the Decapolis, on the east side of the Jordan (Yarden) River. Sometimes called Bashan in antiquity. Major towns included Kochaba and Beth-Ani, the latter sometimes called "Bethany beyond the Jordan." It became the home of Israelites returning from Babylon after the captivity, and a possible birthplace of the Mandaean religion, which claims as its main prophet the man the Bible calls John the Baptist.

Damaskos: Greek for Damascus; Yehuda calls it *Darmsuq* in Aramaic. An important trade city in southern Syria, capital of the Roman province there, and occupied probably as early as the third millennium BCE.

Empire of the Parthoi: The ancient Iranian empire of Parthia, which ruled an area extending from the Euphrates river in Syria to the Indus River in modern Pakistan for about five hundred years. The Parthians were the only serious rivals to Rome at the time and never defeated by them.

Gaulanitis: The modern day Golan, an area ruled as part of the 'tetrarchy' of Herodes Philipos, son of Herod the Great.

Iudaea: The Roman province that, at the time of the story, included the geographical regions of Judea, Samaria and Idumea, but not Galilee, Gaulanitis, Perea or the Decapolis. The latter areas were held by the Roman's clients, the two Herodes brothers, Antipas and Philipos. The capital of Roman Iudaea was in Caesarea Maritimus on the Mediterranean.

Idumea: the biblical land of Edom, stretching from the Judean hill country south to the Negeb (of which the modern Negev desert is a part). At the time of the story, it was included in the Roman province of Iudaea, and was populated by both historical Edomites as well as the semi-nomadic Aramaic-speaking Nabateans, who had intermarried with them and taken control of the area around Petra in present day Jordan. Herod the Great's father was Idumean and his mother Nabatean. The daughter of King Aretas of the Nabateans had married Herod Antipas.

Jezreel Valley: *Yizra'el* meaning "El scatters," named after a nearby town where the ancient Israelite kings used to live. Sometimes also called the "Great Plain" and part of the larger valley the Greeks called Esdraelon. The valley connected the Roman Via Maris, which ran north-south from Egypt up through the coastal cities of Tyre, with the "King's Highway" leading east to Damascus and caravan routes to India. The valley provided a natural border between Samaria and Galilee and descended one thousand feet eastward until it reached the Jordan River.

Mare Nostrum: "Our sea," Latin for the Mediterranean Sea.

Megiddo: Originally a royal city of the Canaanites in northern Samaria, at the southwest edge of the Jezreel Valley. At the time of the story Megiddo is a ruin of the remains of many previous towns and cultures. The name means "place of troops." The town was located on a major pass leading from the coastal plain into the Jezreel Valley separating Samaria from Galilee. Megiddo has been the site of many major battles. The most recent was in September 1918, between British and Turkish forces, which helped decide World War I. The name was transmuted from the Hebrew *har megiddo* into the Greek *Harmagedon* and mentioned in the book of Revelations (16:16) as a gathering place of battle before the visionary final judgment. English usually renders it "Armageddon."

Natzara: sometimes called Nazara or Nazrath (little Nazara), a.k.a. Nazareth. A village of about five hundred people at this time. Destroyed during the Assyrian conquest in the eighth century BCE, it was rebuilt during the Hasmonean (Maccabean) era in the late-second century BCE. The etymology of the name is disputed, but this story takes the point of view of researcher Fr. Bargil Pixner, who derived it from the word for *branch*. See the afterword below.

Paneas: a.k.a. Caesarea Philippi, a town in northern Gaulanitis, near a small valley of springs, cascades and waterfalls dedicated to Middle Eastern 'green man' figures such as Elijah or Enoch. At the time of the story, the shrine was dedicated to Pan, the ruins of which still exist. The home of Shemuel ben Yahayye and his adopted son Yehuda Tauma.

Phoenike: Greek for Phoenicia, a Canaanite land bordering the Mediterranean coast west of Galilee and extending north. The ancient Phoenician empire rivaled Rome and extended through northern Africa, southern Spain, northwestern and western Sicily, as well as the islands of Malta, Gozo, Sardinia, Majorca and Minorca. The most important of the Western Phoenician states was Carthage in present day Tunisia, which was defeated by the Romans in the second century BCE.

Zippori: Sepphoris. A city strategically located in the center of Galilee on a hill overlooking the Beth-Netofa Valley, which connects the Sea of Galilee with the Mediterranean. The Romans made Sepphoris the seat of their administrative capital of Galilee in 57–55 BCE and then burned it to the ground after a revolt began there in the wake of Herod the Great's death in 4 BCE. Herod Antipas refounded it as the capital of Galilee shortly thereafter, but then relocated the capital to his newly built Tiberius in 20–21 CE. Sepphoris was a leading regional city for centuries and remained pro-Roman even during the war against the Romans in 66–73 C.E.

Tyros: Tyre, a two-part port city (shore and island) in Phoenicia on the Mediterranean, important from ancient times for trade to the interior and for its great wealth. All trade routes from ancient Asia—south, north and east—ran through Tyre.

Yaphia: a medium-sized village of about eight hundred people about six miles south of Sepphoris.

Yerushalaim: Ancient Hebrew name for Jerusalem; in Aramaic, *Urushlem*. The earliest derivation of the name seems to be based on the Canaanite god of dusk or sunset, *Shalem*, who is mentioned in the Ras Sharma texts. His twin sister is *Shahar*, the goddess of the dawn, both of whom are associated with another Canaanite sun goddess. Perhaps in representing the end of the day, the word *shalem* becomes linked with the idea of peace, completion and reconciliation. In Genesis 14, the figure of *Malki Tzedek* ("the one who empowers right action," anglicized as Melchizadek) is named as the ruler of the city of Shalem, possibly a part of what later became Jerusalem. *Ur* could be rendered as settlement or foundation. *Ya(h)* is the sign of the Hebrew sacred name for Life Energy and a particle of the "unnameable name." The first century CE population of Jerusalem was probably around 80,000, according to Israeli researcher Magen Broshi.

Afterword and Historical Sources

"This is a story, a work of fiction. Any resemblance to characters living or dead is purely coincidental."

You will find this standard disclaimer in many historical mysteries. It also applies to this one. To distinguish this from my other nonfiction books, I have chosen to write it under another name. I mean to remind the reader: Please don't tie yourself into knots either finding offense or trying to decide if the plot could be true. Relax and remember: it is just a story.

The book's use of various languages arises from my own previous work with ancient Middle Eastern spirituality and mysticism, particularly with Aramaic translations and interpretations of sayings and stories of Jesus in the Gospels. It is also an attempt to provide an admittedly fictional, yet plausible "back story" for the figures of Thomas, John, Judas and Mary Magdalene, whose ancient communities produced the very different "gospels" bearing their names. Scholars often forget that it is a human characteristic for people to remember the same events very differently and selectively, depending on the "eyes" through which they see.

While the common spoken language in the area was Aramaic at the time, some people who needed to bridge different cultures, like the scribe Yehuda, would have also spoken Greek, Latin and probably some form of late, ancient Hebrew, at least for ritual purposes. For this reason, various languages are mixed in the book, not always consistently. That's the way life was (and is today, in the Middle East, for that matter).

Also, readers who are looking for an accurate scholarly transliteration (or spelling) of the characters' names (from Aramaic or another language) will be disappointed. Because this is a story, I compromised spelling for understanding. I wanted readers to be able to recognize a given name and then remember it. So the biblical name usually spelled in English as *Elijah* becomes *Eliyah*, *David* becomes *Dawid*, *Josiah* becomes *Yoshiah*, and so forth. (As a key, neither ancient Hebrew nor Aramaic had "j" or "v" sounds, so you can work out the usual English spelling by substituting "j" for "i" or "y," and "v" for "w." That's as much linguistics as the persnickety among you will get!)

One caution: History has already built some confusion into the names of various characters. For instance, the names that translations of the Gospels spell as Judas and Judah are the same name in Aramaic, which can be spelled in English either Yahuda or Yehuda. Gospels and later story traditions also talk about different people with the same or similar names, such as John, James, Thomas and Mary. Who is meant when? The "Thomas" part of Yehuda's name derives from a transliteration of the Aramaic word *Tauma*, meaning "twin, which was later rendered into the Greek *Didymus*. In the first and second centuries CE, different groups told various stories to explain this confusing cast of characters. Which John, James or Judah/Judas/Jude did what and when? And who was the twin or look-alike?

I left the names of selected groups (such as Judeans, Samaritans, Levites and Galileans), regions (Galilee, Samaria) and places (Jezreel Valley) in English, as I didn't want to risk losing everyone without a GPS. Hopefully, the readability of the story makes up for this level of inconsistency.

The renditions of the various books of Enoch in Yehuda's visions are my own, as are the various translations and versions of the prayers the characters use. So are the visionary statements of Yohanan ("the baptizer"), which are inspired by the sacred texts of Mandaeans. The Mandaean tradition, with roots in Batanea, survived in Persia and modern Iran into the twentieth century and claims John the Baptist as its founder. The Qur'an approved of the Mandaeans as "people of the book," calling them the *Sabians*. Exponents of the tradition still survive today in various countries, including the United States. For further information and methodology of the translation, see one of my other books, like *The Hidden Gospel* or *Desert Wisdom*.

The scroll with the inventory of Herod's supposed treasure is based on the "Copper Scroll" found in the Dead Sea Scrolls at Qumran in 1947. I have changed some of the wording to point to Megiddo. (Please don't go digging there and disturb the archeologists!)

In some ways, this book also results from an earlier collaborative research project in the late 1990s entitled "Jesus and Ecology," in which historians Dr. Joe Grabil, Deborah Oberg and myself sought out the natural sites in Galilee where Jesus lived and taught. It was, understandably, often difficult to find the "nature" under all of the building that various Christian denominations had constructed in the area over the centuries. However, due to excellent research by many ecologists, one can visualize what the land would have been like. Many of the descriptions of the natural world that the characters inhabit stem from this work and my visits to the places involved. (And yes, there were lions in the Merom/Huleh wilderness in the first century CE.) My gratitude to both Joe and Deborah for their collaboration in an adventure that still bears fruit.

One final large disclaimer: The history, culture, language, politics, archeology and even architecture of first century Roman Palestine remain conflicted, to say the least. Because various branches of Christianity use the Jesus stories in different ways, mainstream scholars dispute the interpretation of even very basic evidence. Nevertheless, I would be remiss if I failed to give the sources I have favored. Although I am not trying to convince anyone of anything, I definitely find the authors below much more convincing than others who may be better known.

First among my favorites is Dr. Richard A. Horsley, Professor of Liberal Arts and the Study of Religion at the University of Massachusetts, Boston. Horsley's *Archeology, History and Society in Galilee: The Social Context of Jesus and the Rabbis* corrects many basic distortions that stem from the tendency of previous scholars to over-theologize the available evidence. Among the many distortions is the idea that villages in first century Galilee had purpose-built "synagogues" for the "Jewish" residents. As he shows convincingly, a "synagogue," Greek for a *knesset*, was simply a village meeting, which likely took place in the largest house in the community.

Even more important is the misassumption that all, or even most, Galileans, were "Jews" in the modern sense of the word or supported the Judean Temple in Jerusalem. Most scholars now admit that the word *Jew* used in the New Testament Greek version of the Gospels is a mistranslation of the word *Judean*, that is, a person residing in the geographical region south of Galilee and Samaria. What we have come to call the "Jewish" religion did not exist until after the destruction of the Jerusalem Temple by the Romans and the reformation of the tradition by the early Rabbis. All of this occurred a generation after the time of Jesus himself. What we find in the first century are multiple competing forms of late Hebrew religion, with a variety of contenders who believe themselves to be the real inheritors of Moses and the biblical prophets. Various groups even contested the status of the Judean kings like David and Solomon. Many Galileans and Samaritans, as inheritors of the story of the biblical "Northern Kingdom" of Israel, saw them as Judean interlopers and oppressors.

Two other books by Horsley have also influenced my story. His *Bandits, Prophets and Messiahs: Popular Movements at the Time of Jesus* reveals the extreme volatility of the times in question. Various people and groups, under the intense pressures of empire and an oppressive client-patronage system, coped in very different ways, from violent action to visionary prophecy. Horsley's *Scribes, Visionaries and the Politics of Second Temple Judea* likewise opens up the whole world of the "scribe," a hitherto mysterious figure who was not simply a secretary or a copyist, but a keeper of culture, and sometimes a subversive visionary, acting with simultaneously political and spiritual motives.

With regard to the economy of the time, we often mistakenly think of Jesus's contemporaries as buying and selling in a free, open market similar to that in much of Europe and the USA. Several books point out the fallacy of this idea and the extent to which economic life at the time was based on a hierarchal patron-client model. Poor(er) people sought out rich(er) clients for protection and livelihood in "family" structures not un-like various mafia groups. This still reflects the actual situation in some countries today, where bribery and favoritism are matters of survival. Although we may see these systems as "corrupt" in the Western sense of supposed "fairness," how often is our fairness merely a cover for something similar (for instance, the lobbying system in the American government)?

These ancient systems of exchange have nothing to do with our ideas of capitalism or socialism, but in their most benign form are 'gift' economies, in which a group or community takes care of its own members, without keeping track of who owes what to whom. The ancient biblical injunction for a "jubilee year," in which all debts are forgiven and all land reverts to common ownership reflects such an understanding of community. As differ-ent clans and families rub together, however, the issue of who is included in the community rears its head, and rules of trade with outsiders ensue. When large empires get involved, the favors given and received, as well as the loyalties maintained or betrayed, become matters of life and death. An introduction to this whole area is *Palestine in the Time of Jesus: Social Structures and Social Conflicts* by K.C. Hanson and Douglas E. Oakman. For a wise and eloquent reflection on the history of ancient gift economies, see *The Gift* by Lewis Hyde.

On the origins of the Natzara family, I am indebted to the ideas of the late Fr. Bargil Pixner in his book *With Jesus Through Galilee According to the Fifth Gospel*. From his research, following St. Jerome, Pixner proposes that the Natzarans, a lost "branch" of the tribe of David, rees-tablished the village of Nazareth in the first century BCE after returning from Babylon. He points to evidence that some of the clan remained behind in the border area of Batanea in Perea, which became one of the haunts of Yohanan, the Bible's John the Baptist. He also proposes the idea that members of the Batanea group of the clan were expert horsemen who made themselves indispen-sible to various empires. Throughout ancient history various minority groups did survive and often rise to prominence in this way (for instance, the Ottomans). The notion that the Natzarans had formed an under-ground, revolutionary network that planned to unite all of Israel is my own, of course.

In addition to Dr. Horsley's book on scribes, I also appreciated Dr. Daniel Boyarin's *The Jewish Gospels: The Story of the Jewish Christ* for the story it tells of the major influence that the visionary books of Daniel and Enoch held for various countercultural groups looking for a way out of Roman and Herodian oppression. I also recommend Boyarin's other books on the histori-cal evolution of early Jesus movement groups and early Rabbinical (that is, Pharisee) groups into the Christianity and Judaism of today. A good parallel read is Glen Fairen's *As Below, So Above: Apocalypticism, Gnosticism and the Scribes of Qumran and Nag Hamadi.*

In relation to vision and possession, and their so-cial-psychological causes, I found Stevan L. Davies' *Jesus the Healer: Possession, Trance and the Origins of Christianity* both convincing and provocative. That many of Jesus's followers were suffering from what today would be called "liminal disorders," due to extremely abusive social and familial conditions, puts into perspective the uniqueness of anyone who could negotiate "both worlds" in a healthy way.

Finally, in no particular order, I also found help-ful: Charles Pages' *Jesus and the Land*, David Darom's *Beautiful Plants of the Bible*, Sean Freyne's *Galilee: A Study of Second Temple Judaism*, Lesley and Roy Adkins' *Handbook to the Life in Ancient Rome*, and the monumen-tal *Oxford Handbook of Jewish Daily Life in Roman Palestine*.

My special thanks to my friend Rabbi Arthur Waskow for the example of his own inspired renderings of many Jewish prayers, which point toward direct so-cial action for a better world. His version of the ancient Aramaic *Kaddish* prayer of mourning inspired my own in chapter ten. Now over eighty and still working tire-lessly, Rabbi Arthur, a real "God-wrestler," has taken on the mantle of the prophet—one who acts in both the spiritual and social-political worlds for the benefit of the larger community. For more on his work, see www. theshalomcenter.org

I hope that you find some of these leads worth pur-suing. None of it is meant to convince you of anything, since the whole subject of Jesus and his contemporaries has suffered from too much conviction as it is. I accept any mistakes in details as my own, rather than that of any of the authors I have cited.

My real motivation for this book derives from a desire to contribute to readers a few hours of the same storytelling enjoyment that I have received over the years from authors like Conan Doyle, Rex Stout, Tony Hillerman, Agatha Christie, Arthur Upfield, Boris Akunin, L. Adams Beck, Dion Fortune, Kahlil Gibran, Mikhail Bulgakov, George MacDonald and C. S. Lewis.

Afterword and Historical Sources

With enormous gratitude to my wife Natalia Lapteva for her love, support and encouragement over the years of birthing this project.

May all we do return to praise the One!

--Neil Douglas-Klotz, May 2015

ARC Books

Ferrying Ageless Wisdom Across The Ages

ARC Books is a project of the **Abwoon Resource Center** (Worthington, Ohio, USA) and the **Edinburgh Institute for Advanced Learning** (Edinburgh, Scotland, UK). The **Abwoon Resource Center** (ARC), a non-profit, volunteer project of Shalem Center, offers books, recordings, articles and information about workshops and retreats that support the work in this book.

The website of the **Abwoon Network (www. abwoon.org)** includes a library archive of published articles and blogs by Neil Douglas-Klotz, as well as podcasts of his talks and lectures, upcoming schedule internationally, and information about all of his published books and recordings.